Was it wrong to want more?

She wanted Paris. Rome. Venice. The world. She'd taken the first steps by accepting this job, which had brought her here, to this moment, where she was snowed in with a hunky, delicious man whose one kiss predicted a night that would rock her off her axis. His kisses could wipe the slate clean, erasing her previous mistakes. He'd be the second man she'd ever taken to bed, the first being her ex-fiancé. Shouldn't she see what the sexual fuss was actually all about?

She put her hand on each side of his face, his five-o'clock shadow rich beneath her fingers. "How about you kiss me again and we'll see where things lead? Shall we break our rules this once?"

"If at any time you say no, we're stopping. I'll respect your wishes."

She knew he would. "Perfect. Now kiss me."

Dear Reader,

When I started writing, it was because I wanted to create stories like the ones I loved reading—the ones with the happily-ever-afters. I began reading romance during seventh grade when I was on a two-week-long road trip that went from St. Louis to New Orleans, then around the Gulf of Mexico to Key West, then up the Atlantic side to St. Augustine (before we headed back home). It was in a gas station somewhere in Florida where I chose a new book, because I'd already read everything else, that my love for reading romance novels was born.

One of my favorite things to do is travel, so I understand Lana's wanderlust desire. Lana's on her way back to Beaumont, so she can visit her family, when a snowstorm strikes. Her seatmate, Edmund Clayton (the cousin of Jack from *All's Fair in Love and Wine*, Love in the Valley Book 2), travels constantly but never sees the sights. When he secures Lana a hotel room after they get stranded, fireworks fly. Love isn't on either Lana's or Edmund's mind. Lana wants Paris. Edmund must go undercover to win a bet. Trouble is, he's terrible at being a regular guy. He's not only a fish out of water, but soon he's in a love triangle with Lana, who prefers his alter ego.

I love hearing from readers. Reach me through my website, where you can also subscribe to my newsletter, at micheledunaway.com.

Michele

ONE SUITE DEAL

MICHELE DUNAWAY

Harlequin

SPECIAL EDITION

ISBN-13: 978-1-335-59472-3

One Suite Deal

Harlequin Enterprises ULC
22 Adelaide St. West, 41st Floor
Toronto, Ontario M5H 4E3, Canada
www.Harlequin.com

Printed in Lithuania

Recycling programs for this product may not exist in your area.

MIX
Paper | Supporting responsible forestry
FSC® C021394

In first grade, **Michele Dunaway** wanted to be a teacher. In second grade, she wanted to be a writer. By third grade, she decided to be both. Now a bestselling contemporary author, Michele strives to create strong heroes and heroines for savvy readers who want contemporary, small-town adventures with characters who discover things about themselves as they travel the road to true love and self-fulfillment. Michele recently retired from an award-winning English and journalism teaching career. She loves to travel, with the places she visits often inspiring her novels. She's a mom of two grown daughters and several rescue cats. (The cats, of course, completely rule the roost.) An avid baker, Michele describes herself as a woman who does way too much but never wants to stop, especially when it comes to creating fiction, or baking brownies and chocolate chip cookies. Her website is micheledunaway.com.

Books by Michele Dunaway

Harlequin Special Edition

Love in the Valley

What Happens in the Air
All's Fair in Love and Wine
One Suite Deal

Visit the Author Profile page
at Harlequin.com for more titles.

To all my former students
over the past thirty-five years, especially those
who've become good friends: Chris Waldo,
who flies around the world for a living;
Michael and Katy Gulledge, who make me so proud;
my yearbookers, who daily change the world,
Sarah Rue, Alyssa Juris, Quentin White,
Maddie Villeneuve, Lexi Romeril, Kristen Granquist,
Alison Bacon and Emily Aiken; and to the late
Peter Waggoner (1988–2013), who always
teased me and asked when he'd see his name
written fully in one of my books. (I miss you daily,
Peter. I'm sorry it took so long.) And to Tina Medley,
Sue Robison, Mike Storm, Maren Leonard,
Loretta Wylie and Kim Linneman, who made the
last twenty years some of the best of my career.

Prologue

"I doubt you could succeed even if you tried."

Only two people could speak to Edmund Clayton III like this, and thirty-six-year-old Reginald Justus—a man one year Edmund's senior—didn't qualify, because he wasn't Edmund's mother or sister. Edmund leveled his most haughty glare at his nemesis. Justus, whose tux made him more penguin than cover model, had the gall to add a belated laugh to his taunt.

Edmund tried not to respond with a sneer—the two men were at a New Year's Eve charity gala, after all. Edmund made his tone as smooth as the two fingers of bourbon he held in his left hand. A gold cuff link winked from beneath a tailored sleeve. "I always succeed. When have I not?"

"Perhaps in business. Your love life, however, is quite another story." Justus chuckled boldly, something he wouldn't dare be doing had he and Edmund been alone. But with people around he took the risk, reveling in the fact they glanced over. "Plenty of stories, actually. What's that word? Viral. But not in a good way, of course."

Edmund's broken engagement making headlines was a sore spot, but he certainly wasn't going to concede that point to Justus. Edmund relaxed clenched fingers. "What's that old saying? That there's no such thing as bad publicity?" Edmund sipped his whiskey, letting the smoky heat with hints of oak and vanilla slide down his parched throat.

"You were everywhere. Still are," Justus persisted. "Not in the best light either."

Edmund set the empty whiskey glass on a round, bar-height table covered with white linen. A tea light burned in the center. "I'm well aware of my broken engagement."

And the fact that a mere two weeks later his social media influencer ex, Veronica, had started dating someone else. She'd made Edmund out to be the villain to her one million followers, and six months later, the fallout from the viral breakup still followed Edmund around. The whole thing had been mortifying for a man of his stature.

"So that means you lost at something. Love." Justus, who'd never beaten Edmund at anything, laughed even longer, as if he'd told a great joke.

Edmund refused to let Justus under his skin. He kept his tone even, bored and dismissive. "Well, it's like Oscar Wilde said, 'There is only one thing in the world worse than being talked about, and that is not being talked about.' So let them talk."

"Aww, I hit a sore spot."

If Edmund didn't despise the man, he might just have admired Justus's courage for daring to keep prodding the snake. When Edmund struck, no one saw it coming. But Justus couldn't help that he was so full of himself, which meant he kept going. "Here's another one for you. I'm making the acquisition of Van Horn Hotels my business. They'll be mine by the end of January."

Ah, there it was. The gauntlet. Justus was so damn predictable that Edmund had been waiting for it ever since Justus sought him out from across the ballroom.

"I don't know why you're so smug. Those hotels won't

ever be yours. As you just admitted yourself, I always win in business."

"I did not say that," Justus protested. Then realizing he had, he puffed out his chest. "There's always a first time. You're going down."

Edmund zeroed in on his longtime rival, tuning out the low hum of guests' chatter and the more distant musical notes of a string quartet. He was at yet another high-priced, black-tie charity gala for some do-gooder cause demanding the appearance of Portland's A-list—his third event this holiday season. It was a tiring but necessary burden—the price of doing business in Oregon. "No, I'm not, but feel free to think that."

With a liquor-loosened tongue, Edmund's bitterest rival scoffed. "Been almost a year and you haven't closed the deal for Van Horn. I'd say my chances are better than good. You've lost your touch, golden boy. Can't get to the altar. Can't get a signature on the bottom line. The sharks are circling, and you're chum in the water. I can't wait to take a bite."

Competitors had sensed an opportunity when Edmund's cousin Jack had permanently relocated to Beaumont, Missouri, after he'd fallen in love with former naval lieutenant Sierra James during the acquisition of her family's winery. A happily married man with a baby on the way, Jack had decided investing locally in his own pet projects was far more important than running Clayton Holdings, the firm founded by both Jack's and Edmund's fathers, or as the business world called them, the Conquering Claytons. Starting with almost nothing, the two brothers had built a hospitality business that was worth billions. Now that Jack had abdicated, the responsibility for keeping the company profitable and at the forefront of success fell fully on Edmund's shoulders. He was more than up for the task.

"You know I'm not the only one ready to take a bite out of your market share," Justus added, his glee obvious. "You're slipping, Edmund. You don't have what it takes. Not for the long haul. You're already a has-been."

Edmund gritted his teeth, biting back a reply not fit for polite company. He'd never had an extended period without success, minus Van Horn, whose acquisition had been Edmund's first order of business after being named VP of Clayton Holdings, a promotion that had leapfrogged him to the highest level in terms of company succession. The Van Horn deal should have been signed, sealed and delivered already, but lately it was like he'd walked under a ladder—not that he was superstitious. Both Edmund's dad and his uncle Jonathan, Jack's dad, were rumbling that they wanted to retire, and if Edmund could close this deal, he'd be a shoo-in for the company presidency. And after that, CEO.

Edmund refused to be a has-been. He most certainly would not let Justus see how close the barb came to hitting Edmund's greatest fear. Edmund had big shoes to fill. He wasn't as likable or gregarious as Jack. Or as adventurous and carefree as his two brothers, or as fun and witty as his sister, Eva. No, Edmund was too studious. Too serious. Too formidable. Too focused on the prize. Well, he'd always won the prize, hadn't he?

As for Edmund's inability to close the deal on love, he'd decided that—at least for him—love wasn't worth it, especially after his very public breakup. The bachelor life suited him just fine. Business first. Look at what had happened to Jack. He'd given up his birthright. Edmund refused to do the same.

Edmund watched Margot Van Horn approach, a glass of

bubbly in her ruby-studded right hand. She'd been his late maternal grandmother's best friend. At seventy-five, Margot was one of Portland's most beloved and generous matriarchs, also known for her various eccentricities. Today she wore a glittering black gown with a flared skirt. "Gentlemen, good to see both of you. Fighting over me already?"

"Of course," Edmund inserted smoothly. He saluted her with a champagne flute he artfully plucked from a passing waiter. "You *are* the most beautiful woman here, after all."

Margot's cheeks pinked. Because her white hair was in a chignon, that flush was visible as it traveled down a neck that somehow defied aging. "Ah, Edmund, your mother raised a delightful cad. I shall scold her when I next see her. I wish she'd been able to attend tonight."

"I'm here in her stead, and your wish is my command." He kissed the back of the white-gloved hand she offered.

Margot trilled her pleasure. "Oh, if I were younger..." Then she waved a finger at them. "Gentlemen, I must tell you that flattery won't get you anywhere. A donation, however, will at least keep you both in my good graces."

"Then I will make a hefty one," Edmund said, beating Justus, who added a hearty, "Me too."

"Good." Margot gestured toward the glittering collection of who's who. "This is my favorite event, as it helps raise funds to reduce our homeless animal population."

Edmund had heard the rumors that Margot's four-thousand-square-foot mansion housed at least fourteen rescued cats and two rabbits. "A worthy cause."

"Speaking of worthy, you remember my grandson Lachlan, don't you? The one who went to NYU? He's in California working as a producer for a TV show."

"That's nice." Justus played along, but Edmund's gaze

narrowed. Margot might appear dotty, but she remained sharp and quick. She planned to drop Thor's hammer.

Margot beamed, and Edmund braced himself. "It's his big break. One of those shows where bosses go undercover. He's recruiting talent."

Edmund's internal radar flashed danger even before Margot said, "I fully support him in his new endeavor, so I've decided each of you should do his show."

"What?" Justus appeared stunned, and Edmund wished he held something stronger than France's best bubbly.

"You'll each do one week undercover, and whoever has the highest Nielsen ratings and subsequent social media exposure wins the right to purchase Van Horn Hotels, with mutually agreeable terms to be discussed at the appropriate time, of course," she added with a breathy rush. "But you have my word that, should we reach fair terms, I will sell. Besides, doing this show will be great publicity for your respective brands. It's a win-win."

More like a week of misery, Edmund thought. But he'd do whatever it took, including keeping his mouth shut, unlike his rival, whose mouth dropped open as Justus stared, agape.

"A friendly wager, gentlemen, and an end to all this speculation and bickering. What do you say? You're in, right? Of course you are. You both want my hotels and will do whatever it takes."

Margot's laugh tinkled as she lifted her champagne. Automatically the men did the same, and their glasses clinked together. Margot smiled, satisfied she'd won this round and all future ones. Both men would do whatever it took to please her. "This is going to be such fun. May the best undercover appearance win!"

Chapter One

It is a truth universally acknowledged, that a single woman in possession of a good job and who has her own money, must still be in want of a husband.

No offense to paraphrasing Jane Austen, but what Lana Winchester really wanted was to make it to her next plane, which was why she was running through PDX.

She cursed the fact she hadn't changed into her favorite flats. After traveling for work the last two years, she considered herself an expert traveler who definitely knew better than to wear suede boots with heels to the airport. But she'd wanted to look good for her last client meeting, which had run over. She'd made it to the Eugene airport with hardly any minutes to spare. Once aboard, her plane had sat on the tarmac.

And sat and sat while passengers with connecting flights, like Lana, kept glancing at their watches and wondering exactly when the plane would leave the gate and taxi toward the runway.

What was that about best laid plans? The first flight from Eugene had arrived late, putting her even more behind. Double curses to the airline app that told her she must check in with the gate agent in order to change her second flight. What good was technology if it didn't allow her to do things?

She had to get on this specific flight from Portland—
Oregon, not Maine—so she could make it home to Beau-
mont before a big snow storm hit St. Louis and the entire
Midwest. If not, she might not make it at all.

Everything had conspired against her today, including
Mother Nature. If it hadn't been for a text from her mother
telling her that the storm was moving in early, Lana would
have been stuck in Oregon. If she didn't get on this exact
plane, every later flight to St. Louis would be canceled.
The odds stood at 100 percent.

One bright side? She had one of those tickets that allowed for no cost, same-day changes as long as seats were
available. According to the app, there were two left.

While she liked her time working in Oregon, she had to
get home. Normally she might not mind being stuck in such
a pretty location, but her younger brother Ryan's eighteenth
birthday was tomorrow. She had to be there.

With eight years between her and her sibling, she'd been
in college before he'd even reached middle school. Engaged
and disengaged before Ryan had started his freshman year.
Now he was three months from graduating high school,
and she refused to miss his birthday, especially as she'd
already missed so many.

Even though they talked, with her constant travel, her
brother was more stranger than friend. She'd never seen
him play high school basketball. He was a shooting guard
on varsity, whatever that meant. In a recent video chat,
her mom had told her he'd received calls from coaches as
far away as Gonzaga in Washington State, Duke in North
Carolina and the University of Connecticut. Even the non-
sports-watching Lana knew that meant her brother was
good. He hadn't yet committed, preferring to wait until
the end of the season and hopefully a state championship.

His one birthday wish? That she attend at least one of his games. She had determined that she would be there, Mother Nature be damned.

Refusing to disappoint her brother or her family again, Lana double-timed it through the thick crowd and tried not to crash into any of her fellow travelers. Today was the first Saturday in March, too early for the spring break travel crazy, but not too early for those who didn't understand that airport etiquette meant they were supposed to stand to the right and walk on the left. She bypassed people on the moving walkway, yelling, "Excuse me," and ignoring their surprised or miffed glances.

Pushing through with the fastest power walk she could manage without triggering an asthma attack, she felt her quilted, waterproof tote bag slip from her shoulder, the computer inside clipping the arm of someone who didn't step out of the way soon enough. Without even looking back, she called, "Sorry," and kept going.

Seriously, she could always tell the casual tourists who gave themselves hours to make their flight from the business travelers who knew how to get where they were going with better efficiency and far less luggage. Lana was in the latter group.

Once she'd taken the quality control job with Cederberg Interiors, she'd quickly learned how to fit two weeks' worth of clothes in a hard-sided carry-on. Her iPad and her laptop were in the tote on her shoulder, along with a king-size bag of peanut M&M's candy and a liter bottle of smartwater she hadn't opened on the previous leg.

While many might not find her job as an installation supervisor interesting, Lana loved the challenge. As someone who lived inside hundreds of hotel rooms a year and oversaw the renovations of the rest as her daily job, the work she did mattered. She was the final sign-off after hotels upgraded their guest rooms and communal spaces. She ensured the decorative and installation work Cederberg Interiors performed exceeded expectations. In the case of Clayton Holdings, one of Cederberg's longest clients, the standards were exceptionally high. Clayton Hotels made luxury and service synonymous, a fact proven by the company's high number of repeat bookings from discerning clients.

Lana's next assignment was the first time her work would bring her home for an extended period. She'd be in Beaumont for at least a week, staying on-site at the Beaumont Grand, the top-tier golf course resort hotel Clayton had opened last year as part of its master plan to revitalize the entire county. She'd be close to her family as she quality controlled the final finishing work on the Grand's neighbor—the smaller, pricier and far more exclusive Chateau. The luxurious boutique hotel opened in April. Lana would double-check the installations of the fixtures, the furniture—pretty much everything from floor to ceiling—before signing off that Cederberg's part in the project was complete. She'd get to spend some quality time with her family. Even if she wasn't staying with them, she'd be in the same town and spend her nights visiting. Catch a game as Ryan wanted.

That was, if she could get a seat on this plane.

The gate was just ahead, on the left, and Lana saw two attendants behind the counter. One agent appeared to be talking to a tall man who had his back to her. Unlike him, Lana carried her coat, probably the only reason she wasn't sweating from sprinting through three concourses. The other agent miraculously appeared free, which was never a good sign. Travelers always needed something. *Please let me not have run all this way and be hyperventilating for nothing.* Lana sent a prayer to the heavens and pushed forward.

The first thing Edmund noticed was her legs. Which made him a total cad, he knew. His mother had definitely raised him better. But as if he'd been captured by the pull of a powerful electromagnet, his gaze followed endless sheer black tights upward, from their start in black suede boots until the silky fabric disappeared beneath a red and green corduroy tartan hem that skimmed mid-thigh. He rationalized that he couldn't help but stare—the woman had made quite the entrance by approaching the service desk like a mini-tornado. Her chest heaved and her boots clicked on the worn linoleum while her four-wheeled, hard-sided carry-on whirred in its attempt to keep up the frantic pace. As she came alongside him at the service desk, her bag rolled over his left foot.

"Sorry." She gasped out the word as she spared him one of those automatic, yet polite, apologetic smiles strangers give one another. Still somewhat breathless, the words gushed out. "I need to get on this plane." She shoved her phone forward toward the gate agent, her boarding pass visible. "It's not full yet, is it?"

Without waiting for an answer, she leaned over the counter, the interesting gap forming under the top button of her red silk shirt revealing a peek of black lace. "Please tell me you have a seat."

The agent offered a, "Let me check," and then a, "Yes. I can make the change."

A husky, still-catching-her-breath voice conveyed relief. "Thank you. Whatever it is, I'll take it."

As she stopped leaning and straightened, her soft shoulder bag slipped. Whatever hard object was inside smacked his funny bone with a thwack. He grimaced, and her wide-eyed amber gaze caught his over the bottle of water she was sipping. She readjusted her shoulder strap and shoved the bottle into a side pocket. "I'm so sorry."

"Sir?" the gate agent asked. Edmund's attention snapped back to the representative helping him. "This is the best I can do. I'm sorry we didn't have anything better. But at least it's not the middle of the last row."

"Which I appreciate." He fingered the paper-thin boarding pass and checked his frustration. He could do this stupid undercover week. Even if it meant the VP of Clayton Hotels flew economy rather than on a private plane. What was four hours plus a two-hour time zone change on a commercial carrier in the grand scheme of things, if it meant beating Reginald Justus? Peanuts. A minor inconvenience. A small price to pay to own Van Horn Hotels.

Thankfully, Edmund hadn't had to wear his ridiculous "Peter Waggoner" costume on the flight. The mouth partial that changed Edmund's voice took several minutes to adhere. Then there was the rest of his disguise…

Her bag clipped his arm again, and her lips puckered into a perfect pink O that sent a jolt through him. She looped the strap back onto her shoulder. "Sorry. I don't know what's gotten into this thing today."

"It's fine." Edmund uttered some of the most meaningless words in the English language. He stepped away, but not before committing her to memory, same as he'd do with any guest or business associate. Sizing someone up and filing information away was an ingrained habit. Good business acumen. A winning tactic. Never mind the fact that he found her interesting, despite her lack of control over her luggage. She was pretty too, in that natural, fresh-faced way.

Her skin rivaled milk. A light smattering of freckles graced a perky petite nose. He had a Roman nose, the same one his father, his grandfather and his brothers Michael and Liam had. It was something the show's producers had argued over how to hide, and since the on-site producer was going to be Lachlan Van Horn himself, Edmund had sided with whatever Lachlan wanted. In the end, they'd decided to make it larger, meaning Edmund would have to glue a prosthetic to his face every morning.

Lachlan, who'd also serve as director, had suggested getting into character immediately, but Edmund had pushed back on that. While Edmund would forgo the company plane and fly coach, he'd drawn the line at traveling as Peter. Oh, and no way was Edmund sitting in the row directly in front of the aft lavatory. A man of his stature had his limits. Bad enough he had to settle onto one of those too-small chairs lining the gate. After trying and failing to make himself comfortable, Edmund sent his younger sister a text: I'm traveling economy.

Seconds later Eva replied, All part of being a common man, and punctuated her text with a laughing emoji. The baby in the family, she took liberties like that.

Unamused, Edmund sent back the vomit emoji. He didn't care if the action was childish. He considered his Gulfstream an extension of his office. A place to work and get things done. Instead, he languished in the waiting area along with the general public while the clock ticked away the wasted minutes. He studied the crowd, his gaze again landing on the woman at the counter before he received two more laughing faces from Eva and, You'll beat Justus.

His phone pinged with an additional text: You'll do great. When don't you?

He appreciated Eva's confidence. She'd told him Reginald Justus had already completed his undercover week at one of his Florida adventure resorts. Until she had shared that news, Edmund had held out hope that Justus would back out of the wager. Since he hadn't, Edmund was locked into completing his week. Both his father and uncle had loved the undercover idea, not that they'd ever consider doing it themselves.

As for the show, once it aired, as the company's VP of PR, Eva planned to use the program as the capstone for her latest social media and advertising campaign. "Think of it as a working vacation. Like going to camp," she'd told Edmund as he'd packed his suitcase. "I mean, how hard can performing various hotel jobs be?"

Edmund would soon find out. He stretched tense fingers and shifted on the hard plastic. He hated reality TV, hated gossip. Thankfully no one took notice of him, which allowed him to relax somewhat. In hindsight, dating a popular social media influencer had not been one of his best ideas. But when he'd first met Veronica, she'd seemed perfect. Sweet. Kind. He simply hadn't realized until too late that she'd been two different people—the pretty popular girl in public, and in private, the insecure, high-maintenance woman worried about her numbers, clicks and having Edmund's complete attention.

Despite this, he'd tried to make the relationship work, including asking her to marry him. He realized now he'd been unable to wrap his brain around the fact that he couldn't fix things and make them better. Marriage should make her more secure, right?

Once the veneer came off, all they did was fight. Then

Veronica had asked him to dinner. Had he known the video of Veronica tossing his ring at him over their crème brûlée would be even more popular than an imploding pop star, Edmund never would have agreed to meet. Trusting Veronica was one of his biggest mistakes.

A harried gate agent announced Edmund's boarding group, and because Edmund refused to lose even more pride by failing to land Van Horn Hotels, he joined the queue and shuffled his way down the jet bridge. He stowed his luggage and folded his six-foot bulk into seat 10A, sighing as his knees touched the seat in front of him.

"I see we both got seats," a familiar voice said. Shoulder-length hair the color of sunset swished as she opened the overhead bin. The red silk of her top inched upward, providing a tantalizing view of the pinky-sized dip of her belly button. She handed him the overcoat he'd stowed. "Hold that a second, will you? I need to make this fit."

Her shirt climbed farther, exposing a good three inches of creamy skin as she shoved her suitcase overhead. She replaced his coat, clicked the bin closed and dropped into the aisle seat. Edmund pressed against the window as her deadly tote came close to taking out his arm.

"Sorry." The tote wobbled in her lap, her bottom gyrating as she withdrew a paperback novel, a bottle of water larger than the one he'd carried on and a yellow package of peanut M&M's. She shoved the tote under the seat and extended her right hand, the gape at the vee of her breasts providing clear confirmation of black lace. "How about we start over? I'm Lana."

Fingers tipped in hot pink firmly shook his hand, creating an electric jolt that had nothing to do with winter static. Not ready to reveal himself, but not ready to trot out his TV alias Peter before he was in his disguise, Edmund gave her his childhood nickname. "Trey."

"Nice to meet you, Trey." Long lashes lowered over soft amber irises a man could drown in, shielding her interest. He noted the zing ceased as she withdrew her hand. "You seem familiar. First time headed to St. Louis or are you from there?"

He shook his head. "No to both. And we've never met. I'd remember."

He liked her light and airy laugh as she said, "True. I'd certainly remember you too. I'm from St. Louis. Sort of. About an hour west-southwest. Beaumont."

She didn't wait to see if he'd heard of the town, which he had, as that's where his cousin Jack lived and where Edmund was headed. Her skirt inched upward, exposing more black material, and he settled his business magazine in his lap and listened as she told him how she was from Missouri, where half the state pronounced it *Missouree* and the other half *Missourah*. He had ten total hotels across the state, including the Beaumont Grand located off Winery Road near historic Beaumont and its neighbor, the soon-to-open Beaumont Chateau. When he acquired the Van Horn collection, he'd add twelve more.

"Are you traveling for business or pleasure?" As the word *pleasure* rolled off her lips, Edmund clenched and unclenched his left fingers. Seated this close, his right arm hovered near hers, creating a strange heat that traveled through both his sport coat and his white oxford. Her floral scent drifted into his nose.

How long did it take a commercial flight to take off anyway? His pilot, Chris, would have had him in the air within minutes. Edmund really should work. Take a nap. Put in his noise-canceling earbuds. Rustle a few pages of the magazine to indicate this conversation was over. Instead, he reached to turn on the overhead vent and answered her question. "Business. You?"

Her Midwestern girl-next-door smile lit the space. "Both, well, sort of. I always wanted to travel, so working for an interior design firm that does renovations and installations all over the continental United States is a good way to do it. The trouble is, all I've seen lately are a lot of hotel rooms. Not quite the world, but it's a step along the way."

"You have to start somewhere. Sorry. I don't mean to sound condescending."

Her smile never faltered. "No. I agree. That's what I keep telling my mom. She wishes I was home more."

He liked the sound of her sigh. Her hand bumped his, and she blushed. Unlike the polished women who dominated his social circle, Lana wore her emotions. Interest and awareness oozed from her pores, and he decided there was no harm in talking. Wasn't that what normal travelers did? After they deplaned, they'd never see each other again, and he didn't have a Facebook account. Anyone he needed to keep track of worked for him. "Where have you been lately?"

"New York. Boston. Philadelphia. Pittsburgh. Portland. A lot of *P* towns." She gave a light laugh. "And a bean town. Exciting places like that."

He had ten hotels in New York, eight in Boston, seven in Philadelphia and three in Pittsburgh. "Is Pittsburgh really that exciting?"

Mock horrified indignation spread as she faced him. "Of course, it is. The Andy Warhol Museum is there, and he's one of my favorite artists. I loved seeing the display of soup cans at MOMA. That's in New York. I love museums. They're always on my must-visit list."

Edmund had attended private events at MOMA, and if he wasn't careful in choosing how he responded, he'd bomb being undercover the moment the cameras started rolling. He'd met the cameramen, Ben and Larry, at the test shoot. While nice guys, they'd been everywhere and underfoot. "I'm partial to 'Starry Night.'" Edmund named one of MOMAs most popular works.

"I liked that one too. It was all I'd hoped it would be. But I saw the painting when it was on loan to the Met for a special exhibition, along with other Van Gogh works. One painting was from a private collection. There was a guy guarding it. His whole job was to make sure that no one took any pictures." She tapped her forehead. "I have to remember it up here. It was beautiful. Can you imagine owning a painting like that?"

She tore into the candy and crunched into a blue M&M. His breath hitched. She shook the bag. "Want some?"

"Thanks, but I'm good." Actually, he wasn't. Her eating candy should not have an effect on him.

She popped another candy, her mouth rounding into a kissable O before she bit down. "I like art. Sightseeing is one reason I took this job. When I arrived in Portland a few days ago, I visited the art museum. Sadly, I didn't make it to the Saturday Market, since I was in Eugene this morning. Maybe next time."

She wiggled in her seat and dug out yet another piece of candy. "This flight will get me home in time for my younger brother's eighteenth birthday dinner. We have an eight-year age gap, and I'd like to know him better now that he's all grown up. Do you have siblings?"

"Sister. Two brothers. All younger, but much closer in age than you and your brother. My sister and I are pretty close."

"I wish Ryan and I were."

The plane lurched into the air, and she gripped the aisle armrest. Her right sleeve inched up, revealing a small butterfly tattooed on the inside of her wrist. He put his hand atop the magazine in his lap and listened as she chatted about her family and growing up in Beaumont.

Because of his upcoming undercover job, he didn't tell her he'd been to the historic small town located west of St. Louis several times. His first visit had been for his cousin Jack's wedding to Sierra James. Jack had shown him all the wineries Clayton Holdings owned, including the one that had belonged to Sierra's family. The wineries were part of the master plan Clayton Holdings had for the region, to change it into something like Napa or Sonoma, but in the Midwest.

Edmund's next visit was the grand opening of the Beaumont Grand, a premier golf course resort, which had been built to be on par with courses such as Pebble Beach and Augusta National.

The flight leveled out and beverage service began.

"Are you doing anything fun while in St. Louis?" Lana asked.

When she blinked those long lashes, he wanted to tell her everything, but instead he shrugged. "Not much. Working mostly."

She chewed another candy, drawing his attention back to her mouth. Edmund yanked his gaze away. He prided himself on his self-control. He liked everything compartmentalized, including sex. He set the clear plastic cup down—like a thirsty man in the desert, he'd already drained his cola dry. He'd skipped buying alcohol, wanting his head clear.

Lana sipped her ginger ale. "You really should be a tourist while you're there. You can't go to St. Louis and not do something."

"No time for side trips."

She frowned. "That's terrible. Have you ever visited the Arch on any of your previous trips?"

He'd flown over it. Did that count? "No."

Her eye roll emphasized her disappointment in his lack of tourism initiative. "Take two hours and go. Tickets sell out, so order them online to reserve a spot. You're tall, so take the middle seat."

Because he'd never see her again, he made a rare admission. "I don't usually do touristy things when I travel and certainly not by myself."

She side-eyed him. "That's sad. It's easy. You buy a ticket and go."

He didn't want her pity. Instead, he wanted to taste that mouth mere inches from his. He shoved that thought aside. For a man who prided himself on his iceman control, he was like a randy teen. "I'm really busy when I travel."

"You should stop and smell the roses."

Like her perfume? Whatever she wore was an intoxicant that made him desire to sample her neck. He shook his cup and sipped the few remaining drops of cola hiding beneath the ice. Until he'd secured Van Horn Hotels, he could not be distracted by his libido, especially with a Midwestern sweetheart whom his brutal, competitive world would destroy.

She popped another M&M, and Edmund hoped the bag would be empty soon. How long was this flight? He glanced at his Rolex, finding instead a bare wrist serving as a reminder that he'd left his prized watch at home. His persona as Peter Waggoner certainly couldn't afford a Rolex. Edmund shoved his hand back into his lap.

Lana studied him, and he tried not to squirm. It bothered him that she found him lacking. "May I be bold?" she asked.

Hadn't she been all flight? "Sure, why not?"

"I predict you probably haven't lightened up in a decade."

He laughed at that. "More like two."

Being the nephew of the Clayton Holdings CEO and son of the hotel division CEO, Edmund had been on the fast track by age fifteen, if not right out of the cradle. He rattled the cup, sucked an ice cube into his mouth and crushed through the hole in the middle, breaking it into two pieces. "My life is complicated. There's pressure at work. I was also engaged. It didn't end well."

He wasn't planning on telling her that last part, but it slipped out. She touched his arm, her fingers sending heated awareness through his veins. "Neither did mine. What happened to yours?"

Social media gold digger. "Long story not worth rehashing. Suffice to say, if I don't deliver this project…" He caught himself before mentioning the TV show. "I have a big project on my proverbial plate. It's on my shoulders whether it succeeds. Once I'm done, I'll take a long vacation." Or he'd at least think about it. "I'll lighten up then, like you said." He highly doubted he would.

Lana continued to face him, that butterfly tattoo flashing whenever she moved her hand. "Tell you what, if you start with the Arch, I'll be your tour guide. As friends," she amended, glancing quickly toward the aisle to hide her interest. "I don't pick up men on planes."

"Thanks. I appreciate the offer. And no worries. I didn't think you were that type."

No need to say more. They both knew this seatmate banter meant nothing. He was one more person she'd meet during her travels, someone she'd never see again, whom she might tell her friends about. It couldn't be any other way. He'd soured on the idea of happily ever after, and he could tell she was that kind of girl. Whoever'd let her go was an idiot.

Besides, he and Lana weren't going to be one of those "I met my forever on the plane" stories that CNN often posted. Instead, Edmund purposefully moved their chatting into less personal topics. Conversation continued to flow easily, which made the time slide by. The intercom announcement letting them know the flight attendants would be making a final pass through the cabin to collect trash came as an unwelcome jolt. They'd land soon. The past four hours would become nothing but a distant memory.

She leaned over, her tantalizing scent directly under his nostrils. She was practically in his lap as she tried to peer out the oval window as they approached St. Louis. "Can you see anything?"

He ventured a glance. "Too cloudy and dark."

She craned her neck. He pressed as far back as possible before his libido got a mind of its own. He'd never given into his base urges. Everything he did he calculated to the nth degree. He was hardwired that way.

Her left breast brushed his chest as she shifted back into her seat and put the armrest down. "Bummer. Depending on the approach, you can see the Arch or the confluence of the rivers. I'd hoped to see it, but there's a snowstorm on the way. St. Louis can use the precipitation. The region has been in a drought for the last two years. The river is so low that shipwrecks are visible. Last year, we had fourteen inches of snow the last weekend of March. It was gone by Easter though, and this year we've had nothing worthwhile. Until today, I guess." She settled back and closed her eyes. "Oh, well."

He inhaled a deep, cleansing breath, but her perfume lingered. His joints ached from the torturous lack of legroom. Never again would he fly commercial. Once was enough.

Buffeted by the wind, the plane shook, and she gripped both armrests. Instinct made him cover her hand. "We're almost there. Hang on," he told Lana.

Her lashes fluttered, but her eyes remained closed. "I hate takeoffs and landings. And just so you know, I'm still not hitting on you. I once fell asleep on a stranger. The flight attendants had to wake us up."

He shouldn't be experiencing jealousy at the thought, or the desire to wrap her in his arms. His brother Liam had been right. Edmund hadn't dated Veronica for the right reasons, especially if Edmund kept experiencing zings when he touched Lana. He tried to play it cool. "It's all good. This is me simply trying to be a good seat buddy. You seem nervous."

"I am. Keep talking. You'd think after all the miles I've flown I'd be used to it by now, but I remain firmly anti-turbulence, and this is getting bumpy."

As the plane dropped and so did everyone's stomachs, Edmund told her about a childhood Christmas memory. "My brothers and I were so disappointed. Santa was to bring us another brother so we could have even numbers for games. Instead, we got a girl. My dad told us we didn't get to order siblings like you did fast food or meals at restaurants."

The anecdote made her laugh, which was good as the descent continued to jostle the plane. Then the ground came into view and the steel bird landed with a large, hard *thunk*. The brakes squealed, and the jolt jostled open one of the overhead compartments behind them. Finally, after a side-to-side shudder, the plane slowed and passengers began to clap. Edmund gave her hand one final squeeze. "Relax. They deliberately land hard so that if there's any ice they break through and hit pavement. More traction. Safer."

"Good to know." Lana disengaged her fingers.

As the plane taxied, they retreated into themselves, as passengers do upon landing, severing the temporary connection humming between them. Edmund sent Eva a text saying he'd arrived. Lana's fingers flew over her phone's keyboard. Outside on the tarmac, big wet flakes fell faster and heavier, creating a layer of white. The plane rolled past multiple gates with parked planes already coated in a layer of snow.

The intercom crackled as the pilot spoke. "Howdy, folks. Sorry for that bump, but welcome to St. Louis. We're glad we're on the ground, because the tower tells us we're the last flight in or out because of the weather. If you have connections, please see the gate agent. As soon as we get to our gate, we'll get you inside where it's warm and dry."

Edmund noted Lana had paled. "What is it?"

She stared at him wide-eyed. "I'm stuck here."

He frowned. "Isn't this your last stop?"

She clutched her cell phone. The screensaver was a picture of her family. "My mom left a voicemail saying they're already snowed in. The road crews can't get the snow cleared fast enough." Her lower lip quivered, and she gave a short, hysterical laugh. "I ran all that way and can't get home."

"You can't take a cab?"

She gave him a blank stare. "To Beaumont? Not when the roads are closed so that people don't slide off and die."

Which meant he wouldn't be traveling out there tonight either. No big loss. Beside him, the woman who'd charged through the airport to change her ticket shook her head at the irony.

"On the bright side, I would have been stuck in Portland for several days if we get the eight to ten inches they're predicting. At least I'm here. I'll get a hotel room. Sleep on a bench if I have to until the plows clear the roads. Tomorrow's another day. My dad drives a snowplow. He'll get me at some point."

Edmund admired her optimism. Veronica would have already been shrieking at her assistants and blaming them for being unable to control the weather. He tried to reassure Lana. "Hopefully, it won't come to that."

The plane came to a stop at gate C23, and Lana reached under 9B for her tote bag, providing Edmund with one final view of that breathtaking black lace. She was on her feet, both bags in hand. "It was nice meeting you. I hope you visit the Arch. Seriously, don't miss it."

He checked the urge to give her his business card, especially as he'd told her his name was Trey. Besides, he wasn't going to Beaumont to socialize. He let her go with a simple, "Thanks for being a great seatmate."

"You too." She moved with a single-minded determination to be one of the first ones off the plane.

He couldn't blame her. He'd seen news reports showing how closed airports could turn into pure chaos and madness. He rose, grabbed his carry-on and stepped into the aisle once it was his turn. Then his mother's voice was in his ear reminding him she'd taught him better than this. When you were fortunate enough to have it all, as they did, you gave back. Helped others. Edmund allowed himself a deep sigh. He was Edmund Clayton III. He could perform miracles. All it took was one phone call.

Chapter Two

What good was a smartphone if it couldn't provide any answers? Lana gritted her teeth as she paced the concourse. Or the phone number of a hotel with availability? At this point, any room would do. Even a conference room with a pullout couch. Or a rollaway in a closet.

But calls to the closest airport hotels had revealed that the probability of finding even a sliver of space was nada, zip, zilch. The apps on Lana's phone had yielded dead ends as well. She was stuck at the airport, completely at Mother Nature's mercy, along with the dozens of other passengers milling about, most of them frantically talking or texting. The truly fatalistic had already commandeered the cell-phone charging stations, surrounding them like pirates staking out treasure or piranhas surrounding prey. One of those airport golf-cart-like vehicles whizzed by with an annoying beep, beep, beep, its back end stacked high with travel blankets. Over her right shoulder, the rest of her flight still exited. Trey hadn't deplaned. No way would she have missed him.

Trey—they hadn't shared last names—had been her most interesting, most attractive seatmate to date. She'd liked how his dark hair, with no hint of gray, had swooped over his temple. His jaw tapered to a hint of dimpled chin—

a little crease begging for a woman's touch. Those gray eyes—Lana wondered what worldly sights he'd seen on his travels. Then again, when he'd mentioned he'd visited Rome and Paris, he'd also told her he hadn't seen much since he'd been working. Because of that, she'd glossed over the fact those two cities were on her bucket list.

Despite his lack of solo tourism skills, his aura of supreme confidence had impressed. He knew exactly who he was and where he fit into the world. Lana was iffy on both counts, but finding herself was what taking this traveling job had been all about. She simply wished it had led to more exotic locations, than yes, Pittsburgh. Or Pottsville, Pennsylvania. She had to admit those cities weren't London, Sydney, Berlin or Milan. Neither was Beaumont, for that matter, and she still called it home, even though her permanent address was only used for taxes and bills that couldn't be paid online.

She guessed Trey to be in his midthirties. That made him older than her twenty-six. He was also out of her league. She'd seen the label of his overcoat, recognizing a designer often featured in fashion magazines. Then again, he was flying coach. Perhaps he'd bought the coat secondhand. Her designer clothes and purse came from a high-end, online resale shop, purchased for a fraction of the original price. Either that or she rented her special occasion clothes. But really, odds were he'd bought his coat new. One did not do business in Italy in used, out-of-fashion clothing.

Her phone rang, and she collapsed into one of the many empty seats surrounding a deserted gate a few down from where she'd deplaned. "Any luck?" Lana asked her mother when the call connected.

"Nothing. Honey, I'm so sorry. Your dad's already out

plowing or I'd have him come get you. He says the roads are a mess and to stay off them."

Her dad worked for the highway department, so he'd know. "Thanks for trying, Mom. I guess I'll see you all tomorrow."

"We'll do Ryan's birthday then. He's okay with it since your dad had to work. He's online playing video games with friends."

Movement caught Lana's attention, and there Trey was. Easily topping six feet with impressive broad shoulders, Trey walked toward her with a powerful stride, his expensive overcoat flapping against well-cut trousers. She sucked in a breath.

"Mom, don't worry about me. I'll join one of those airline clubs for the night or something. Stop worrying. I excelled at primitive camping with my Girl Scout troop, remember? The airport has indoor plumbing and heat. I'll be fine."

Trey's shadow fell over her, her face suddenly eye level with his stomach. A little lower and *ooh la la*. Her imagination fired. "Mom, gotta go. Love you too."

Lana ended the call and leaned back so she could see Trey's chiseled face. Even harsh airport fluorescent lighting didn't diminish his attractiveness. "You stuck here too?" The beeping cart whizzed by, devoid of blankets. Hopefully it would return so she could get one.

"Follow me." Firm fingers created a tickling sensation as he drew her to her feet. He picked up her smaller bag and draped the strap over her shoulder. "Walk fast, like you did at PDX. You got one more sprint in you? There's a shuttle waiting. If you want a hotel room, it's all yours. But you have to hurry."

"What? How?" Spurred on by the hope of getting out of

the airport, Lana started walking. Their gate was nowhere close to the exit, and she again cursed the fact she'd chosen to wear these boots. But who had expected the cold front to come in early? Probably every St. Louisan. Her own fault for not paying better attention. "How did you manage to find rooms? Every place I called is sold out."

"I got lucky." He hoofed it on the moving walkway, and she found herself practically running as they passed the people thankfully standing to the right. "They can't hold the reservation forever, even for me."

She tripped over the end of the walkway, and he caught her. He lifted her to him and set her steadily on her feet. Common sense then kicked adrenaline to the curb, and she paused. "Look, while I'm grateful for the reservation, I think I gave you the wrong impression."

To her chagrin, he kept walking. She sprinted after him, her carry-on zipping behind her.

He didn't look back. "I'm not hitting on you, and this isn't a pickup. We already established that on the plane, right? Consider this my pay it forward. It's your room if you want it. I have my own. Do you want to sleep in a real bed or would you rather find a spot out here? Decide quickly. We're keeping people waiting and the roads are getting bad."

When he put it that way, a bed sounded divine, especially compared to the airport floor or sleeping upright in a chair, but Trey wasn't slowing for her answer, so Lana raced onward. They passed the TSA security agent manning the exit. When they reached the sliding doors, Trey cupped her elbow and propelled her outside. Wind and snow hit her face, and he snagged her carry-on and double fisted their respective luggage as they walked toward the shuttle labeled Clayton St. Louis Airport Hotel.

"I called them. They were full." She'd called them first, because that's the hotel chain's renovations she'd been overseeing. The family-owned global chain rivaled Marriott and Hilton, or in Missouri, Drury Hotels. The front desk clerk had been sympathetic, but firm that the airport hotel was completely booked.

"I must have gotten the last room. It's a suite. It has a dividing, lockable bedroom door with its own hallway exit that will be perfectly safe. Or you can sleep in the hotel lobby. But we need to get on that shuttle before it can't make it back. Consider this one of your grand adventures."

Even sleeping in the lobby would be an improvement over sleeping at an empty airport gate. "Okay, I'm in."

Trey passed the bags to the driver, who stowed them in the rack. Lana plopped down onto one of the last two seats. When Trey sat, her thigh pressed against his and subsequent sensations sent danger signals that her sense of adventure decided to ignore.

The hotel was directly across Highway 70, and the shuttle discharged them underneath the protective portico before the driver parked the vehicle for the night. Lana knew a huge Missouri storm when she saw one. No one would be going anywhere tonight, but if MoDOT snowplow drivers like her father worked around the clock, the main highways would be clear sometime tomorrow morning. She followed Trey into the warm and welcoming lobby, where a line had formed before the front desk. Trey set his bags next to Lana. "Wait here."

He bypassed the crowd and approached a uniformed clerk who seemed to appear from nowhere. Trey returned with two small paper sleeves containing room keys. Lana blinked. She'd been living in Clayton Hotels for over a year and didn't rate that type of personal treatment. They hadn't even swiped his credit card for incidentals. "You must be important."

He was already lifting their luggage and walking toward the lift. "I'm a top-tier frequent guest whenever I come through town, so don't give it another thought. Did you want a digital key? I figured this was faster."

"This is fine, thanks." She clutched her tote before it slid off her shoulder.

Once inside the elevator, he pressed the packet to the sensor and pushed the twelfth-floor button. The doors slid closed. He passed her a paper packet. "Your key."

She palmed the plastic card he handed her. "Tell me how much I owe you so I can pay you back."

He leaned against the wall of the elevator, staying on the opposite side like a perfect gentleman. "Don't worry about it. My company paid. Pay it forward for someone else sometime in the future. That'll be enough."

Lana was skeptical. No one was ever this nice. "I don't know you from Adam and you're giving me a room. With no strings."

Big shoulders shrugged as if releasing tension. He tilted his neck from side to side but thankfully it didn't make one of those annoying cracks. "You seem surprised. Don't be. The room isn't costing me anything extra, and seriously, I have zero expectations. Work always comes first. Let me be the good guy for once. It's rare, so let me enjoy it."

She wasn't certain if he was joking. "Surely you're not always like that."

His gray-eyed gaze held hers through the reflective surface of the mirror. "Trust me. I'm a selfish workaholic who at least owns it. As much as I'd like to blame my ex for calling me a heartless iceman, I have to own that I made the mistake of proposing knowing that things were broken. We were ill-suited and I wasn't going to change my ways either. It's better for me to stay focused on business, on my goals and winning the prize. I don't have time for anything else."

"Including sightseeing."

"Exactly." The set of his jaw revealed his seriousness.

"All work and no play." She puckered her lips and shook her head, the thick strands slightly damp from the intense snow. "You travel alone and you never see the sights. That's sad."

"You said that before. The only thing I truly mind is eating alone."

Lana tilted her head. "I've never felt that way. I do it all the time."

His mouth edged downward. "Well, I don't." As if aware he was appearing formidable, he gave her a smile. "As such, I'd be honored if you'd join me for dinner before we go our separate ways. Unless the peanut M&M's were enough?"

Her stomach rumbled, and she laughed. "No, not even. Tell you what. I'll go with you if you let me buy dinner."

"I can agree to that."

"Then it's a date." Her face flamed. Where had that flirtation come from? "I didn't mean…"

His brow arched. "I got it. No worries. Just dinner. Because you're a good girl."

"Exactly." The way the words good girl had rolled off his tongue had made her want to be very, very bad. Her skin prickled with awareness. His close proximity made her body tingle the way it did before she rode a roller coaster. She knew the ride was going to be dangerous and thrilling, yet somehow, she also trusted it would be safe. Going on adventures was about enjoying the adrenaline rush. The elevator gave an imperceptible lurch when it reached their floor. The doors slid open. He motioned with his arm, indicating that she should go first. They stopped outside the door to her room. Trey set her suitcase by her feet.

"Dinner in twenty minutes? Is that enough time? Meet you downstairs?" he asked.

She wasn't sure she would ever be ready for dinner with a man like Trey, but why not? She never refused an opportunity, especially when it was safe to accept said opportunity and experience something new. Besides, she did need to eat. She waited until he'd moved to his own door before she pressed her card against the lock. He was already halfway in his room when she turned the handle after the green light blinked. "Trey?" He glanced back. "See you soon."

Edmund stepped into the living area of Room 1208. He shrugged out of his new wool overcoat and hung it in the closet so it could dry. Besides the foldout couch, the suite's living area had everything else he'd need: desk, TV, small dining area and full bathroom. He had his regular clothes in his carry-on; Peter's outfits had already been delivered to the Beaumont Grand. Edmund changed into a fresh shirt and a pair of dress pants—thankfully not too wrinkled. He'd put his toiletry bag in the bathroom and finished using the facilities when he heard a knock on the interior door. When he unlocked his side, Lana stepped through, and he drank her in. He found the fact she sincerely had no expectations of him so refreshing and unique. He wondered if that was part of her appeal, why she affected his libido so much.

She gave him a smile. "Hi. Sorry, my stomach said it didn't want to wait twenty minutes. I'm starving. Am I interrupting? Do you need more time?"

"No. I'm ready." He was extremely impressed that in a mere ten minutes, she'd brushed that fiery red hair, refreshed her rosy lip color and changed into flats, black jeans and a blue-and-black-striped crewneck sweater. Veronica would have needed hours and then still complained she didn't look right.

Edmund took a step back. He didn't want Lana to think he was expecting a hookup. Even if his sexual radar wanted to send out all the right signals and convince both of them otherwise. "Your room's satisfactory?"

"Yes. Thank you. Much better than the airport, but you should have put me out here. I didn't realize you didn't have your own bedroom."

"My mother raised a gentleman. The sofa bed's a queen, but it's fit for a king." Okay, that sounded lame, but not needing to be thinking about beds any longer, he opened the door leading into the hallway. "Shall we go?"

Downstairs, they found a line of people waiting for a table. "Looks like everyone had the same idea," Lana told him as they approached the hostess stand. She gave the woman a warm smile. "Two please. The name's Lana. How long is the wait?"

The hostess glanced up, her eyes widening as she recognized Edmund from his frequent stopping through St. Louis. However, one fast shake of his head served as an immediate warning not to say anything or acknowledge him.

"Reservation under Lana," Edmund confirmed, pleased when the hostess nodded. "Thank you."

"Of course," the hostess said. "It's at least a half hour, probably more like forty-five minutes. We're slammed because of the storm."

Normally Edmund didn't wait. Not at his hotels. Not at any restaurant in Portland. Not anywhere, really. Tonight, however, he was Trey, of no last name, with Lana, also of no last name. Unlike Hilton hotel ads, which lately featured Paris Hilton, the Clayton family had never made themselves the face of their brand. While his staff might recognize him, the travelers in his hotels shouldn't, especially as his viral breakup video hadn't been as popular in the Midwest as on the West Coast.

"That's fine," Lana said, not once losing her cheeriness, proving yet again how different she was from the women of Edmund's world. "As long as there's food, it's all good."

"Oh, there's plenty of food. No worries there." The hostess smiled, but Edmund could sense how nervous she was. Her hand shook slightly as she typed Lana's name into her computer. "You know, if you want, you could sit in the bar until a table opens. I see several available seats."

"That sounds great." Lana strode off, giving Edmund a great view of her backside. He paused before following and leaned toward the hostess. "No special favors. Make sure everyone understands not to call me Mr. Clayton tonight. Spread the word. Do it now."

"Yes, sir." The hostess summoned her assistant to the hostess stand and scurried off.

Edmund went after Lana. Deep down he knew he should tell Lana who he was. He promised himself that he'd tell her after dinner. Until then, he wanted to enjoy himself. Whenever women found out who he was, their attitudes changed. He liked that Lana was treating him like an everyday guy. Would she be as open and honest if she knew he owned the hotel? No one else was. They immediately wanted something.

He and Lana were having too much fun to ruin the evening now. They were sharing a meal, and he was enjoying being incognito. What was the harm if he came clean later?

Lana's bottom wiggled onto a bar stool, and Edmund slid onto the stool next to her. "What do you want to drink?"

She swiveled toward him. "I'm thinking a glass of red wine. You?"

The bartender hustled over, a huge smile on his face. "Good evening. How can I help you, Mis—"

Edmund interrupted him. "Hi, Bill. I'm Trey. This is Lana."

Bill, who'd tended bar for the past ten years at this establishment, recovered quickly. "Nice to meet you, Trey. And Lana." He placed two beer-themed coasters down on the polished wood. "What can I get the two of you?"

"May I see your wine list?" Lana asked. Then she turned to Trey. "Trey? What do you think? Wine? Something else?"

When Lana directed that power punch of a smile at him, wine didn't sound nearly strong enough. Straight bourbon wouldn't cut it either. "Wine list," he confirmed, his brain short-circuiting.

Sensing Edmund was deferring to Lana, Bill passed her the drink menu. Lana glanced at the wines and frowned. "I never know what to choose. I wish they had some of the Beaumont wines. Ever since Jack Clayton bought out Jamestown, the region has really been taking off. Oh, here's a Clayton vintage. It's a pinot noir."

She gave Edmund another one of those smiles that kept making him weak in the knees. What was it about her? "Does that sound good? Or are you more of a white wine guy?"

"The pinot noir is perfect. But the wine's on me," Edmund insisted.

"You can't keep picking up things," Lana protested. "I said I'm buying dinner."

"This isn't dinner," he pointed out. "Bill, wine on my tab."

"Yes, sir." Bill moved away.

Lana pouted and shook her head. "You're splitting hairs. That's not fair."

Edmund grinned. He liked teasing her. "Funny how that works."

"Fine. This time." Lana relaxed, and as their legs pressed against each other, he shifted before heat consumed him.

"If it helps your sensibilities, it's one bottle of wine. Two glasses each, paid for by my company. I won't even feel guilty if we don't finish the bottle. So allow me to stick it to them."

"In that case, why not? They are having you stuck here in a snowstorm." She tucked a glossy strand of hair behind her left ear. Edmund itched to set the lock free, but one invasion into her space already had his body abuzz. "I have to admit that I love adventure, but tonight seems truly surreal," she added.

Surreal described her impact on him. He never stepped out of his comfort zone, and certainly not with someone he'd just met. "As long as you don't think I'm one of those guys who buy women drinks because they know they're traveling alone."

Lana's response burst forth. "No, I know you're different. I hate that though. They always want something out of it, and it's annoying." She paused. Considered. "My gut says I can trust you, but my head wants to know exactly what you're getting out of this. Why are you doing all this for me?"

Why? Because for once, someone wasn't with him for what he could do for their career or social aspirations.

"I told you. I hate dining alone. That's the honest truth." He certainly wasn't lying about that. "Now, instead of eating room service, I'm enjoying the company of a beautiful woman for a few hours before we go our own ways like two ships in the night."

Another lame remark. He really was out of sorts tonight. She laughed and rolled her pretty amber eyes, but she didn't seem too upset by his awkwardness.

"Please. No need for false flattery. I am not that interesting. Especially when you consider that I've hit you with my luggage several times and chatted nonstop on a four-hour flight. That's more annoying than anything else."

"Don't sell yourself short," he told her.

"I'm not."

She was, but as she continued speaking, he let it go. "Ah, I know what your motive really is. You've adopted me like the stray kittens I used to bring home."

Hardly. Edmund wanted to kiss her. "I can guarantee you I don't think you're a stray kitten I found in the airport."

Her cute, perky nose wrinkled at the seriousness of his tone. "Are you married? I probably should have asked that hours ago. Just because you were engaged… I mean, you could have gone to Vegas."

Her babbling made her even cuter. "No. Never married. No intention of getting married."

Relief had her let her lower lip go with a soft pop. "I've had married men hit on me before. It's rather rude."

"Which pisses me off, as it reflects badly on the rest of us." Edmund's anger flared at the thought. "Cheating is one hundred percent wrong. Marriage is for life. All vows meant. Hence the failed engagement and my usual routine of eating dinner in my hotel room."

"I'm sorry if she cheated. It sounds like she did."

That had been a mere drop in the bucket and just one more way he'd been foolish. "Trust me, so was I. But at least I found out long before we walked down the aisle. We hadn't even picked a date."

"Sounds like we both had close escapes," Lana said.

"I'd agree with you there." When she didn't elaborate, Edmund contemplated what it was about Lana that made him share his past so willingly. Thankfully he saw Bill bringing their wine, a Clayton vintage from the Willamette Valley.

Edmund turned toward Lana and gripped his bent knees. "Before Bill gets here, let me tell you what I want besides a good meal and a decent night's sleep. I have an upcoming week from hell on that project I mentioned. It's unlike anything I've done before, and that makes me nervous. Tonight, I don't want to think about the future. Tonight, since we're snowed in and I can't get where I need to be, I want to forget the outside world exists. Instead of working twenty-four seven, I want to relax, drink some wine and enjoy conversation that isn't related to my business or my project. That's it. Good food and good company. Nothing more. Just two strangers killing time until we finish dinner and you lock yourself inside your room, alone." He drew a deep breath. "Sorry that came out so abruptly. But I meant it and wanted to clear the air."

"I appreciate your honesty. It sounds like a good plan that I can live with." Her trusting smile hit him like a punch in his gut, and he realized he didn't want to be locked in his room alone. He wanted her. Plain and simple. But he'd never once failed in being a gentleman. Tonight would not be an exception. Edmund did not do one-night stands.

"Your pinot." Bill held up the bottle for Edmund's inspection, and a few minutes later, after sampling, Edmund lifted his filled wineglass. "Here's to good food and even better conversation."

"To being snowbound," Lana added, clinking her glass to his before bringing it up for a sip. Her lips molded around the edge, and the way her throat moved made his groin ache. Around him, the noisy bar faded. She was the type who would steal a man's heart while he wasn't paying attention, although Edmund wasn't worried. He had no heart left to steal.

Chapter Three

The night was going far better than Lana had imagined. When she'd first realized that her family couldn't make it into St. Louis to pick her up, she'd panicked. Now she was almost to the bottom of her first glass of delicious wine, and a tingly warmth reached every pore. She and Trey still waited for a table, but Bill had dropped off an on-us, we're-sorry-for-the-wait appetizer sampler filled with potato skins, toasted ravioli, chicken wings and mozzarella sticks—traditional St. Louis favorites. She lifted one of the toasted ravioli squares, dipped it in marinara sauce and closed her eyes in appreciation as the flavor hit her tongue. Nowhere else toasted ravioli like St. Louis did.

"Good?" Trey asked.

She gave a contented shiver. When she opened her eyes, she found him watching her. "Try one. It's delicious. You don't find these anywhere else. You'd have thought T-ravs would have caught on nationwide. But no, this is a regional thing."

Trey took one of the fried ravioli squares, dipped it in the red sauce and bit into it. "Not bad."

"I know, right? I mean, who was the person that thought, hey, let's bread meat-filled ravioli and toss them in a deep fryer? I guess we can google the answer. But this food is to St. Louis as sweet tea is to the south. In the Midwest, you have to ask for sugar. Although it's always on the table here. Both real and fake. See?"

She pointed to the tiny container filled with colorful packets that rested behind the bar. She lifted her glass and studied the way the light reflected on the deep red wine. "Is it wrong that I love to travel? I mean, I can settle down later, right? I just want more." Her cheeks heated. Where had that admission come from? But she and Trey had been talking like this for hours, sharing things with each other that they'd admittedly never told anyone else. She'd even broken down and told him about Paris being the number one place she wanted to visit someday.

Trey set down some eaten-clean chicken bones. "There's nothing wrong with more. I excel at wanting more. Wanting more makes you ambitious. Why stop until you're satisfied?"

"What if you're never satisfied?" Lana voiced one of her greatest fears. She felt safe to do so, as she'd never see him again.

Trey licked spicy wing sauce off his fingertips, the movement making her watch his mouth. "Then you keep going until you are. There's nothing wrong with having ambition. More isn't always a bad thing."

"Sometimes I worry that it might be. Aren't there times when more is simply more?"

Trey sipped his wine. "Maybe. But you know that saying? If you're green you're growing? If you're ripe, you rot? I refuse to rot. I won't rest on my laurels. I like to solve business challenges. My personal life might be in shambles, but business is my forte. It's what I'm good at. Who I am. Why question that? Why change what works?"

"Because at the end of the night you and I sleep alone?" Lana felt the need to point out.

"Are you suggesting we sleep together?" A millisecond later he added a wicked wink, lightening the mood. "You know I'm joking, right?"

She laughed. "Of course. We said no hookups." Even though part of her wanted the exact opposite. She dipped another toasted ravioli square. "I think I'm nervous about being home and facing everyone. I shouldn't be, but what do I have to show for myself? I'm not married. I don't even have an apartment or house. My mom thinks I should be settled down, and I live out of a suitcase."

Trey lifted another chicken wing. "Those are false social constructs everyone else puts on you. What do you want?"

"Not sure yet, but I know that I didn't want to be in a small town forever. Maybe later, but not without seeing the world first. I'd been engaged to this guy I met in college, and I got dragged along with the wedding preparations."

Trey nodded. "I can understand that."

"Then I realized I was more in love with the idea of being married then with him. I wanted adventure. Excitement. Before I took this job, it was like I was watching my life from outside, and it was the most boring movie ever. I'm young. We don't live in our parents' world where people married early."

Trey wiped his mouth. "No, it's ours. We have options. Just think, had you gone through with the wedding, you wouldn't have been to the Empire State Building, or to whatever you saw in Pittsburgh." Then he remembered. "The Warhol Museum."

"Or here in a snowstorm with you," she pointed out.

He grinned, drawing her in with an innately sexy smile that made her weak at the knees. "Exactly." He saluted her with his wineglass, and Lana swore her toes tingled. "How'd I get so lucky?"

She laughed. "I was stranded and desperate and so were you."

"Ah, the real reason." His grin was wicked. The only word for it.

"I'm always honest. I'm not one to pull my punches." She grasped for some control over her desires.

He nodded his agreement. "As you shouldn't. I haven't known you long, but that's probably one of your strengths. It's a good one to have."

"Thanks. It's been fun getting to know you." One glass of wine had been like drinking truth serum. "My meals aren't usually this fun."

"Agreed. I'm enjoying myself. Do you know how rare that is? Very."

"Aww. That's sweet. Sad, but sweet." She bit into more ravioli to give herself a minute to think.

How long had it been since she'd been in the presence of a man even half Trey's caliber? He wore an open-collar dress shirt that accented a sexy, broad chest. Tailored slacks and loafers offered a casual yet classy vibe. With their bar stools swiveled toward each other, his legs wound between hers. His gray eyes darkened whenever he listened intently, which with her was all the time. She'd had plenty of men hitting on her during her travels, but Trey was different. "Where are you off to after this?" she asked.

"Once I finish this weeklong project, I'm headed back home to Portland. I grew up there, but I'm on the road most of the time, like you."

Lana's brow creased. "Dumb question, but if your company can afford a suite and this wine, why did it fly you in coach?"

"First class was already full. Last-minute change, remember?" He set more chicken bones on his appetizer plate.

His logical answer made her relax. She reached for a blue corn tortilla chip but didn't dip it. "I was glad to get on the flight. I'm off to either California or Arizona next. I haven't been to either, so I'm excited."

"More museums," he teased.

She laughed, same as she'd been doing most of the night. He was easy to talk to. Fun. She was having a good time. She dipped the chip and set it on the square white plate in front of her. "Of course. I collect pressed pennies. I've got four filled books. I need more."

He laughed. "And I'll be back to working my typical seventy-hour weeks."

He covered her hand. Heat powered through her. It would be silly to pretend otherwise. The two of them had chemistry. "I'm glad you were my seatmate. I find you fascinating. You're not jaded. You see life as a grand adventure. A brass ring to be seized. Another day in paradise is paradise, not a slogan full of irony. I appreciate that."

Was the room getting hotter? Lana glanced around. Maybe the hotel had turned up the heat since it was snowing outside. Her skin cooled when he withdrew his hand. "I'm exactly what you see," she protested.

Those gray eyes studied her over the rim of his wineglass. "Which makes you the realest woman of my acquaintance."

"If true, that's sad. Oh, I keep using that word. It's rude. I should stop. I'm sorry." She shoved the chip in her mouth so she didn't say anything more.

Unoffended, he shrugged. "I'll admit it. Work is my real love. The rest? They all want something from me, including my family. Even my sister, who's my best friend. Since I'd do anything for her, here I am."

"Everyone should be friends with their siblings. It was one of the reasons I ran through the airport to be there for my brother's birthday. The party will be tomorrow now. I'm glad I'm in state and not relying on getting a flight. But I understand what you mean. Being on the road all the time sort of keeps you from having deep friendships. I wouldn't consider myself a loner though, more a nomad."

"A nomad. That's a good word. There's nothing wrong with wanting to chase your dreams. Ultimately, you're the one who's responsible for your happiness."

His words hit home, and Lana changed the subject by asking, "Should we go check on our table?" That was safer than her sudden desire to close the gap and kiss him, which was not a good idea. She shouldn't feel this way about someone she'd just met.

Trey didn't seem inclined to move. He reached for another chicken wing. "They won't forget us. Besides, I'm in no rush to go back upstairs. I'll just get on my computer and work."

"No work tonight, remember? Just play." There was a Freudian slip for the ages. He'd flustered her. Turned her into something needy. "Oh, you know what I meant. Because that's what you said. Or meant, yourself." Yes, it had definitely gotten hotter in here.

"Exactly." His deep, timbral voice washed over her, making those anticipatory little tingles roar to life. Her nerve endings powered up to high voltage like she'd had a caffeinated energy drink. No man had impacted her quite like this. In days gone by, he'd have been a conqueror. Lana noted that he'd already attracted the attention of every woman sitting at the bar. Several stared openly as if they'd like Trey for their main course instead of the food in front of them.

Lana couldn't blame them. The way Trey's lips wrapped around a wineglass should be illegal. If she leaned forward, she could taste his mouth for herself. She hadn't misread any signals. He wasn't hitting on her. Flirting, yes. But trying for a hookup, no. He'd respect her boundaries. However, should she want more, it was clear he'd be willing. The choice was hers to make. The ball was in her court, so to speak.

Wine, mixed with low barometric pressure, addled her sensible brain and short-circuited her common sense. She grabbed for her phone and swiped. The weather was always a safe topic, right? "Six inches of snow already on the ground with more coming down. The weather forecasters are calling it a snowpocalypse, a repeat of last March."

"Good thing we're in here and safe," he said.

Safe being a relative term. The blustery storm was nonexistent inside the darkened bar. However, she was inches away from the sexiest man alive and fighting the urge to become one of those wanton, eager women, the kind who would find some excuse to take her seat should Lana leave it. The rebellious part of her nature clamored, petitioning her sensible brain to throw caution to the wind. *Come on,* it begged. *Taste the forbidden.* Experience a man way out of her league. Wasn't that the fantasy? For one moment, to let herself go and say to hell with the consequences? How many romances had she read with that exact premise? Time to slow down before she staked a claim and did something stupid. They'd set parameters for a reason. Tonight was not about a hookup. It was dinner. That's all it could be.

Two hours and one delicious steak and seafood meal later, Lana felt like she and Trey were old friends. Perhaps that's why she followed him into the living area of the suite instead of closing her bedroom door and checking email.

The living area had a complete set of furniture, including a love seat, an arm chair and a queen-size sofa bed that remained closed. She frowned. "Shouldn't housekeeping have opened that?"

"They will when I call. I didn't want you to think I was trying to get you into bed. I thought you might like to watch a movie or something. If not, I'll just say good-night and work."

"It is still kind of early. I could watch a movie." Her gut told her she was safe with him, and her gut had never been wrong. Well, maybe about saying yes to marriage with her now ex—but that really hadn't been a gut decision. That had been going against her gut, actually.

She walked to the window and peered at the parking lot.

Outside, snow glittered and blanketed everything in a pristine layer of thick white, draping the streetlights so they glowed softly. The city slept—there was nothing to be done until the storm passed. Trey moved to stand a few inches to her left. She didn't mind.

"There's something about untouched snow," she told him. "Out in Beaumont, the world becomes mythical. Miles of unbroken whiteness. It's calming. Silent. Almost magical. When the historic streets get covered, even being in town is special. Not that I want to go back and live there. I didn't do well in school, and I..."

Trey stopped her. "Do grades really matter in anything besides restaurant health inspections or meat? The answer is no. You've done well. You're a successful career woman. Focus on that."

Warmth spread through her. "You're good for my ego."

"You're worth the compliments."

Side by side, they watched the snow fall. Highway 70 was

a sheet of white, making the world seem a winter wonderland of possibility.

As Trey stood about half a foot taller than her, she leaned back to study him. Magnetic poles couldn't have more pull. Amber-colored eyes met gray, and a telepathic understanding passed between them.

Trey shifted. "Don't look at me like that. I meant what I said earlier. I have no expectations. I'm not a guy with a woman in every city he travels. Quite the opposite. No one since the ex."

Which he'd told her had been six months ago. "Same. Which is why I think I'd like you to kiss me, if doing so wouldn't make me one of those women who want things from you. Or if kissing me would violate your code of ethics."

"To hell with it. I can deny you nothing. You had me at peanut M&M's. Take whatever you want."

His mouth found hers in the softest, most tentative, feathery touch. He drew back, those fathomless gray pools questioning, wondering…waiting. Then he put his forehead against hers. "It's important that you know I didn't bring you here for this."

"I know. That's why this is happening." She appreciated his honesty, just as she appreciated the fact she was on the adventure of a lifetime. She'd left behind an ex-fiancé who'd wanted her to settle down and do nothing but have babies—a man whose idea of a vacation meant boating on Lake of the Ozarks and drinking himself to oblivion in Party Cove. He'd gotten someone pregnant a month after Lana had called things off, and she'd left town a week after his subsequent courthouse nuptials and enough sympathetic glances from townspeople to last a lifetime.

Was it wrong to grab the brass ring just this once? Was

it wrong to want more? She wanted Paris. Rome. Venice. The world. She'd taken the first steps by accepting this job, which had brought her here, to this moment, where she was snowed in with a hunky, delicious man whose one kiss predicted a night that would rock her world off its axis. His kisses could wipe the slate clean, erasing her previous mistakes. He'd be the second man she'd ever taken to bed, the other one her ex-fiancé. Shouldn't she see what the sexual fuss was actually about?

She put her hands on each side of his face, his five o'clock shadow rich beneath her fingers. "How about you kiss me again and we'll see where things lead? Shall we break our rules this once?"

"If at any time you say no, we're stopping. I'll respect your wishes."

She knew he would. "Perfect. Now kiss me."

As Trey brought his mouth to hers, she threw herself over the cliff. Even after the snowplows cleared the way for tomorrow's reality, the mystery of who he was wouldn't matter. Tonight, she'd lose herself in the only thing a man like Trey could promise—the pleasure and memory of his lovemaking.

One tiny touch sent powerful, tantalizing tingles teasing their way to her toes. She quivered, her body ready and willing. The decision of how far to go was hers. It was evident in the way he held himself—tightly bound—ever the gentleman, refusing to cross the line and afraid he already had. They may not have intended to end up in bed, but now she could think of nothing else.

Her fingers traced a hard jawline. She caressed full lips with her index and middle fingers, memorizing every ridge, until he groaned and drew one of the digits inside. "Lana."

She enjoyed the way he murmured her name, rediscovering the womanly power she'd long ago thought lost. His shudder indicated he held himself on the tautest of strings. She respected him more for his restraint. His tongue licked her fingertip.

She closed the remaining gap and threaded her left hand into his wavy brown hair, the strands like fine silk. She captured his lips, sending waterfalls of pleasure spreading from head to toe. She'd never thought that cliché of "time stood still" could be real, but she swore time froze. Sound muted. The world reduced to a pinpoint.

She felt the thump of his heart, inhaled his musky after-shave, heard the sharp hiss of his breath and sensed the full size of him pressed against her stomach. Their kiss consumed everything in its path, including all doubts, until, overwhelmed by the new sensations, she slid her mouth from his. A sense of loss immediately intruded, and wanting to reconnect, she touched her lips to his jaw and whispered against his cheek. "The movie can wait. I can't. As long as you respect me in the morning."

"I wouldn't dream of doing otherwise." His lips slid along her neck in long, delightful nibbles before he scooped her into his arms and carried her into her bedroom. He sat beside her, cupped the back of her head and brought his mouth back to hers.

He palmed her breast, and she ceded the lead. His hand pushed the soft cashmere fabric of her sweater aside. He slid fingers underneath her bra and circled, making her brain short-circuit. If one touch sent this much heat pooling, tonight would be incredible.

"You are so beautiful, and before you question that, I never say anything I don't mean." Trey pressed a kiss to her skin and she shuddered.

She leaned against the pillow as his free hand tugged at

the hem of her shirt. "Let's get this out of the way." He fingered a bra strap. "Do you know what this black lace has done to me all day? Teasing me right here…"

He pressed the valley between her breasts before he pushed aside the lace and captured her nipple with his tongue. Her eyes closed as ripple after ripple grew into intense pleasurable waves. She reached for him, but he deferred. "Let me touch you."

Touch he did, and overcome by sensation, Lana could do nothing but follow his directive of, "Let go, beautiful." She fisted the bedding as he gave her the best orgasm of her life.

Sated but desiring more, she helped him shed his clothes. He truly was magnificent, tall and perfectly proportioned. All those silly romantic clichés of coming home and being complete felt totally appropriate, but suddenly they weren't enough, for no words could describe the dizzying sensations overpowering her senses as he lifted her to the sky and beyond.

"Tell me what you like."

"*This*. Everything." Her thoughts frazzled when she splintered and saw stars. Maybe heaven. Her whole body sang. Shook. Trembled. Her fingertips ran along his back until they both drifted down and momentarily held each other tight.

"Be right back." Trey wiped her forehead with his hand, kissed her cheek and climbed out of bed.

Trey left the bedroom to remove the condom and do his business in the living area bathroom. The kindness touched her, as it left her bathroom free for her own use. She'd climbed back under the covers by the time he'd returned, still gloriously naked. He lifted the sheet and cradled her to him as he dropped kisses on her neck. "That was incredible."

"It was." Shaken by exactly how good, and not wanting to examine why the sex had been so transcendent, she shifted her hand lower. Morning would arrive soon enough, and being with her second ever lover had proven she'd been right to leave home. Life was meant to be lived. To be explored and reveled. Enjoyed.

For one night, she could do things she would never do again. Trey would be a pleasurable pit stop on her grand adventure, and she wanted everything he could show her. Years later, tonight would be nothing but a fond memory, a special, secretive moment to smile over. This was all they could be, would be. The night was just getting started, and she refused to waste a single minute of the brief time they had left.

It had been a glorious evening. Mind-blowing. The type of sexual awakening that made Edmund question everything, including all the rules he'd set and his vision for the future. For one epic night, he'd been free to be himself. Lana—she'd been perfection.

Edmund rolled over, already knowing he was alone. He'd heard the exterior door open and close several hours ago, the soft click and subsequent thud rousing him from a deep sleep. By the time he'd registered the noise, it had been too late to stop her from sneaking out. Besides, after going viral with Veronica, his one-bitten, twice-shy self was not about to rush after Lana, as giving the security cameras something fun to capture was not an option. *Edmund Clayton runs naked through his hotel*—he could picture the headlines now. No matter how loyal his employees, things leaked.

Despite his initial disappointment, her leaving was for the best. His waking alone saved them from having one of those awkward goodbye conversations. She'd made the choice for them, and deep down he was grateful.

But for a short moment he threw his arm over his eyes, as if the tiny hints of sunlight creating slivers around the heavy blackout curtains could actually harm his vision. He'd closed the drapes sometime in the early hours so that he and Lana could catch at least an hour or two of real sleep. Every time they'd tried, one of them had initiated something else.

Facing the inevitable fact that it was probably far later in the day than he liked, he reached for his phone, which he'd left charging on the bedside table. Flipping it over, he groaned. He'd slept until almost noon and had at least sixteen messages and countless other notifications. He needed to get out of bed, shower and shave, scrounge some food and pick up the rental car. He rose, pushed aside the curtain and held up his arm to ward off bright winter sunlight streaming in.

In the parking lot below, a plow piled snow high. St. Louis was digging out. He sent a text, letting Lachlan know he'd arrived in St. Louis and would be on the way to the Beaumont Grand soon. Lachlan and his two cameramen had been in Beaumont since last week. They'd filmed another candidate, one who was a paid actor. That fake week of production was part of an elaborate ruse to hide Edmund's true identity and make his appearance as Peter Waggoner more credible to those with whom he'd work.

To make things even more realistic and help hide his identity, Edmund Clayton would also be in town. He'd be there to oversee the final preparations of the Chateau, one of his first of several trips before its late-March soft opening. He'd make enough appearances as himself to reduce any doubts he and Peter might be the same.

Edmund did have work to do. The Chateau's official grand opening gala occurred the second weekend of April, and because travel writers had dubbed the Chateau the latest "it destination," the boutique hotel was already completely booked for the months of May and June. The Grand would handle any guest overflow. However, the Grand was at 90 percent occupancy with those arriving to play spring golf.

Having a visible Clayton Holdings VP created a more realistic smoke screen—even if Edmund and Peter were never in the same place at the same time. Edmund still didn't buy the fact that someone wouldn't put two and two together and recognize him at some point, but then again, he'd be even more disguised as Peter, including wearing the mouth partial that changed his voice.

And it was too late to tell Lana who he was. He'd never see her again. She was visiting her parents in Beaumont and then heading back on the road to destinations unknown. What would it be like to have that type of freedom? To simply go where the job took you, have no responsibilities beyond that, and have a chance to stop and see the sights? When you had numbers behind your name, like he and his cousin Jack did, you had a responsibility to live up to that legacy. To achieve greatness. He vowed that someday his son—number IV—wouldn't feel so much pressure.

Jack had carved out his own path. However, before Edmund could stray down that dangerous path and imagine that he might be able to somehow do the same, he shoved that thought back into Pandora's box and closed the lid tight. Jack's defection had opened the door to Edmund's ascension. He couldn't let one night of lust and admittedly great sex throw him off his game. The stakes were too high. He and Lana had both understood that from the moment they'd shared their first kiss. One night. Nothing more.

He refused to accept that something inside himself had fundamentally shifted. Edmund's role was to secure the purchase of the Van Horn hotel group, not wonder if he might, by some chance, run into her again.

Edmund ordered a room service breakfast, had the concierge check on the roads and his rental and began answering the texts and emails he'd ignored during the blissful time he'd been with Lana. He'd let work slide long enough, as evidenced from a text from his sister: Snow didn't interfere too much, did it? We can't let anything get in the way of winning.

He didn't tell Eva about last night and his straying-from-normal behavior. He might eventually, but for now he wanted the night to remain his memory alone. He sent back a vague text. Yeah. Headed out soon. Roads are already cleared.

Her reply came quickly. You got this.

He had to, because Edmund did not fail. His workaholic nature refused to consider that he would, and certainly not to Reginald Justus. Edmund had a grueling week ahead and a competition to win, but he *would* win. Of that there was no doubt. Time to return to the real world.

Chapter Four

She'd never left a man sleeping before. Not even her ex-fiancé. Crawling out of the bed of some man she'd met on an airplane and whose last name she didn't know—and then leaving him alone in his hotel room—was definitely a first. And something she didn't plan on repeating. This hadn't been on her bucket list, but now she could say she'd checked off "Have an incredible one-night stand."

"Lana, you seem a million miles away," her mom chided, jolting Lana from her thoughts and from leaning on the elbow she'd propped on the ancient kitchen table.

"Just tired." Not necessarily a lie. She and Trey had slept very little, their time occupied by other, more pleasurable endeavors.

"I'm sure the anxiety of not knowing if you'd get home had something to do with that," her mom said. "But your dad drove into St. Louis the minute his shift finished. He didn't even go home first."

"I already told him how much I appreciated that."

After manning a snowplow all night, her dad had arrived at the hotel in his pickup truck, one also outfitted with a plow and chains. He'd even brought a thermos of hot coffee. Now he napped on the ten-year-old living room couch while her mom bustled about a kitchen not updated since Lana was in middle school. Home was a place where little changed. Sure, there was a new stove and microwave. New carpet in a living room used only when company visited. Her dad had shoveled off the deck—the floorboards and joists replaced last year. The house itself was over one hundred years old, and radiators hissed and a fire crackled in the hearth near where her dad dozed. The pumpkin bread baking in the oven filled the space with a spiced cinnamon scent.

She'd missed this. Even missed Beaumont, at least a little. Her family lived three blocks west of historic Main Street, and because the plows might damage the cobblestones, even after clearing, the streets retained a thin layer of snow. On the way home, her dad had given her a tour of downtown. Not much had changed from the last time she'd been in town, although it seemed everything had.

The outside of the historic buildings might remain the same, but the occupants had changed. Instead of a college bar, there was a community makerspace. South Main now boasted a self-serve wine bar. Several new stores had opened. The historic inn the Bien family owned featured shamrock wreaths on the door. Mrs. Thornburg's soap and sundries shop was right next door. Lana's parents had attended Luke Thornburg's wedding to his childhood sweetheart, Shelby Bien, as had the rest of the town.

So many weddings, her mom had told her via texts and emails. Sierra James had married Jack Clayton, and Sierra's sister Zoe had married Nick Reilly less than two years later. Lana had been in elementary school at the same time as Shelby, Sierra and Zoe, but they'd been a few years ahead. Despite this, Lana's mom had kept her abreast of town gossip and how Sierra and Zoe's husbands had settled in Beaumont, and how Beaumont had maintained its charm and small-town feel even as the town drew more and more tourists lured by the changes Clayton Holdings had made. Her mom had also stressed how nice Beaumont was to settle down in. Raise a family.

Hint. Hint.

Even if the words had never been spoken directly, Lana had heard them and the guilt grew. Her parents had never understood her wanderlust or her need to get out of town, or why she never popped in beyond a day or two here or there.

Her mom removed the Bundt pan from the oven, the steam from the pumpkin bread wafting upward. "That smells good," Lana complimented. She'd never found a place that served pumpkin bread as good as her mother's.

"Is that ready?" Still wearing flannel pajama pants despite it being afternoon, Ryan's huge bare feet padded into the kitchen. Her six-foot-three brother had slept until after two. He pointed to the pan and rubbed his stomach. "Can I have some?"

"Not until dinner. It has to cool." Her mom set the pan on a rack.

"That's fine. I'll wait." Ryan grabbed two chocolate chip cookies from the honeycomb-shaped jar Lana had found last year in Atlanta and shipped home as a Mother's Day gift.

"Eat something real," her mom called after him. His mouth full of cookie, Ryan gave a backhand wave as he left the room. "Teenagers." Her mom added a teasing roll of her eyes.

"I guess." Lana had never been one to sleep in. Even after a long day on the road, she'd rise early. Be ready to go. It was one reason why she'd been able to wake and leave Trey's bed.

"When's Kyle's next game?" she asked.

Her mom opened the dishwasher and added a few baking tools. "Tuesday night. The snow should be gone by then."

"Aren't his games usually on Friday nights?" She remembered how fun Friday night football and basketball games had been when she'd been in high school.

Her mom opened a refrigerator covered with magnets documenting Lana's travels. "Some are. The rest can be whenever. Over Christmas he played in a tournament in downtown St. Louis. It was four or five games."

"That's an intense schedule for a high school kid."

Her mom's expression grew dreamy. "He loves it. You should see the coaching emails. And the letters and phone calls he gets from people wanting him to consider their school. It's unbelievable. He's got the athletics and the grades. We're constantly going through the offers. He should have a full ride somewhere."

"That's great." Lana had been a B student at best. Despite going to a local four-year college, she'd never earned a bachelor's degree. With a wedding to plan and promising herself she'd get back to finishing her degree, she'd left college with a semester to go. Then once her engagement had ended, she'd left to see the world. She knew her parents loved her, but she'd never made them as excited as they clearly were with Ryan and his prospects. Lana brought her empty glass over to the sink. "You're sure there's nothing I can help you with?" She didn't want to feel like a dead weight.

Her mom made a shooing motion and took the glass from Lana's hand. "I got it. Go relax. Get a nap before everyone gets here. We said five, but you know that Grandma and Grandpapa will be at least a half hour early because they want to see you."

"Okay." What else was there to say? Besides reading and touring museums, Lana didn't have hobbies. She didn't golf. She didn't garden. She liked cooking, but when you lived out of a suitcase, that wasn't an option. She'd tried cross-stitching and knitting and failed at each. The adventure of traveling was seeing the sights, but at night, back in her hotel room, she watched movies or read.

She felt like a guest in her childhood home. Most of her possessions, those she still owned post-breakup, were in three plastic storage tubs in the basement. The room she'd sleep in tonight didn't look anything like when she'd decorated it with celebrity posters and framed pictures of friends.

She pulled her phone from her front pocket and checked her email. Her boss had emailed her and cc'd the hotel manager. Seemed that Cederberg Interiors had joined Clayton Hotels for one of those reality TV competitions. Wendy, her boss, had promised that filming shouldn't be a distraction. She'd also written that Lana should let the hotel manager know if filming the show became problematic.

Lana shoved her phone into the back pocket of her jeans. She climbed the stairs to the second floor, where she could hear background music coming from a video game Ryan was playing. She raised her hand to knock on his closed door but changed her mind. No sense in bothering him while he was busy. She didn't play video games. Never really understood how people could sit in front of a TV all day and shoot at aliens. She also couldn't talk to him about college life since she'd never lived in a dorm.

She loved her family. Knew they loved her. But being home showed that she didn't have much in common with them at this juncture. Her mom wouldn't have had a one-night stand. She felt like she'd let them down. First with throwing away her studies and then with her choice of fiancé. At least Ryan would fulfill their collegiate dreams. As for Lana, she'd get back on the road where the next adventure was only a new city away.

* * *

Monday morning, after a long evening spent trying to explain to her grandmother why she loved traveling and why she wasn't married, Lana strode into the Beaumont Grand Hotel bright and early. If it weren't for the eight inches of snow covering the ground, she could almost believe the storm had never happened. The main roads were clear and dry, and her brother had groused that no school had been canceled.

"Tough break," Lana's mom told Ryan before pressuring Lana one more time to stay at home for the duration of her work on the Chateau. "We'd love it if you were here. Can't you say?"

"No. It's easier for me to stay on-site. And it might snow more." However, she'd promised to visit several more times, and yes, she had Ryan's Tuesday night high school basketball game on her calendar and promised not to miss it.

She knew her mom didn't understand, but the moment Lana stepped up to a front desk decorated with fresh flowers and friendly, welcoming smiles, some of her stress dropped. Was she running away? Absolutely. But it was far easier to stay on-site and be able to immediately address any problems that might arise. Especially as, in this case, she'd drive a heated utility vehicle each morning about a quarter mile to the Chateau. In the summer, most of the staff would use golf carts to traverse the service road between the two hotels, but because it was winter, she'd use one of the maintenance vehicles: a side-by-side with HVAC.

"Nice to have you with us," the front desk clerk said as she passed over Lana's keys, completing what had been perfect check-in service. "You have some packages, Ms. Winchester. Shall I get them for you?"

"I'll pick them up in a few minutes. I'm going upstairs

first." The contents, which were mainly picture hanging supplies and small containers of spackle, needed to go with her to the Chateau. Lana took a smooth elevator ride to the fourth floor. She wheeled her suitcase into a posh guest room and stared. If this was a regular room, what did the rest look like? Unlike Saturday night's stay in an upscale airport hotel designed to make business travelers' lives easy, the Beaumont Grand radiated understated elegance. Her bed had bolsters, for goodness' sake. The hotel's decor certainly created an environment that urged guests to indulge in the lap of luxury.

Opened last year as a key part of Clayton Holdings' comprehensive plan for the revitalization of Beaumont County, the six-story Grand boasted large rooms featuring huge windows overlooking either the golf course or the surrounding woods. With full banquet facilities and meeting rooms, indoor and outdoor pools, a world-class spa she hoped to try but most likely wouldn't have time for, and an exclusive fine dining restaurant, a visitor never needed to leave the grounds.

However, if they chose to leave, the Grand chauffeured guests in a bright red trolley to Clayton Holdings' six wineries. A complimentary bike rental meant guests could cycle the Katy Trail, a rail-to-trail state park that stretched across most of Missouri. She'd once ridden twenty-five miles with her friends, had lunch in a nearby town, and then cycled back. For those guests wanting private transportation options but not wanting to use rideshare apps, the hotel had a fleet of limos and town cars.

Lana set her suitcase on the luggage rack. Her room overlooked the third green, not that the golf course was visible under a blanket of snow already sprinkled with animal tracks. Deer, most likely.

Lana glanced at the bedside clock and checked her watch. The clock was five minutes fast, meaning she had enough time to unpack. Toiletries went onto the bathroom sink. Some clothes moved to hangers while others remained in her carry-on. Lana never put anything in the drawers—she'd learned that lesson the hard way after leaving her t-shirts behind in Milwaukee. She swapped snow boots for steel toed. For this particular job she was performing quality control over the initial installation of furniture and decor, instead of a room refresh or remodel.

She couldn't wait to see the Chateau. As a boutique hotel, it promised its guests an even more upscale luxurious experience than the Grand, and the Grand had spared no expense. If she weren't working here, there would be no way she could afford ti stay one night, much less a week or more.

On a normal day, she'd leave via the employee entrance, but this morning she made an exception to retrieve her packages. Before she reached the front desk, Mr. Smith, the sixty-something manager, greeted her. Mr. Smith would be moving to the Chateau as general manager, and he currently divided his time between the two hotels. "Good morning, Ms. Winchester. The valet is retrieving your UTV. Do you have a minute?"

Lana paused. Mr. Smith was buttoned up in a blue suit jacket, his white shirt pressed and topped with a yellow polka-dot bow tie. "Of course. How can I help you?"

"Did you see my email?" Seeing her frown, he pushed on. "The one I sent last night? I know it's a rather unusual request, but like I indicated, we had a television crew filming last week, and they'll continue this week. The decision to approve the filming came from Ms. Eva Clayton herself."

Now she understood what he meant. The show. "Yes, I read your email, and it's fine. I'll work around whatever is happening." She glanced toward the door. If she didn't get going, she'd be late. She believed supervisors should lead by example. As she still needed to load the boxes into the UTV, she worked to extricate herself. "I signed off on the production specs. I'm fully up on the details."

Mr. Smith peered through his wire frames. "I personally want to stress how important this is. The hotel must look good. It's one of those reality shows where they help a down-on-their-luck person get a new job. They teach them new skills or something like that."

"I don't really watch TV. Well, Cardinals baseball. A few movies." Actually, far too many movies. She frowned as a thought occurred. "This isn't one of those undercover boss shows, is it?"

Mr. Smith appeared suitably horrified, and his face reddened. "Do you think Edmund Clayton is the type to go undercover? You may see him around, as he's in town for business. The opening of the Chateau must be impeccable. I won't be satisfied with anything less."

"Of course. I can guarantee it will be." She could understand Mr. Smith wanting to protect his job. When open, the Chateau would be Clayton Holdings' flagship property in Missouri. And Jack Clayton now lived here. While she'd met Jack once, years ago, she'd never run into his cousin Edmund. Why should she have? He hadn't been promoted to VP until recently.

She worked to reassure the manager. "As long as the camera crew stays out of my way and the job candidates remain on task, everything should be fine. But they cannot create a distraction, because if my crew gets behind, then Clayton's paying overtime. Increased costs will definitely not make any of the Claytons happy. Mrs. Cederberg agreed we could add the new hire, Peter, to the mattress installation crew since you had nothing available at the Grand." Lana checked her watch again. "Nothing will go wrong on my watch."

His Adam's apple bobbed. "That's all I ask. I'll have the bellman load your boxes."

"I'd appreciate that." Lana went outside where a valet waited with the utility vehicle. Because of its bigger tires and stronger construction, the side-by-side was more rugged than a golf cart. Lana drove the short distance down a cleared service path to the Chateau, the vehicle making short work of any residual snow and puddles. Even though Lana had seen pictures of the exterior of the hotel, as she rounded a curve, she gasped. Photos didn't do the structure justice. In a nod to Beaumont's French settler roots, the Chateau's exterior features had been inspired by French castles such as Versailles, Fontainebleau and Chambord.

The Chateau was certainly not as large as Versailles's twenty-three hundred rooms or Fontainebleau's fifteen hundred. In terms of scale, Clayton's Chateau more resembled Vanderbilt's Biltmore, located in North Carolina. The Biltmore, another Renaissance-inspired landmark, had forty-three bedrooms. Clayton's Chateau had thirty-seven, with the smallest the size of a junior suite.

Lana parked, and one of her crew came to unload the boxes. She entered through the back construction entrance, but couldn't resist taking time to take a peek at the ornate foyer and common rooms that would greet guests upon their arrival. The public spaces were a gorgeous testament to the beauty and grace Clayton Holdings had created. In several weeks, the place would be full of travelers coming to enjoy the last of winter in Missouri's premier wine region. They'd stay in luxurious lodgings designed to feel like they were stepping into a private home, not a hotel.

Lana greeted one of the architects before taking the freight elevator to the top floor. After she stepped out, she pushed through a service door and entered a hotel corridor filled with chaos.

"What the…" She bit back the expletive. Towering lights shone bright everywhere. Her workers seemed starstruck being in the presence of two cameramen, and it wasn't even 8:35 a.m. What would the rest of the day be like? She needed to get her crew moving.

Where was the construction project manager? Or Keith, the Cederberg Interiors foreman? She dodged a plastic-wrapped box spring going by and did a tiny who's-going-which-way dance with someone carrying artwork. The sound of drills, hammers and tearing plastic also added to the cacophony. "Am I being filmed?" someone called.

"They don't care about you," someone else yelled.

To avoid being hit by a passing armchair, Lana ducked into the bathroom of Room 25. This spacious spa-like retreat contained an earth-tone walk-in shower with an oversize rainwater showerhead. Other amenities included an extra-large, high-end marble countertop with a seamless inset sink. Minus the final cleaning and placement of towels and toiletries, everything gleamed. Figuring the coast was clear, she stepped out, only to hear a shout. "Hey, careful!"

"Wha—ow!" The corner of a mattress clipped her arm, and she jerked back as the king-size mattress tumbled, blocking the door and her escape. Her tote bag slipped from her shoulder and yanked her arm. While the bag hit the floor, she caught it before any of the contents rolled out.

"You okay?" a voice called through the sliver of open space near the top of the doorframe.

"Yeah." She brushed some lint off her jeans and Henley. She rubbed her arm to stop it from throbbing. She reached for her tote bag and checked to ensure her iPad wasn't damaged. It had survived better than her pride.

"What happened?" someone called.

"New guy tried to kill the lady supe," the same, younger voice said. Then he added, "Dude, you have to hold up your end or this isn't going to work out. You don't look that out of shape. It's a mattress. Sheesh. Get it together."

Lana didn't hear the second muffled answer as the mattress shifted and moved into the room, freeing the opening to the bathroom. She began to step out, but froze as a man carrying a video camera charged past.

"Are you kidding me?" She gripped her iPad to her chest as she tried to get out of the way. So much for safety first. "Really? What the heck? This is a work zone!"

She inched around the bathroom door frame, hesitated, but when no one else seemed inclined to crash into her, she stepped into the room.

And saw what the commotion was about.

A huge man standing at least six foot four used a box cutter to slice and remove the outer wrapping of plastic from the mattress that had clipped her. Like the rest of the crew, the huge man wore blue jeans, an orange t-shirt emblazoned with the words Cederberg Interiors, and a long-sleeve flannel partially buttoned on top of the tee. As his surprised gaze locked on to hers, she felt a start of recognition, but she knew she'd never seen those brown eyes before. He wore rectangular black plastic glasses. His hair was shaggy blond and bowl cut, and he had a thick mustache and soul patch surrounding lips that protruded slightly, as if he'd needed braces as a kid but hadn't gotten them. The mattress wobbled before dropping onto the bed with a crooked thud. The man yanked it straight. Then his gaze found hers, his eyes widened, and Lana felt a sense of awareness through her from head to toe. Which was impossible. She'd never seen him before. She wouldn't have forgotten him.

"Here you are." Keith, Cederberg's job foreman, appeared behind Lana. A married man with two grown kids around her age, Lana considered him her work dad. He'd shown her the ropes when she'd started and watched out for her ever since. "I see you've met Peter Waggoner, the TV show's latest job candidate."

"Met him, no. Been almost knocked over by a passing mattress he carried, yes."

"Yeah, that wasn't good," Keith said.

"He's a bit rough," Lana noted as Peter gathered up the plastic.

"Understatement of the year." Keith turned, and Lana followed him into the corridor. Various hotel room doors stood open as Cederberg crew members moved furniture in and packaging out.

"What's his deal anyway?" Lana asked. "Aren't they supposed to give him a makeover? That mustache can be seen from space. It's almost as big as your beard."

Keith laughed and automatically touched the silver-streaked beard that reached his collarbones. He currently wore it braided. "Maybe they already did. I don't care about his looks as much as I do the fact that he's not very competent at performing basic manual labor tasks."

"King-size mattresses are awkward, and we *are* using California kings."

Keith scoffed. "Not that awkward. He's been on shift since eight, and he's a mess. At least the last guy had some semblance of a clue. Not much, but far more than this dude."

"He'll get better."

Keith rubbed the back of his neck and came away with drywall dust on his palm. "You always see the best in everyone. Some people are simply incompetent. Trust me, I can size up someone in an instant, and he's one of those."

Lana always protected the underdog. "I'm giving him the benefit of the doubt, as Mrs. Cederberg once gave me. You too."

"Yeah, but I could tell that you had heart. He's on reality TV. That stuff is always fake. Rigged. Have you seen the producer yet? He's a jerk."

Lana tried to keep the peace. "Well, we have to deal with it and find a workaround. Before I drove over here, Mr. Smith emphasized how they want the candidate to do well. The hotel will get great exposure from the show, as will our boss. Besides, you have to be desperate to go on a TV show to get a job, especially when you can't do it very well."

"Not when it's also a competition for a hundred thousand dollars. It's ridiculous. Last guy didn't want to get his manicure dirty. Complained when he broke a nail." Keith held up fingernails that already had dirt under them. "What were the Claytons and Mrs. Cederberg thinking, allowing this disaster? And giving that producer free rein?" Keith practically spit out the words, making his feelings on the situation clear.

"You know Mrs. Cederberg. She'll do what it takes to make Clayton Holdings happy. They're her largest client. If one of the Claytons wants something, we do it. We'll make it work. Even if the guy is awful."

"I doubt the people who watch these shows can even afford to stay here. The pricing is obscene." Keith shook his head, the bead at the end of his beard swaying. "It's a dumb idea, but what do I know?"

"If the new guy wins a hundred thousand, he'll be able to stay here," Lana pointed out.

"Still doesn't mean filming won't make our lives miserable."

"Surely it won't be that bad." Lana ignored the residual tingle of having her funny bone bumped. It had been an accident—and one that thankfully hadn't required an incident report.

Keith turned back to the matter at hand. "I just don't want them in our way. Did you get the specs for this floor? I emailed you which rooms are complete."

"I have everything. I'll spot-check Patsy's work before tackling the rooms you've finished. Text me if you need me."

"Will do. Lana, whatever you do, stay out of that guy's way," Keith warned as he strode off.

Determined to get her work done, Lana stepped into a completed guest suite. Decorated to feel like a luxurious personal bedroom, each guest room had different decor. Some suites had modern, clean vibes while others bent more historical. The one she stood in had a four-poster canopy bed. Lana opened the software on her iPad. Each room had its own checklist, and Lana ran through each item on the inspection sheet before exiting, closing the door and making her way to a lower floor.

Patsy had already inspected these completed rooms, which meant Lana could audit her work quickly. Each guest room Lana entered was truly beautiful. She ran her fingers lovingly over a mahogany dresser and dreamed that one day she could stay in a place like this, before locking up Room 12.

"What do you think?"

Lana jumped and pressed the iPad to her chest. Peter, the new hire candidate, stood about ten feet away. He gave her a friendly smile that showed lots of huge teeth. "Sorry.

Didn't mean to scare you. I'm on break. Wanted to take a better look around the place."

Lana pointed to his shoes. "Good you aren't tracking dirt. These floors have been cleaned."

He laughed. "I wouldn't dare mess anything up. Pretty posh place." His repetition of the letter *p* came out with a lisp, as did the "ace" sound. Poor guy couldn't even speak well. Still, something drew her to him, and she smiled.

"Want to know a secret?" she asked. "It's so high-end that even I'm afraid to touch anything. I like it though. It's classy yet subtle."

He shifted side to side as if his boots rubbed him wrong. "I guess you stay at a lot of hotels."

"Not like this. A bit rich for my paygrade. I'd add it to my bucket list, but I know I'll never be able to afford it."

"Here you are." A man Lana hadn't met before rounded a corner. He seemed to be somewhere in his midtwenties. "We need you back upstairs," he told Peter. Then, seeing Lana, he extended his hand. "Lachlan Van Horn. I'm the producer and director."

"Nice to meet you." She removed her hand from his, not liking the snake-oil salesman gleam in his eye. No wonder Keith disliked him.

"Move it," Lachlan told Peter.

"Bye," Peter said. After a nod Lana's direction, Lachlan left without a backward glance.

Lana inspected a few more rooms and made her way back upstairs. As she moved throughout the hotel, she'd occasionally see Peter and the film crew, who kept getting in the way. Once Keith shot her an exasperated "get me out of here now" look, to which she'd returned a sympathetic smile.

Her crew usually moved like precision clockwork. Today they tripped over themselves trying to avoid the two camera operators and Peter, who fit that old adage of a bull in a china shop. Or a deer in the headlights, which was a far more common sight on the rural roads surrounding Beaumont.

Having an extra hand should have been a huge help, but by lunchtime Lana had to agree with Keith—Peter's bulk kept getting in the way. For such a large man, he didn't have good spatial awareness. He also dropped things, or bumped them into the walls. He'd more or less failed the task of hauling mattresses, so Keith now had him carrying artwork and smaller items, like television sets or lamps. How any of these tasks would make for good TV, Lana had no idea. People actually watched this stuff? Shaking her head at the absurdity, she scurried toward another guest room so she could ensure it was ready. Studying the room layout on the iPad as she walked down the hall, she rounded a corner and ran smack-dab into a solid wall. One made of flesh, not drywall.

"Careful. Don't worry. I got it." A hand shot forward and grabbed the iPad before it fell from her grip.

"Thanks." She stepped back, her senses on high alert. She seemed to be getting a static charge from everyone lately—first Trey and now Peter. She bit back the automatic "You should watch where you're going," because technically she'd run into him. She plucked the iPad from his fingers. "You have a good day."

To her surprise, Peter fell in step beside her, making awareness power through her. The last time she'd felt this sensation had been Saturday night, with Trey. Trey was a large man, but compared to Peter, Trey was shorter and thinner. Peter had more inches on Lana and seemed broader. "I wanted to apologize for almost clocking you with that mattress. And now I blocked your path. I'm really sorry if I hurt you," Peter said.

She craned her neck and tried to place his accent. Somewhere southern. Atlanta maybe? There was a hint of something about Peter that reminded her of Trey, but Trey didn't have a lisp or extra-large teeth. She wondered where Trey was and how he was doing, and if he still felt the same afterglow she did. That had to be the reason for her hyperawareness of Peter. Just oversensitivity caused by a weekend of great sex with a total stranger.

"Today I've learned I'm not very good at this and I keep getting in the way," Peter said.

Lana let him somewhat off the hook. "Just do your job right and all will be forgiven."

"I'm trying. I need this job to be a success."

She kept walking and swiping, trying to ignore the fact her body wanted to go haywire. Had one break of her self-enforced celibacy caused a short circuit in her programming? "Or do you need the hundred thousand that comes with winning?"

His hair didn't really move when he tilted his head so he could glance her way. "Who doesn't? You can't fault a guy for trying."

"True." She bought a lottery ticket every so often, especially when the jackpot got in the triple millions. She and her coworkers would joke that even one hundred thousand would be enough. "Is this truly a competition?"

Big shoulders shrugged, making the t-shirt stretch across his chest. "At least between me and one other guy here. Another guy was in Florida. My family is depending on me, and me injuring the inspector means I'm not off to a strong start."

"I'm fine. Nothing that warrants safety documentation, thank goodness." She gave him a friendly yet professional smile, with the same level of appropriateness as she'd give any of her coworkers.

"That's good. What do you think of my chances so far?"

She stopped so she could face him. Being five seven, she had to tilt her head back. "I have no idea. The show is slowing down my crew, so what I really need for you to do is stay out of the way and allow us to do our job. This hotel needs to be perfect and open on time."

"Have you met Mr. Clayton?"

"No, but I heard he's in town." Feeling someone else behind her, Lana turned. A cameraman was filming the entire encounter. She pointed at the man, whose name she'd learned was Ben. "Seriously? You don't have my permission to film me. Turn that off."

Ben stood his ground. "Actually, you'll find that the paperwork you signed with Cederberg Interiors gives us permission."

Lana blinked. She'd signed an addendum a week ago that said if any images of her were used she'd be compensated, but she'd thought it was for the Cederberg website or promotional materials. Not for a TV show. She should have read last night's documents better. She glared at Ben, and reading her puckered lips and serious expression with deadly accuracy, the cameraman lowered his arms and backed away. "I'll take five."

"How about ten? Even twenty?" Lana suggested. That would at least buy her crew a few minutes of respite. "A half hour might be fine too. Take your friends with you."

She and Peter watched the cameraman walk off. Then Peter turned those deep brown eyes toward her. "I didn't think he'd actually leave."

"Take these few minutes to regroup and get yourself together," Lana instructed. "You've at least tried to do the work, unlike the last guy who thought this was an easy job. It's not. We're in the business of making people happy.

There's a lot of behind-the-scenes stuff that goes into open-ing a hotel."

He nodded solemnly. "I can see that."

She studied him with a critical eye. A better haircut and a mustache trim—and shaving off that dumb soul patch—would do wonders for his on-camera appearance. The pro-ducers should have made him more camera ready so that viewers wouldn't laugh at him or turn him into a meme. Then again, maybe that was the entire point of the show, allowing viewers to make fun of the people the show fea-tured. If that was the case, Lana didn't think the show's intentions were very nice.

"Tell me, out of curiosity, why do people agree to be on shows like this? Especially when you have no control over how you'll be presented? Surely there was another way to get gainful employment? Unless you really think you'll win the money."

Peter heaved a sigh and stopped himself from jerking a hand through his blond hair. "It wasn't my first choice. Last one, actually. I guess you can say this is a Hail Mary pass to get what I want."

A notification flashed on her iPad. "Good luck then. I've got work to do." Intent on answering her email, Lana strode off. As she turned another corner, she glanced back. Peter stood there, staring after her with a strange expres-sion that seemed like longing. Surely not. When she caught his gaze, he turned the other direction.

Hormones, Lana thought. That must be the reason for this hyperawareness of a man who looked like the guy em-blazoned on that one brand of paper towels, or at least how he looked before the manufacturer gave their packaging and the man a makeover. Lana yanked on her ponytail to ensure it was straight and not falling out. She wasn't in a hard-hat-required zone, but maybe she should get one. Or maybe she just needed to hope some sense got knocked into her.

After dating one man most of her life, perhaps her one-night stand with Trey had been like cracking the seal on a water bottle and releasing the contents.

Whatever this desire was, having a second fling with yet another man she'd never see again wasn't on her agenda, even if something about Peter made her stomach flip. Even if all the atoms in the room seemed charged whenever she was near him. Not that she could fathom why.

She did have one thing in common with Peter—he wanted a job and so did she. She had a huge, midyear bonus riding on the completion of the Chateau. With that money, she'd finally be able to go to Paris. Not first class, and definitely on a shoestring budget, but Paris, early next November.

Paris, the stuff of fantasies. She refused to let anything—or anyone—get in her way.

Chapter Five

Edmund let loose a breath as he watched Lana walk off. The disguise had held. She hadn't recognized him. Not one glimmer of suspicion, even after they'd been up close in the hallway. She'd believed the man she'd bumped into to be Peter Waggoner, job candidate. Her lack of recognition shouldn't bother Edmund, but it did. As Trey, he and Lana had been skin-to-skin for almost twelve hours. But she'd had no flicker of recognition. Perhaps she'd forgotten him already.

Not that he could forget her. He could still remember the sound of her sighs. Hear the kittenish cries she'd made when he'd nibbled her delicious, supple skin. It had been a shock seeing her this morning, made worse by clobbering her with a wayward mattress.

He shifted from foot to foot before the erotic memory gave the foreman, Keith—he had to remember his name—another reason to dislike him. Edmund rubbed the back of his neck to loosen tight muscles. Edmund had believed he was in great shape, but after a few hours carrying mattresses, every muscle ached, including ones he didn't even know he had. The end of his week undercover couldn't come soon enough.

Was this what other company presidents or CEOs felt like when they went on this show? Like they were incompetent? If so, Edmund didn't like the feeling. He'd been a bumbling idiot today, and the entire world would see him at his worst. Was that why Lachlan had insisted he wear boots that added three inches to his height, even though they made Edmund's legs feel off balance when he walked? He'd appear like a gangly, dorky giant traipsing through the footage. Edmund hated this.

"You okay, man?" someone asked as they went by.

"Yeah, all good." Edmund pressed on the thick fake mustache in a futile attempt to relieve the itch caused by the adhesive. He lifted his bulky jet-black glasses and rubbed the bridge of his prosthetic nose. The cheap plastic frames pinched and the latex irritated. The colored contacts turning his gray eyes dark brown either dried out his eyes or made them water. The watering was definitely worse, as then it made his nose run. He looked awkward enough. He didn't need to appear sickly as well.

"Peter." Lachlan came into view. At a mere twenty-four, Lachlan's youthful face made him pass for a high schooler rather than someone who'd graduated film school. The jury was out on whether Edmund liked the guy. Lachlan's grandmother had clearly told her grandson about the bet, because Lachlan had brought up the wager several times during his and Edmund's first production meeting. Lachlan glanced around and frowned. "Where's Ben?"

"Taking a break," Edmund said.

From the firm set of his lips, Lachlan didn't appear pleased. "Who gave him permission to stop filming?"

"No clue." Edmund refused to tell Lachlan that it had been Lana.

Lachlan tapped his watch. "Doesn't matter. It's lunchtime. Larry can film the next scene. Time to have your conversation with Jimmy."

"The kid who keeps calling me dude?" Edmund had not been able to relate to Jimmy in the slightest, or understand Jimmy's belief that calling any male older than twenty made the term "dude" somehow socially acceptable. Edmund had stopped counting the number of times Jimmy had used the word when the number reached fifty.

"Yes. That's him. And he's not a kid. He's twenty-one."

Edmund didn't know what he'd done to irritate Lachlan, but he'd gotten the impression that Margot's grandson didn't like him very much. Edmund prayed Lachlan hadn't liked Justus any better or Edmund's quest for Van Horn Hotels might be over before the TV show aired. He made a mental note to follow up with Eva as to whether she'd heard any gossip. She always had an inside track and various ways to discover secrets.

"So we'll eat lunch and chat about Jimmy's career plans." Edmund clarified the instructions he'd received.

"Yes. He's a local boy. Be kind to him so he gives good answers. I want him to look good."

Edmund noted Lachlan didn't mention making Edmund look good. And Edmund was always nice to those who deserved it. Hadn't he gotten Lana a hotel room? Just because his lack of ulterior motives had turned into mind-blowing lovemaking didn't change the fact he'd done a good deed. Sure, sometimes he had to be ruthless in business, but only because if he wasn't, his business would fail, and then the people who depended on him would find themselves out of a job. Over Lachlan's shoulder Edmund saw that the second cameraman, Larry, was headed in another direction. "What am I supposed to be asking Jimmy?" Edmund asked. "Do you have a list of questions?"

"Let's walk and talk." Lachlan gestured impatiently, leading the way toward the employee break room located on the first floor. "I want you to ask him about himself and actually listen. Each person you'll meet has been chosen for a specific reason. With Jimmy, it's about his dreams for the future. His vision. Do you think you can handle that?"

Edmund's patience was wearing thin, and he was already tired of Lachlan's patronizing attitude. "Yes. You don't get where you are in my world without being able to talk to people."

Lachlan didn't appear convinced. "Sure. Whatever. What were you saying to Lana?"

Edmund bristled at the interest he heard in Lachlan's tone. While he didn't know Lana's type, he was confident in what she wouldn't like—guys like Lachlan.

"I was apologizing for hitting her with a mattress this morning." Edmund couldn't believe he'd done that. However, he'd been more surprised when members of Lana's crew had reassured him she would not hold the accident against him. They'd told him she was a great boss who saw the best in everyone. That part he could believe, although he had his doubts she'd forgive him if she knew he was actually Trey from Saturday night, and that Trey was actually Edmund Clayton III. Lana may have broken her rule of one-night stands, but Edmund knew her integrity was 100 percent intact. She was not going to be happy with his deception as either Trey or Peter.

"As long as talking is all you're doing," Lachlan said. "Lana's not part of this. At least not yet."

"She doesn't need to be part of it at all," Edmund said, glad Lachlan didn't know that two nights ago Lana had worn Edmund out in the best possible way. He'd expected never to see her again, but here she was, in his hotel, working for one of the subcontractors Clayton Holdings used. When they'd discussed their jobs on the plane, they'd done so in general terms with no real specifics. He never would have guessed she worked for Cederberg Interiors, or that she'd be staying at the Grand instead of with her family. But thanks to a few text messages he'd sent to Mr. Smith, Edmund had those details, along with an even stronger desire to kiss her again. The latter, of course, would not occur. He couldn't take the risk of being discovered. But after he was finished with this week? As much as he was tempted, he shook off the idea. He had to return to Portland.

"Besides," Lachlan said, oblivious of Edmund's tension, "I might ask her out myself."

That outlandish idea caused Edmund to raise one of Peter's thick blond eyebrows. "You think she likes you? That you're her type?" Edmund asked.

"Girls always like TV producers and directors."

Lachlan's LA confidence got on Edmund's nerves. He couldn't help but scoff. "Yeah, good luck with that. Doubt she likes being called a girl either." Somehow Edmund managed to make his tone nonthreatening and noncommittal.

They'd reached the break room, already cleared of other workers so that Jimmy wandered around by himself while Ben and Larry busied themselves with setting up lights and discussing camera angles. Jimmy kept stopping to peer over their shoulders.

"Dude, this is going to be so cool," Jimmy said as he approached Edmund and Lachlan. "Me on TV. My mom was thrilled when I told her. I get the check today, right?"

"Yes," Lachlan said. "Two hundred fifty for your appearance, as outlined in the contract you signed."

That was all? Seemed like a bargain, Edmund thought as he threaded his way through the break room's combination of square and round tables. Edmund rolled his neck and flexed his fingers. He was going to change his gym workout when he got back to Portland. Today had proved how soft he was compared to the guys who built his hotels.

"Peter!" Lachlan called Peter's name. Deep in thought, Edmund needed a moment to register that Lachlan was calling him. The producer was even more impatient the second time. "Peter? Hey, earth to Peter."

"Yeah. I heard you the first time." Edmund tried not to snap but wasn't quite successful. Lachlan, however, ignored the jab.

"This is Jimmy. You're both sitting at this table." Lachlan pointed to a square, four-top table with two lunch coolers already staged. Edmund took his assigned seat, and Jimmy sat to his left.

"Hey, Jimmy," Edmund greeted.

"Hey." Jimmy's leg shook and bounced nervously. He wore blue jeans, work boots and a Foo Fighters concert t-shirt that he'd covered with a red-and-black-checked flannel shirt.

Edmund tried to put him at ease. "Foo Fighters, huh? Great band."

"Yeah. Can't wait until they go on tour again. Saw them a few years ago." Jimmy adjusted his shirt sleeve to cover his forearm. "I'm practicing keeping my ink covered. Dress code, you know, once I'm permanently over here. Do you have any tattoos?"

"No." Edmund thought of the butterfly on Lana's wrist.

"I got like thirteen. What I really want is to have my neck done. Like maybe a vampire with top and bottom fangs surrounding my Adam's apple. But I can't. Dress code. Might scare the guests."

Edmund really tried to relate to Jimmy but couldn't. "Too bad. Sounds interesting."

"I know, right?" Jimmy grinned from ear to ear.

"Yeah," Edmund agreed, still not understanding why people tattooed their faces or necks. Lana's wrist made sense, as did some places on the arms, legs and backs. Edmund couldn't imagine sitting still for the inking process, much less enduring whatever pain came with permanently coloring such tender skin. Larry finished testing the lighting, moved the camera tripod one final time, and gave a thumbs-up.

"Jimmy, this is your big TV debut. Don't screw it up." Lachlan stepped out of the frame. He patted his shirt pocket. "I got your check right here for when we're done."

Jimmy grinned wide. "I'm ready. I'm amped on two Red Bulls."

Great, Edmund thought.

"No product placement unless it's paid for," Lachlan called out. "Peter, let's start with you talking. Action."

"Hey, Jimmy." Edmund unwrapped his sandwich from its plain white wrapper, the paper crinkling.

"Cut." Lachlan moved to the table. "The wrappers are making too much noise. Let's start after they have their food. Lay the wrappers flat, put the chips on them and then start talking. Whatever you do, don't eat. It's too much noise for the mics. We need at least ten minutes of usable footage."

Edmund and Jimmy began following Lachlan's directions as to how to set up their food. Edmund and Jimmy also had plain white fountain sodas, with straws sticking out, and Lachlan couldn't decide where he wanted the cups placed. As Lachlan had them move the cups once more, Edmund gave a quick shake of his head, making Jimmy smile. The kid was clearly nervous. "We got this," Edmund told him. "I'm the one who will look foolish if this scene doesn't go well, not you. You're in the clear, and you'll get your money."

"Cool. Thanks, dude. I'm saving up for an engagement ring for my girlfriend."

"No talking until I say action," Lachlan commanded. He circled the table and then moved to stand by one of the cameras. "Okay, action."

Edmund began to speak. "Jimmy, I heard that you'll be on the maintenance staff here once the place fully opens. You went to tech school, right?"

"Yeah." Jimmy reached to finger the edge of the wrapper now serving as a place mat but jerked his hand back when he saw Lachlan's scowl. "Beaumont Tech. I studied HVAC and electrical."

Even with working with architects and overseeing his hotel construction, Edmund knew nothing about either. But he had interview skills. "Do you like one better than the other?" he asked.

That question got Jimmy talking, and he explained he preferred electrical. "At one point I wanted to be an engineer," he told Edmund. Lachlan rolled his hand in a gesture to keep the conversation moving.

"Why didn't you?" Edmund asked.

"Trade school in high school got me to the workforce at nineteen," Jimmy said. "I didn't think I was college material."

"How old are you now?"

"Twenty-one. Most of my friends went to college. They're always going to parties and things." He shrugged. "I also had to take care of my mom. She needed me. She had cancer and, well, I'm the oldest. The medical bills were pretty big, so my working here on install helped out. The docs say she's in remission because she's been two years without symptoms of the disease. But the bills, man. They keep coming no matter what."

"I'm glad she's healthier," Edmund said, understanding why Lachlan had chosen to feature Jimmy.

Jimmy grinned. "She's tough, you know? She's going to beat it. What about you? What's your deal?" Jimmy clearly wanted the spotlight off himself and his mother's remaining medical expenses. "Today you looked as if you could have used some sort of hands-on school."

"Yeah. College didn't teach me how to haul mattresses."

"College can make you soft, especially if you sit behind a desk all day. Hopefully you're not in debt. Got friends who are, and man, I already make more than many of them ever will, you know? Where'd you go?"

Stanford, the western Ivy equivalent, was the university of choice for the Clayton family. Jack had gone there, as had Edmund. And no, Edmund wasn't in debt. "Somewhere out west," Edmund hedged. "College doesn't have to be for everyone. What's important is that you're happy."

Jimmy considered that. "Sometimes I regret not going and getting my engineering degree. Maybe if I had I'd be designing bridges or something. I qualified for the A+ Scholarship Program. That's a thing where I'd get two years of community college paid for because of stuff I did in high school. But I needed to be there for my mom, you know? And I didn't want to leave Kayla. Been dating her since middle school. I'm gonna pop the question. Just can't afford a nice ring yet. Don't want one of those fake look-alikes you can get at the superstore, you know? She deserves something real."

"Probably a good idea," Edmund agreed. "If you love her, she deserves the best you can afford."

"Yeah, she does. I've been saving. You know what they say, dude, two months' salary. Hard to do when I'm still paying medical bills. Mom's working from home, but it doesn't bring in much. I keep stopping by the jewelry store on Main Street, but I haven't had the nerve to go in yet since I don't have enough cash. I don't do payment plans."

"You'll find the right ring." Edmund tried to be encouraging, knowing he'd probably be funding Jimmy's engagement ring as part of the show. He didn't mind. One good thing about the show—it allowed Edmund to pay some things forward.

Edmund could still remember how Veronica had thrown her fifty-thousand-dollar diamond engagement ring back in his face, screaming that he was a no-good lowlife... Something anyone could watch on the internet. Once he'd had the ring back, Edmund had asked his jeweler to remove the precious stones. Edmund had sold them and donated the proceeds to charity. The only good thing—at least he hadn't given Veronica his mother's engagement ring. His mother had offered it to Edmund, but he'd turned her down, knowing that Veronica would find the design too old-fashioned. Maybe someday he'd find someone worthy of it, but probably not before she gave it to one of his brothers.

"I'm proud of Kayla," Jimmy said, reminding Edmund that Peter should be paying better attention to Jimmy and not his own problems. "She's going to be an elementary school teacher. She's doing her student teaching this spring at Beaumont Elementary. Once she gets a job, she'll have some student loans, but we'll pay those off."

"That's great," Edmund said. "I'm happy for you both."

Jimmy reached for his cup and sipped, much to Lachlan's displeasure. "Thanks, dude. You know, you're really cool. A lot cooler than I thought you were. Let me know if I can help you. I could probably think of a few things you could do to improve, and you need to learn some skills."

"Appreciate it. That'd be great."

"Cut!" Lachlan shouted. "We got what we needed."

"Great. Can I eat this now?" Jimmy pointed to his food. "I'm starving, and I gotta be back on the clock in a few minutes."

"Eat," Edmund urged. His turkey sandwich had been sliced in half, and he lifted one section. He figured it was safe if Jimmy had already bitten into his.

"It's good," Jimmy confirmed after swallowing a bite. "They told me to bring two lunches today so I did."

"Let me at least pay you back."

Jimmy shook his head, his long hair swishing. "Nah. They're giving me two hundred fifty bucks, remember? I can buy you a sub. Besides, my friend works at the sandwich shop and always gives me a discount."

"Thank you. It's been great getting to know you." Edmund, jaded from business dealings with cutthroat competitors, found that he meant every word.

"Me too. You're okay, dude. Even if you don't know what the hell you're doing, I'll teach you."

Edmund knew during the reveal portion of the show the boss always gave employees some sort of grand gesture. Edmund planned on rewarding Jimmy handsomely. The guy was honest and decent. And the sandwich wasn't bad.

Lachlan placed a check on the table next to Jimmy. "There you go. Thanks for your help, Jimmy. Peter, you finished?"

He'd had three bites. "I just started eating."

"Time is money." Lachlan pointed to his watch. "Clock's ticking."

"Sorry, dude," Jimmy said. "Don't worry. I'll eat the other half."

"Fine." Edmund shoved the rest of the sandwich in his mouth, leaving the other part for Jimmy. Edmund took a long pull from the straw and discovered the contents were room temperature tap water.

Lachlan tapped his Apple Watch again, a habit that was becoming more and more annoying. "We've got other shots to film, and your next coworker is waiting. You can eat later."

"Sure thing." Edmund passed Jimmy the untouched portion. He tamped down a temper made worse by the fact that he was hangry. Breakfast had been hours ago, and that had been half a bagel with a swipe of cream cheese and grape jelly. He figured he'd actually get to eat the lunch during filming.

But Edmund decided not to complain and piss Lachlan off, not when Edmund knew the producer could easily sabotage Edmund's show and his chances to buy Van Horn Hotels. Justus's show was already in editing. Edmund had no idea how it had gone.

"Where are we going next?" Edmund asked. "Not near Lana, are we?" He couldn't risk her finding out who he really was. He had too much riding on winning these hotels to complicate matters.

"I don't need to stalk her to get her to like me," Lachlan said with a pride that grated on Edmund's nerves. He glanced Edmund's direction. "Besides, why do you care? You hit her with a mattress so I'm not sure she likes you much. Now maybe if you were Edmund, but then, you're not, are you? Was there any other reason you asked such a dumb question?"

"No reason," Edmund said he trudged after Lachlan. "No reason at all."

Chapter Six

By 3:00 p.m., Lana's frustration reached a boiling point. Like a steam kettle, she might go off at any moment. Her fingers tapped an agitated staccato against the back of her iPad. She'd accomplished far less than she'd hoped thanks to a film crew that kept interrupting what was normally a well-oiled operation.

Lana teetered on the edge, that place where any outburst she'd held back might suddenly burst forth without restraint. The entire day she'd either had to move out of the room she was in, or she'd had to dodge crew members trying to get out of the way of cameras. Mrs. Cederberg was not going to be happy with her progress on the quality control auditing, which meant Mr. Clayton wouldn't be happy.

Worse, Lana remained highly aware of Peter's location, like he had some form of homing beacon that her body couldn't resist. She had no idea why her radar pinged whenever he was near. The show hadn't given Peter a makeover. He had an oversize nose that appeared to have been broken once or twice. Not that Peter held a candle to the hotness of Trey. Who could? Trey had been perfect.

Hearing shouting, Lana found her gaze straying to Peter, who was once again struggling and making her job site an unmitigated disaster. Not that she could do much about it.

Whenever either she or Keith had asked Lachlan to move the cameras out of the way—and to have Peter do anything else but whatever he'd been doing badly—Lachlan Van Horn had said no. He'd told her to take it up with Edmund Clayton. "He's on-site at the Grand, and he's approved everything. You could march right over there if you'd like." Then Lachlan had had the nerve to flirt with her, as if he thought his Hollywood job was some sort of female aphrodisiac.

Several times Lana had wanted to wipe the smirk off Lachlan's face, but she didn't want to jeopardize Mrs. Cederberg's contract with Clayton Holdings. Lana decidedly disliked Lachlan, who kept peering at her with open interest. Finally, during one conversation, she'd lost it and snapped, "Hey, my face is up here," before adding, "and whatever you're thinking will happen, it won't. Let's be professional, okay? This is a no harassment zone."

Maybe that was one reason why Lachlan was acting like more of a pompous, entitled jerk than before.

At least Peter hadn't ogled her. He was hanging pictures in one of the guest rooms. He'd misjudged the height from ceiling to picture hanger, and one frame was hung a good two inches below its mate, which was too great of a distance for the wire to simply be shortened. Lana sighed. He'd have to patch the hole, spot paint and rehang the offender. Add an inability to use a measuring tape to his long list of failings. Lana noted on her iPad that her crew would need to come back and fix things. "Where's your film crew?" she asked.

Peter set a hammer down and gave her one of his toothy smiles. "Hey, Lana. How's it going? They're on break, I think, now that they've got enough footage of my screwups. I'm not sure why I agreed to do this show. I'm doing terrible."

She imagined he was thinking about all the money he

no longer had a chance to win. She felt sorry for the guy. He had bad hair. A bad lisp. Bad carpentry skills. He was batting zero. No one deserved that. Well, maybe Lachlan. "Perhaps you'd do better at some other tasks. Have you asked the producers about switching to something else?"

When his brows knit together, they almost touched. "Lachlan enjoys my failures. I have no idea what else I can do. I never realized exactly what went into putting hotel rooms together. Been interesting to see."

Lana lowered the iPad. "What did you do before this? I'm genuinely curious."

"Office work, actually. I see you don't believe me." He tried to pry open the tub of Spackle, and she stretched out her hand.

"Give me that." Balancing the iPad, she popped the top, took the putty knife from his hand and used it to stir the pink-colored substance. Then she dipped it into the container and handed him a knife covered with the correct amount of fluffy hole filler. "Dab it on the wall. No, not like that."

Lana set the iPad down and stepped forward. "Let me show you. Do it like this." She covered his hand, guiding his. "Use this motion. See?" With their hands joined, she demonstrated how to spread with one side of the blade and then the other, filling the hole and removing the excess.

She released his hand, her fingers tingling. Must be static. Either that or she still had a hyperalert body caused by one night of passionate sex. That had to be the reason touching Peter warmed her insides and made her feel gooey.

Peter passed her the putty knife. "Better?"

"Almost." Lana finished the repair. Once the Spackle dried, it would need a light sanding and a dab of paint.

"How'd you learn to do that?" Peter asked.

"I helped my dad build our basement. When this is dry, the pink will turn white. That's how you know it's ready to be painted, and our painter will finish the repair and hang the picture correctly. Why don't you try another hole?"

Peter dipped the putty knife into the tub. He applied the Spackle. "How's this?"

Better, but nowhere close to perfect, and they both knew it.

Lana tried to remain positive. "You're getting the hang of it. I can't believe they assigned you jobs you don't know how to do. That seems rather unfair of the producer."

Peter shrugged broad shoulders. "I think that's the whole point. When I signed up for this project, I didn't expect to be shoved in over my head, but here I am. In for a penny, that sort of thing. Doesn't matter how dumb I look as long as it's good TV."

"I'm hating that for you. What if you fail?"

His half laugh, half choke made her wonder if he'd swallowed wrong. "I already am. It's not good for a man's ego to learn he can't do everything. Lachlan says humility makes for a good show."

"Which is why I don't watch reality TV," Lana said.

"You're more the Hallmark type."

"And proud of it," Lana said. "I'm about the happy endings."

Peter's mouth twisted, making the caterpillar above his top lip wiggle. "My family needs me to win for our happy ending. Have you ever wanted something so badly that you'll sacrifice almost anything to get it?"

"Sort of." She'd broken an engagement to travel, leaving her family behind. With her next bonus, her goal of making it to Paris was finally in reach.

"There's a lot on the line for me," Peter said.

"Surely there's another way you can get what you want."

She was such a softy, the type who hated when people or animals were in trouble, even if it was of their own making. She'd always been the one to cry whenever she saw a lost pet poster hanging on a utility pole. Peter stirred her heartstrings.

"Sadly, this is it. Believe me, if there was another way, I would have found it. The future depends on my performance."

Before Lana could respond, Keith entered. "Here you are."

"Me?" Lana retrieved her iPad. There were no messages saying he'd been looking for her. Next to her Peter groaned as the cameraman entered the room. A flickering red light indicated Ben was taping.

"Not you." Keith pointed to Peter. "I need him."

Peter stepped toward the two men, the open tub of Spackle and putty knife still in his hands. "What's up?"

Lachlan came in and waved at Lana. "Could you clear the room?"

"I'm working." She used the iPad as a shield. "You can go elsewhere."

He made a shooing motion. "We're shooting here. Go."

Lana shot him a death glare, but Lachlan had the audacity to roll his eyes and give her an exasperated "Time is money" expression and another shooing motion.

Irritated, Lana gritted her teeth, kept her head held high and worked on keeping calm. Refusing to lose her temper, she stepped through the doorway and into the corridor. Instead of walking away though, curiosity made her hover. Keith assessed the spackled hole.

Lana tensed when Keith folded his arms. She knew that stance. It never meant anything good. "Peter, look, this job isn't really a good fit for you," Keith said.

Lana frowned. The wall needed some sanding. The

patched hole would be hidden behind a picture. No one would ever notice. She'd already pinged the painter.

Peter stood frozen, putty knife still in one hand. "Then what else can I do?"

Keith shook his head. "Nothing. We're too far behind, and that's on you. Hopefully something else will work out better, but this job's not it."

Peter's frown twisted a knife into Lana's gut. Like watching a horrific train wreck, she knew what was coming next.

"You're fired from room install," Keith said.

Peter appeared incredulous. The hand holding the plastic container tightened. "I'm fired? Like, I'm actually being *fired*?"

Lana cringed but couldn't look away. Peter set the container down. "I'm supposed to be on-site at the Chateau for another few days."

A smaller man than Peter, Keith crossed his arms and widened his stance. "Not on the install team. You can't do the work correctly, and I don't have the time to train you. Not when you don't have the basic carpentry skills necessary to even spackle a hole. You can find something else."

Keith spun around and exited. "Don't tell me that seemed too harsh," he warned her as she followed him down the hall. "The producer said not to go easy on him, so I didn't."

She knew Keith was right. "Fine, I won't criticize your performance as long as you're okay with being on TV looking like a bad guy. Because that's how you came across."

Keith lengthened his stride. "I did what I was told. I followed directions."

"But now Peter can't finish his show," Lana protested. "You're the one who'll be blamed."

Keith paused. "No, I won't. It's not my problem. He and that producer-slash-director can work it out."

"The producer's a jerk. How much were you paid for your performance?"

"A thousand. Look, you may not like it, but you should be glad he's gone. He was a distraction. Need I remind you that we're now behind? Do you want to lose your chance at our bonus for finishing on time?"

"No." The bonus meant booking a ticket to Paris. "But it's not fair."

"Sometimes things aren't." Keith strode off, and Lana returned to the hallway outside the hotel room. While she couldn't hear what was discussed, the conversation between the cameraman, Peter and the producer appeared animated.

Her parents had raised her to help people. To do what was right. She stepped back into the room just as Lachlan pushed by her on his way out. "Watch it." Clearly she'd lost favor with him. Oh, well.

Lana didn't spare Lachlan a backward glance as her focus was on Peter. She hesitated as she came into his space. "Can I do anything? Help somehow? I might be able to find you a more suitable job."

She felt the full force of Peter's intense, brown-eyed gaze. "That's nice of you, but—" Peter broke their connection as he shoved the putty knife into the Spackle so the handle was sticking out. He pointed to the cameraman. "Turn that off and go."

To Lana's shock, Ben lowered the device and left the room. "You deserve a fair chance," she told Peter. "This is your shot."

"It's sweet for you to defend me, but it's not necessary," Peter said, softening.

"It is when your producer is an ass."

To her surprise, Peter laughed. "He is most definitely

that." He sobered. "He's not high on my list of favorite people."

"Mine either. I'd report him for harassment if I thought it would help. I can't wait for him to be gone. Any idea what comes next? Are they sending you home?" Lana's anxiety warred with her anger. "I hate when bad things happen to good people."

His toothy grin was lopsided. "Thanks for thinking of me as being good people. I appreciate you trying to help more than you know. But I've messed up your schedule enough."

"You aren't good at this work, but that doesn't mean you don't deserve a fair chance."

He reached forward as if to touch her but dropped his hand. "It'll be okay. Lachlan and I will work something out. I don't want to be rude, but I need to go. I'm catching a ride back with them to the Grand."

"I'm staying there. Will you let me know what you find out?" Lana asked. "I'd like to help if I can."

He seemed surprised. "That's kind of you, but you didn't meet your quota because all this has been a pain in the ass. You don't owe me anything."

"I've been behind before. I'll catch up tomorrow. I just want you to get another chance." As Peter stared at her, Lana ignored the butterflies dancing in her stomach.

Peter gave her a smile. "You're pretty great, you know that? Thanks for being you. I'll keep you posted, okay?" When he left the room, it was as if the energy went with him.

Lana had been so aware of him as a person and not just as some guy trying to be on TV. She lifted the Spackle, removed the putty knife and tapped the lid closed. The painter walked in as she was leaving, and she handed both items to him and retrieved her iPad. Her watch beeped, letting her know it was four o'clock. Not her normal quitting time, but close enough for today. Besides, she couldn't deal with any more stress. She was invested in Peter's success, even though she had no reason to be. Her mom always told Lana that she cared too much. Lana found caring to be a blessing and a curse. An idea hit as she headed down the hall. Edmund Clayton was in town. He'd told her boss to approve this disastrous TV show idea, so perhaps he should help her fix it. She drove the UTV back to the Grand and had a front desk clerk show her to Mr. Smith's office. He pushed his glasses farther up his nose as he stood and greeted her. "Lana. This is a surprise. How are things going?"

She shook his hand. "Installation-wise, fine. As for the TV crew, that's another story. I want to see Mr. Clayton."

Mr. Smith sputtered and gestured wildly. "He's not availa…"

Lana cut him off. "You told me this morning he's in town. Call him and tell him Lana Winchester of Cederberg Interiors wants to see him. Explain his hotels will look like the big bad wolf on TV if he doesn't meet with me."

Mr. Smith's hands fumbled as he reached for a fountain pen and a notepad. "This is highly irregular. I'll write him a message."

Lana's stubbornness came in handy at times like these. "A man's future hangs in the balance. Clayton Hotels doesn't need bad PR. I'm not happy with what I saw today. I'm not leaving this office until I see Mr. Clayton."

"I can't solve this problem?" Mr. Smith had paled, and Lana wondered if he feared interrupting Edmund. Was Edmund really this scary?

"I'd love for you to help me, but on something like this I'd rather go directly to the top. I just need five minutes of his time. I know it's valuable."

"Do you mind?" Mr. Smith signaled for some privacy, and Lana paced the small hallway until Mr. Smith opened his office door. He appeared even more agitated than before. Was Edmund really this much of an ogre?

"Mr. Clayton says he will meet you in twenty minutes in the small conference room."

"Perfect," Lana said. No matter how awful Edmund was, she'd get Peter another chance.

Chapter Seven

Lana returned to the main level with two minutes to spare. After leaving Mr. Smith, she'd gone to her room and changed into jeans, a crewneck cable-knit sweater and the suede booties she'd worn on the plane. She'd freshened her appearance, including resetting her ponytail. She hadn't bothered with makeup except for a swipe of lip gloss.

The small conference room had a table that comfortably sat ten. However, instead of taking a seat, Lana moved to study an oil painting of the Missouri River Valley by local artist Bryan Haynes. She assumed Edmund Clayton III would make her wait, if only to prove that he was the boss, the VP of Clayton Holdings and the man in control, not some underling she could summon at will. To her shock, he arrived on time.

"She's waiting in here," Lana heard Mr. Smith say.

"Leave us." The sound of that familiar deep voice sent a chill running down Lana's spine, and she stilled. *It couldn't be.* Instinct made Lana want to close her eyes and pray a hole would open in the expensive carpet and swallow her. She stared at the painting as a familiar aftershave she would recognize anywhere reached her nostrils. Her skin prickled. The hair on the back of her neck rose and stood at attention. How, oh, how had she been so naive? How could she not have known? Looking back—the appetizers, the wine, the suite—it all made sense. Maybe not flying economy, but the rest?

"Hello, Lana. Long time, no see."

That West Coast accented voice that had begged her to come and told her she was beautiful washed over her. She turned from studying the painting, her control held by the thinnest of threads. "Hello, Trey. Or should I call you Edmund?"

Despite her anger at the deception, Edmund was a sight for sore eyes. He wore a crisp, expensive suit even more posh than the casual one he'd worn the night they met. He spread hands that had roamed her body freely. "My good friends call me Trey. I'd say we're close friends, wouldn't you?"

They'd been as close as two people could get, and her face heated.

"Since I don't have a lot of time, how about you tell me what you need?" Edmund asked.

She caught her breath. Drew herself to her full height. She wouldn't let her shock get in the way. "Thank you for seeing me."

He adjusted his sleeve. "You didn't give me much of a choice. Something about bad PR? You planning on selling our night to the tabloids?"

Lana blinked. "I didn't even know who you were until this moment." She gathered her wits. She'd survived being blindsided before, especially by her controlling ex. By now she should be an expert in handling this type of situation. But this was Trey—*no,* Edmund. She felt as if she'd just stepped off a topsy-turvy carnival ride. "I want to discuss Peter, the man who's being filmed for the TV show. He was fired today."

Edmund arched a brow she'd traced with her finger. "I don't see what this has to do with me."

"He was fired trying to finish your hotel. Think of the optics. I want you to give him a second chance. Find him something here. Convince the producer that he deserves to film the entire week." Those once-tender gray eyes widened in disbelief, but Lana pressed on. "Surely there's some other job he can do for Clayton Hotels. Like working here at the Grand."

Edmund's lips thinned, his expression inscrutable. "I heard he was a disaster. A costly embarrassment. Not Clayton material."

"He's not like you." She took in Edmund's crisp white shirt, the red power tie and the dark stubble on his chin. The stubble he'd been careful not to scratch her with during their 6:00 a.m. lovemaking. He'd been passionate, yet gentle. Trustworthy. The man who stood before her looked like the person she'd spent the night with, but his attitude was hard. Cold. All business.

Trey—no, Edmund—folded his arms. "What is it to you if he continues? Why do you care? You don't know him."

"I don't have to know someone to care. He has a family. Sure, it's a competition, but Peter seems like a nice guy. He's not rich like you. He can use a break. He said he needs to win this."

As if aware of the closed-off nature of his posture, Edmund loosened his arms. "And you want to make sure he does."

She shook her head. "I want you to make sure he has a fighting chance. Manual labor and handyman services aren't his thing. There has to be something he can do. Maybe valet, or front desk? Night audit? He was fired at your hotel. That looks terrible."

"For your foreman, not me," Edmund pointed out.

"One and the same to viewers. I can't believe Mrs. Cederberg signed up for this. She'd be appalled. I can't let this injustice slide."

Edmund stepped closer. "What's in it for me? As you know, I'm the king of bad PR."

Besides getting Peter another chance, she hadn't thought that far. She'd acted impulsively, as she had Saturday night, something she seldom did and had now done twice. "I don't know. As Clayton Holdings VP, shouldn't you know where a man of his talents could be placed? Shouldn't you care about people who aren't in your orbit? Or do you simply like hiding your true self, *Trey*?" Desperate, she threw out that barb to goad him into action.

His gray eyes glittered dangerously, shooting an excited thrill through her. She'd hit a nerve. "Would you put him on your crew? Could he do your job?" Edmund pressed.

"Inspecting hotel rooms?" Lana clarified.

"Yeah. How hard can it be? Didn't you train most of your crew?" He'd edged even closer, and Lana breathed him in.

She jutted her chin. The spot checks she'd done of finished floors of the Chateau revealed how well she'd trained her crew. Almost nothing had been overlooked or needed correcting. "Yes, I could train him. He can work with me."

Both of Edmund's brows lifted. "You'd risk dealing with someone who clearly wasn't suited for today's jobs because..."

"Didn't you tell me to pay it forward? Well, here I am. Feel free to call me the queen of lost causes, but everyone deserves a second chance. He's going to be fired on national TV. That's embarrassing." She thought fast. Tried to find the right ammunition. "You'll personally look bad."

"After what my ex did, I doubt I could look any worse

than I already have. I'm not one of your homeless kittens, am I? Surely you're not trying to save me?"

How had she not realized how pigheaded he was? That night he'd been all about her satisfaction, her pleasure. Then again, they hadn't been VP and quality control inspector. That night, business had been the last thing on their minds. And he had told her his ex had called him a heartless iceman. Lana simply hadn't believed it. Until now.

"You pay my boss, who pays me," Lana tried. "As we have a long-standing contract with Clayton Hotels, it's best for all parties that this show is not an embarrassment."

"Hmm." Edmund crossed his arms across the chest she'd rested her head on while they slept. "Do you care about him?"

Why? Are you jealous? The words hovered on her tongue, but she bit them back.

"I'm sympathetic to Peter's situation," Lana hedged. Like that night with Edmund, she'd had a physical reaction to Peter, and because of that reaction, she was defending Peter in front of Edmund. "He's in a bad spot. My parents taught me that if someone is in need, and I'm in a position to help, then I'm to help. People in Beaumont take care of each other. Clayton Hotels is new to Beaumont, so perhaps you should get with the program."

"I'd say I took care of you just fine."

Heat spread at the memory. She rallied the troops. "I never would have slept with you if I'd known who you were."

The corner of Edmund's lips inched upward. "What would be the fun in that? You wanted adventure and I gave you one, Lana of no last name."

"Trey. Not even your real name," she spat back. "You

could have told me who you were. I'd say you're guiltier than I am of misrepresentation."

Edmund didn't appear too upset. "I honestly had no idea who you were or that you were working here until this morning. But since we said one night, I felt it best not to approach you."

That shocked her. "What? When was this? I never saw you. And not approaching seems like a poor excuse."

Edmund arched a brow. "You wouldn't have seen me because your nose was buried in your iPad."

She acknowledged that truth with an almost imperceptible dip of her chin. "I was consumed with work. I'm always that way. We talked about that."

"We did. We also discussed how each of us wanted nothing more than good food and good company. We wanted one night. No more. You left me without a goodbye. Why would you think that I should rush over and tell you who I was when I first saw you?"

"That's fair. I still don't like it, but I understand your perspective."

His fingers snaked forward, lifted a lock of hair that had escaped her ponytail and set the strand over her ear before his hand darted back into his own space. "I don't do one-night stands, and I admit I didn't know how to handle seeing you again."

"Frankly, I was unsure myself. That's why I left."

He seemed pleased. "Then our actions were a first for both of us. We had powerful, earth-shattering sex."

"I can't deny that," Lana admitted as his fingers came back, this time to trace the side of her jaw with one finger. Her body quivered. He shouldn't have the ability to turn her inside out, but he did.

"Look at us. Whatever this chemistry is, it hasn't burned out. You make my knees go weak."

Hers felt the same, so Lana crossed her arms and stepped back. "You and I, we have to pretend it didn't happen and remain professional. I'm willing to do that if you are, and if you help Peter. He's a nice guy. You'd like him if you met him."

"I have met him and he is. But Lana, what if I don't want to pretend nothing happened? What if I want this chemistry?"

Heat pooled low, and Lana resisted letting him see how he affected her. When his gaze slid over her, she knew he was imagining her naked. She couldn't help but do the same. He was magnificent with or without clothes. If she was one of the wanton and bold women in her really steamy romance novels, she'd be pushing him against the conference table and having her way with him. But that was fantasy, and this was real life.

"We are not repeating Saturday night." Her voice wasn't as steady as she'd wished. "I'm not like your other women. You probably have to pry them off you. Give them fancy jewelry as a parting gift."

A hint of a smile began. He was 100 percent in control and knew it. "You read too many romances. Ah, don't deny it. You told me on the plane."

Blast it. She had.

"And I do not have 'women,' as you said, nor do I buy anyone off with jewelry. As for you being like any woman I've ever known, you're in a class of your own. That's a good thing. I like your refreshing, impulsive nature. You're unique. Challenging. Different. It's one of the things that most attracted me to you. None of that has changed. I'm still attracted."

His words flattered her, and Lana brushed them aside with a false show of bravado. "I'm immune to your flattery."

"For someone who hates lying, you just told a big one."

She had. She remembered more of their conversation. "Were you even engaged? Or was that another lie?"

Edmund shrugged. "Google it. The whole sordid story is on the internet for the world to see. I've not lied to you about who I am. Omitted some details, yes. Absolutely guilty on that count. People always want something from me. That night you only wanted one thing, and I enjoyed it thoroughly."

His lips formed a little pucker, and Lana fought back a blush. She'd research him once she got back to her room, where she'd also order room service and hide away until morning. At least in her room he couldn't push her buttons. "Look, let's stop with the tangents. Will you help Peter or not?"

He ended the suspense. "Since it matters to you so much, I'll find something for him to do so that the show is a success and he has a fighting chance to reach his goals."

"Thank you." Relief filled her. The girl who'd taken in stray cats had saved someone's job. That's what mattered, even if she couldn't exactly explain *why* it mattered. As much as she'd felt a pull toward Peter, Edmund was a death star tractor beam. She was a moth to his flame. If he bent his finger, she might throw herself at him.

Those gray eyes glittered, and she'd pay whatever price he demanded for his help. "You know I hate eating being alone. Have dinner with me tonight."

Heat crossed Lana's cheeks. "Dinner only. Nothing more. I'm here to work. I don't have time to go out. I have family events to attend, and I won't cancel them, not even for you. As for falling into bed again, I won't make the same mistake. I know who you are now." And she knew a fine line existed between like and dislike, love and hate, that sort of thing. She'd already crossed a line in bedding him. Even though she wanted him again. Like maybe on the conference room table.

Edmund ran a finger down her arm. "Great sex is never a mistake."

As if he'd been affected by touching her, he stepped away. "But you have my word I'll be the perfect gentleman. You want more from me, you say the word. That I'll leave up to you."

She was already tempted. However, she knew that in this instance, Little Red Riding Hood was no match for the Big Bad Wolf named Edmund Clayton III. At least he'd done the right thing by Peter. "I should find Peter. Tell him the good news."

Edmund quickly shook his head. "No need. I'll personally make sure he's informed of his good fortune and upcoming career change. Shall we eat at La Martina tonight? Unless you have plans with your family."

La Martina was the hotel's premier restaurant. Her mouth watered at the thought of dining there. "Not tonight. I was going to order room service."

Edmund shook his head. "We can't have that. The chef is debuting his spring menu, and his food never disappoints."

Edmund dangled the right incentives. The chef was a James Beard award winner. Dinner at La Martina was a bucket list item far out of her budget, and even if she could afford it, the tables booked up months in advance. Unless you were the owner.

"Shall we say seven?" Edmund asked.

"Sure. Seven it is." One thing Mrs. Cederberg had taught

Lana—always pack a cocktail dress in case of emergencies. That advice had saved her more than once.

Edmund held out a business card. "Here's my direct number. I'll meet you at the restaurant. Hopefully Peter will thank you profusely tomorrow."

Lana sagged after Edmund left, and she gripped the side of a nearby conference chair for support. Dear God. She had saved Peter's job, but she also had a dinner date with Edmund Clayton, aka the sexiest man alive. *What had she just done?*

After leaving Lana standing in the conference room, Edmund returned to the penthouse and shut the door behind him. He strode directly to the bar and poured two fingers of bourbon. All day he'd been aware of Lana, waiting for her to see through his disguise and call him Trey. But she hadn't. No, she'd bought Peter's disguise completely. She even seemed to like the guy, a surprising and unsettling development, as Lana seemed to like Peter far more than she did Edmund, and he'd been as intimate with her as one could be.

She liked the guy who got fired better than the VP. The world, it seemed, had turned upside down. Edmund admired Lana's gumption. She'd shown the same drive that had gotten her the last seat on the last flight into St. Louis. Her determination had been evident in the way she'd marched into Mr. Smith's office and demanded to see him. Poor Mr. Smith had been so rattled and apologetic that it had taken Edmund several minutes to reassure him everything would be fine.

Edmund sipped and let the liquid fire burn down his throat. He'd found it amazing that Lana actually was the type who fought for the little guy and the underdog. Her crew had indicated such, but he hadn't really believed it until he'd seen the lengths she went to get Peter his job back.

He'd never found people to be generous without having a stake in the outcome. Today she'd been magnificent, kind and wonderful. A true avenging warrior demanding justice. He'd expected some sort of blackmail, but she'd never stooped to underhanded tricks. She'd been real and caring.

He'd never been so turned on in his life. Everything about her did it for him. Her mind. Her drive. Her verve and spirit. Her body. Definitely her body. He wanted all of her.

But he couldn't risk trusting her with the truth about Peter. As much as he'd wanted to blurt out the truth in the conference room, he'd kept his mouth shut. He couldn't tell Lana that the firing had been deliberately staged, even though Keith didn't know Edmund and Peter were the same person. When Lachlan had told Keith he needed to fire Peter, Keith, clearly annoyed by the day's work, had happily complied. Earning one thousand dollars for doing it hadn't hurt either.

Edmund wanted to tell Lana, but the show's rider dictated who he could and couldn't tell. Then again, he was Edmund Clayton, worker of miracles. He'd shared so much with Lana when they didn't know last names; surely, he could find a way to tell her this one thing. But, hearing his sister's voice in his head reminding him how important this show was to their family business, Edmund fought back the temptation.

Lana's being here already complicated things and changed the week's trajectory. He'd have to be even more careful he didn't slip up and reveal himself before the show wrapped.

Lana liked Peter. She'd liked Trey. It was probably safer for all of them if she did not like Edmund, especially since he wanted nothing more than to take her back to bed. He could tell she wanted the same thing—the signals in the conference room had been more than obvious.

But he tainted every relationship. Lana might be enjoying traveling the country, but deep down she was home and hearth. Warmth and sunshine. Edmund's heart was as cold as the weather outside. He could dim the light in a room just by entering it. Lana was bubbly and bright. He refused to take any of her infectious joy away. If they dated, he would. He ruined things. She was a relationship type of girl, and he refused to be another guy who might break her heart.

It was safer for everyone if he stayed the man who got things done, the man currently living a double life this week. To make the ruse even more real, Peter even had his own hotel room on another floor. Mr. Smith had assured Edmund that his secret other—better—half would be safe. No one would know.

Edmund sat at the suite's ornate desk and opened his laptop. He had a plethora of emails that had stacked up while he was playing Peter today, and each one required an answer. His job went on, even if Peter's had stopped for the evening.

Edmund grabbed a cold bottle of water. His phone trilled with an incoming call from his sister. He hesitated for a moment and then guiltily sent the call to voicemail. Eva had a way of seeing right through him. They'd always been this way. Even though he was the oldest and Eva was the youngest, he felt closer to her than he did to his two brothers. Liam was the adventurer, always off climbing some mountain. The sale of his tech startup had allowed him to concentrate on charitable works, and he was usually in some third world country when he wasn't hiking and traveling.

Third in line was Michael, or, as his brother described himself, the spare's heir. Michael drove his parents crazy and had since he'd arrived. He'd never taken anything seriously and was Portland's most notorious playboy. He was warm, gregarious and all about having fun. He had a job with Clayton Holdings, but to Edmund's knowledge, their father never cared if Michael showed up to the office or not. Meanwhile, Edmund had been expected to achieve since he'd been in the womb.

Edmund felt a tremor in his pocket. His phone buzzed with an incoming text from Eva. Hey, called you because I'm dying to know how today went. Tell me!

Edmund texted back, Off to dinner. How about I call in a few hours?

Portland was two hours behind Beaumont, so even if he called her around ten, it would only be eight Pacific Standard Time. The one thing he wouldn't say? *Hey, I slept with this woman I met on the plane, and now she's here and she defended Peter and we just had dinner.*

Eva would call him a fool before warning him that he was going to mess up and make things worse. She'd say Edmund had created the whole ludicrous situation by not controlling his libido. On that, he'd have to agree. Not that he had any regrets. Part of him wanted Lana again. The sane part of him knew what a bad idea that was. Especially when he couldn't come clean until the show filmed the reveal segments. He had to maintain the deception. He couldn't let his family down. That hadn't been a lie.

Edmund checked his wrist. He felt naked without the Rolex that had been a gift from his father, but it was in the safe back in Portland. Edmund's phone buzzed again, and he saw a number he didn't recognize. I'm downstairs, the text read.

Lana. Five minutes early. He smiled, saved her number and shoved his phone in his pants pocket. Showtime.

Chapter Eight

La Martina was a dream destination. Crisp white linen covered the table. The polished flatware had heft. The glassware was crystal, the plates fine china. The luxurious decor featured subdued lighting that created intimacy. Fresh flowers added pops of spring color. The food was presented in perfectly plated portions that created visual delight. She'd assumed she'd have a quiet dinner with Edmund, but so far their meal had been the exact opposite. If this was what it was like to be the center of attention, Lana wanted no part of it.

The best seat in the house made her feel like a fish in a bowl. Lana watched as another of Beaumont's power couples approached to pay homage to the man seated across from her. As he had several times before, Edmund wiped his lips and set his fork down on the white linen. He rose to shake the man's hand and accept the woman's air kisses. Edmund introduced Lana, and she smiled, but as the couple had no reason to include her in their conversation, they shut her out. Same as each time before, the exchange lasted a minute or two before they left and Edmund returned to his seat. After the fifth time, she wondered how he'd managed to get any of the earlier courses into his mouth.

"I don't know why you're worried about eating alone,"

Lana told Edmund as Beaumont's mayor and his wife walked away. "Everyone and their dog have stopped by."

Edmund's forkful of salad suspended in midair. He frowned. "I didn't see a service animal."

"I was being sarcastic."

"Oh." His forehead creased in confusion. "Is there a reason for that? Did I do something wrong?"

Lana lifted her one and only glass of Riesling and sipped. She'd earlier waved off Edmund's offer of a bottle. "Not you, per se. But the number of people popping by makes it feel like I'm at a table with a revolving door."

"Hazards of my job." Edmund set his fork down. "I'm sorry I didn't take you somewhere quieter. I thought we'd be left alone."

Lana rolled the wine over her tongue and carefully chose her words. "Any of these people would have invited you to join them."

Edmund wiped his lips with the cloth napkin. "True, but I don't want to eat with them or have some impromptu business meeting that masquerades for a meal. I wanted good company, that's you, genuine conversation, also you, and fantastic food. You have to admit that it's been delicious."

"It has," Lana admitted. La Martina lived up to its reputation. "I'm certain it will be packed this weekend." This upcoming Saturday the restaurant was serving a seven-course chef's tasting menu with a price point out of her budget.

Saturday would also mark a week since she and Edmund first met. Their snowed-in dinner had been perfect, unlike the constant interruptions this evening, proving that trying to recapture the magic of that night was futile. Trey had been hers alone. Edmund seemed to belong to everyone else. Lana buttered a roll, the texture of the bread light and airy.

"Do you want me to make a reservation for Saturday night for the both of us?" Edmund asked.

"No, thanks. Bucket list item checked off. I'm good. Besides, I'll probably have family things."

Edmund didn't buy her fast excuse. "Okay, but what if I invite them to come along? I thought we were having a nice time."

"We are, but…" She hesitated. As much as she might like the idea, she reminded herself this couldn't be a real date. She was not going to go to his penthouse suite. As much as the idea of making love with him tempted her body, her brain screamed that their one-off should not be repeated. She was drive-through coffee, not French press. Burgers, not steak. While she'd wanted to try the food at La Martina, from the moment she and Edmund had arrived, they'd been on full display. Either everyone stared at her, wondering who she was and why she was with him, or they dismissed her as insignificant. "Never mind. It's not important."

Edmund gave her his full attention. "No, you don't get to wiggle out of telling me what's wrong. You started saying something, so finish it. You're not the type to shy away from anything, and you've always been blunt, especially with me. Where's the woman who made me give Peter another chance? He says thank you, by the way."

"Good. I'm glad." Lana placed her fork on the salad plate. As if by magic, one of the exceptional waitstaff whisked away the used dishes. Lana should be over the moon to eat here. But unlike that night in the airport hotel bar, a tension existed between her and Edmund. This disquiet hadn't been there between her and Trey, Edmund's convenient alter ego.

She focused on Peter. He was the real reason she was here, fulfilling her side of the bargain. She'd agreed to this dinner in exchange for Edmund saving his job. "You did the right thing, helping Peter. Thank you again for that."

"You're avoiding my question." Edmund fixed his gray-eyed gaze on her, and she trembled under the weight of his attention. "Say it even if you offend me. I'm a big boy. After going viral on the internet, I can take it."

She sipped more liquid courage, the Riesling flat on her tongue. "Honestly? I'm trying to reconcile the person you are with the guy I spent last Saturday night with."

The annoyed pucker of lips she'd thoroughly kissed told her he didn't like the sound of that. "I'm the exact same person."

Disbelief raised Lana's brows. "In appearance, yes, but not in how you act. That night no one knew you as Edmund." She leaned back, suddenly realizing a truth. "Or at least *I* didn't. But only because you told your employees not to reveal who you were or treat you differently. That's why we waited for a table. You would never have waited otherwise."

"Guilty as charged. But only on that one point." Edmund spread his hands across the tablecloth in front of where his plate had been. "It wasn't my intention to deceive you, but I was enjoying the fact that I could be a normal guy. That you didn't want anything from me or have an agenda. I wasn't expecting us to fall into bed, because I meant what I said in the airport. I wasn't hitting on you. Even though there was sexual tension between us from the moment you clobbered me with your tote bag."

His words shot a thrill through her. "You felt it that early?"

Edmund nodded. "Absolutely. And then you sat next to me on the plane and I was a goner."

He'd made her feel desirable. Having finished her wine, Lana reached for her water goblet and ran her finger over the rim. "Neither of us expected to see each other after we deplaned."

"No, but I couldn't let you suffer in the airport." He idly moved his entrée fork a few inches to the left. "I wanted you the moment I saw you. Don't forget you told me this afternoon that you wouldn't have fallen into bed with me had you known I was Edmund Clayton. Can you blame me for wanting one meal where I could be with a beautiful woman who saw me as an average Joe?"

"Nothing about you is average. Not your height. Not your innate power. Not your..." Lana trailed off. He knew what she meant. "Stamina," she finally added.

"Thank you. But you know what I meant. Women in my circle see the dollar signs that come along with being me. You didn't. You just felt attraction."

"I felt the pull. I can understand why you kept the secret and used your nickname. But since I deal in truths, I'm more upset that you didn't come find me the minute you saw me and knew who I was. Especially since you're my boss's boss."

"Would you like me to write some legal document that says I won't fire Cederberg or you? Would that help? I give you my word I won't retaliate."

Lana bit her lip, and then catching herself, let it go. "Maybe."

"I like spending time with you," Edmund continued. "I'm attracted to you, and that's the truth. You promised to show me the Gateway Arch, remember? Or have you rescinded that offer?"

Lana fingered the corner of her napkin. "Edmund, as much as I might be into you, you and I have to be honest with ourselves. One night does not translate into any kind of future. Which means we aren't repeating last Saturday."

Releasing the napkin, Lana gestured to the room. "This scene isn't who I am. I'm a simple girl from a small town who's not looking for a Cinderella story. I don't need saving. I refuse to be the subject of gossip, like people saying. 'Oh, there's another woman with Edmund Clayton.'" She stared him down. "And I refuse to be an afterthought."

Shocked by her words, Edmund thumped against the chair back. "Is that honestly what you believe I think of you? That I'm simply after more sex?"

"You wanted the truth. There it is." Lana sipped her water. The moment she set it down, the busboy refilled her glass.

While he waited for the server to leave, Edmund drummed his fingers on the table, the linen muting the sound. "First, I have never thought of you as just a hookup. I respect you far too much for that. Second, I don't want this dinner to be some chore you have to endure so Peter can have a job. It's unsettling that you see me this way. Rest assured, your job, Peter's job, everyone's job is safe."

He savagely pushed some hair off his forehead, something he did whenever he was frustrated. "Third, I pride myself in not being a playboy like my brother. Unlike Michael, I don't cave into my baser urges. Saturday night was a rare exception. That's a credit to you, that you made me lose myself so thoroughly. I have no regrets. You said it's not happening again, so it won't. That's not what this dinner is about."

She didn't believe him. He could see it in the set of her

chin, the crease between her brows and the way her eyelids had lowered. He'd finally met the one girl who wasn't impressed by him, whom he couldn't charm. "I like you. I respect you and your wishes. I asked you to dinner because I wanted to get to know you better, beyond the physical. Did you google my breakup?"

Lana's chin dipped. "It was painful to watch. You stood there while she berated you."

He shrugged. "Fighting her, having any type of reaction, would have made the situation worse. She spread my personal life across the internet. My business rivals had a field day. I'm still mortified, humiliated and frankly, angry at myself. How could I have not seen her true character? Why did I try to fix things for so long? Then I met you, and found I could be the real me, or at least the guy I'd like to be. Saturday was special, and that's why I wanted to see you again when I found out you were here."

Lana wiggled in her seat. "I want to get to know the real you as well. I'm simply having a hard time figuring out who that is."

"I'm sorry this evening has made you uncomfortable. All I wanted was another meal with you. My entire motivation in a nutshell."

She sighed. "It's just that everyone came by and interrupted us. They didn't even want to talk to me. Maybe the fact that bothered me is a sign of my own insecurities. My ex always dominated the conversation, never let me get a word in edgewise."

"Not my intention. I could have had the chef bring the meal up to Penthouse A. But I didn't want you to get the wrong idea because we'd be alone with a bedroom door as our only defense against temptation. I want you, Lana. If anything, seeing your work ethic today has made me desire you even more."

Her skin flushed a lighter pink than the deeper red color of her hair. "I want you too, but I'd be the one getting hurt. I'm invisible to your peers. They looked straight through me. With Trey, I was an equal partner in everything."

Edmund understood power dynamics. He'd grown up observing them. By his teens he'd mastered them. In business, he dominated the competition. However, Lana kept him off balance. She constantly changed the goal posts. Deep down, he knew she might be right. But he cared about her. Liked her too much to give up. Why couldn't they try? Maybe they'd surprise each other.

"You are not invisible. I should have realized, especially since I haven't been in Beaumont since the Grand opened, that people would want to see me now that my cousin Jack stepped aside. It's not an excuse. I didn't put your needs first."

"Apology accepted, as long as you realize that if I'd known dining in a fishbowl would be the price I paid for exquisite food, I would have had room service toasted ravioli instead."

"You would rather have fried food than this?" Edmund didn't know why toasted ravioli was such a popular St. Louis food, even if the meaty squares had been delicious. "Never mind. We're talking in circles. I like being with you, but you don't feel the same. Is that correct?"

"Yes. No. I don't know." She tapped a finger and stopped as she realized what she was doing. "I liked hanging out with Trey. His world and mine seemed the same. Your world and mine aren't. You're too focused on business. But Trey never showed me that side."

"Yeah, because for one night he got to be someone else."

Edmund sucked his lips into his mouth. He wanted Lana to like him and her words had wounded. He wanted her to see him as the man he could be, someone warm and caring, not cold and heartless. "It's okay. We can just be friends. I often bring out the worst in people. I don't want that to happen to you."

"Now who's selling himself short? You're not a bad guy. You did give Peter a job."

Edmund's stomach churned. He should tell her he was Peter. She deserved to know. Hadn't there been enough subterfuge with the whole Trey/Edmund identity? But he couldn't. "Peter's a better guy than me. Even if he can't use a hammer. You probably like him better than me too. Peter, Trey, me." Edmund punctuated the words to show that Peter ranked higher than the other two.

Guilt swarmed Lana's features. "There's nothing wrong with you. I may love romance novels, but I'm a realist. There are reasons people from different social circles don't usually mingle. You're private jets, not burgers and Budweiser."

Lana's hand gestured toward the room. "Fine dining is your everyday, not mine. Your dad runs a corporation. My dad drives a snowplow and repairs highways. We're one hundred percent blue-collar middle-class. I didn't finish my bachelor's degree. You have an MBA. From Harvard or Yale or something."

Stanford, not that he corrected her. Where he went to grad school didn't matter. He reached for his water, the bourbon he'd had earlier long gone and the glass removed. He hated the metaphorical wall she'd formed between them. "You're making me sound like a rich elitist with no redeeming qualities."

Lana leaned back. "I'm trying to explain how different we are. You're wearing a custom suit. I'm in a dress I found on the clearance rack. Half the women who came to the table took one look at me and turned up their collective noses."

"You're beautiful. You'd put them all to shame wearing rags. I don't care about your clothes."

"I'd embarrass you. And don't think about saying you'd buy me clothing. That would be offensive. I'm not a charity case."

"Of course not." Although he had with Veronica, which was another point in Lana's favor despite her constant of throwing up obstacles. Couldn't she see he'd move heaven and earth for her if needed? He was losing her, watching her slip away. "I don't know why you think you're not good enough to sit across from me. I choose my company and I chose you. Shouldn't that be enough? Fate gave us another chance. I want us to take it."

Their server brought a palate cleanser, providing a sudden break in the conversation. Lana rested against the comfortable chair and studied the room, her gaze anywhere but on Edmund. He didn't like it. He wanted her to look at him, to see how serious he was.

"Your entrées will be out in a few moments. Is there anything else you need right now?" the server asked.

Edmund noted the server had addressed him directly, as if Edmund would also answer for Lana. He waved the server gone, irritated by the slight. This is what Lana meant, he realized. She wanted to be seen for who she was. Trey's world had seen her. Edmund's world did not. He'd known being in his world could be cruel, which is why he'd become Trey that night.

Now that he was Edmund, he still didn't want her to go.

Perhaps as Peter he could get to know her better... No, he couldn't. That would be deliberately dishonest.

"What?" Lana broke the silence.

"Our server didn't even ask you if you needed anything. That's unacceptable. I'll be dealing with that."

"Leave him alone," Lana insisted. To Edmund's surprise she didn't appear pleased by his defense of her. "It's hard enough to be a server without having to be the one serving the boss. He's nervous. Don't you know how intimidating you can be? Especially in a small town like Beaumont?"

Edmund's forehead wrinkled. "We only hire experienced servers for this level of restaurant. That type of slight..."

Lana's chest lifted before she gave a great sigh and cut him off. "Edmund, I'm not worried about a server not asking me how I'm doing. It's those in *your* circle who find me beneath them. They're the ones who bother me. Not the poor guy who's trying to make ends meet. That's the difference. Look, you're big city. I'm Podunk. He deferred to you simply because you own the place, not because I'm unimportant. I know the difference."

"Nothing about you is dull or insignificant and never has been," Edmund protested, trying to check his irritation. He'd had this whole meal planned out. He'd wine and dine her, and they'd recapture the some of the magic from the first night they'd met. Then, with things going well, he'd ask her out for tomorrow as well. "How about we drop this and try to enjoy the rest of our meal. Talk about other, happier things." Maybe then he could get the evening back on track.

"Yes, let's do that. I'm sorry, I don't know what's wrong with me tonight." Lana reached across the table. Heat fused her palm to the top of his hand. He enjoyed the tingling sensation far too much. Wanted it to last forever. He was in far too deep already. She'd break his heart in a way Veronica never could, and he'd probably let her.

"I don't know what's wrong with me either." Edmund shifted so his fingers laced with hers and noted she made no move to free herself. "There's a lot of family and corporate pressure on me this week. It's probably making me a bit of a jerk. Peter and I definitely have the stressful week thing in common. Well, minus the fact that you don't think he's an asshole."

She cracked a smile, and relief filled him. "You've been on the internet enough, so I promise I won't tell your story in that 'am I the asshole' online forum." Her expression shifted into seriousness. "I know it has to be difficult having the pressure of the soft opening and then the grand opening on your shoulders. The Chateau has to be perfect, and it will be. That's my promise to you. Luckily I'm really good at my job and I can tell you're good at yours. So nothing is going to go wrong."

"Thanks. I admire and appreciate your optimism. There's a lot going on." He had another perfect opening to tell her about Peter, but let the opportunity pass by. A billion-dollar acquisition was on the line, and he had a legal obligation to keep this role quiet.

Besides, she liked Peter. He didn't want to lose his connection to Lana. He could get to know her as Peter. Even if that did seem wrong and underhanded. But for the first time in his life, Edmund understood desperation. What was that old saying? Do it and ask for forgiveness later? His need to keep Lana in his life outweighed his honesty.

He swiped his thumb over hers. "I'm realizing I sound like some poor little rich boy whining about my problems."

"I don't think that. Having 'the third' after your name probably means certain expectations."

"Especially from my dad and uncle. Once Jack left, it's all on me." He studied their entwined hands, enjoying the heat their fingers generated. Her hand fit in his like it belonged there. "Then again, is my life really a trap if I like it? If I excel at business? If I enjoy solving the problems it brings? If I want to be CEO because I deserve the glory and the spoils of my hard work. Am I really trapped if I'm doing what I want?"

She removed her fingers from his, and he immediately missed their warmth. "I can't fault you for following your passion when I'm doing the same. I wish things could be different for us here, but they aren't. It's like we're trying to fit a square peg into a round hole. You can't force things that aren't meant to be. Ugh, sorry. I speak in analogies sometimes. Bad habit."

Another one of her adorable quirks. "You fit me perfectly," he told her. Lana flushed deeper. "I mean it. Even with the awkwardness of the constant interruptions tonight, I'm glad we've cleared the air. I hope someday you'll give me another chance."

Their server set down their entrées, chicken piccata, one of Edmund's favorite dishes. He used his knife to push the lemon slice garnish off to the side.

They'd ordered the same meal, and Lana picked up her knife and waved it toward him. "How about you tell me more stories, like you did on the plane? Maybe that might help us salvage some of this. Tell me something a friend should know."

"I can do that." Besides, all wasn't lost. Perhaps what he learned about her by being Peter might help his cause. She'd liked Trey. She liked Peter. Surely, she could like Edmund?

As he cut into the lemony breaded chicken, he began telling her about a college escapade. By the end of dessert, they'd talked nonstop, including laughing so hard at one point Edmund's stomach hurt. While the beginning of the meal hadn't had the best start, by the end they each admitted they'd had a good time. He should have anticipated the circus dining here might cause, but no one else came by and the place eventually cleared out.

His desire to kiss her hadn't lessened, and when she took a bite of cake, Edmund had to yank his gaze away. The power she had over him was strong. He waited until they were finished with dessert before saying, "I owe you an apology. I think I was trying to impress you. I won't do it again."

Lana studied him. "Next time, I pick the place. Somewhere you can be Trey and not Mr. VP."

She'd surprised him. "You're giving me another chance?"

Lana nodded. "I'd like to at least be friends."

"Sure." Being friend-zoned felt like something had stabbed his heart, but he'd work with it. Knowing they both were leaving at the end of the week was pressure enough. Friends would be safer. And if they became more? He'd respect her either way.

Lana reached for one of the after-dinner mints as Edmund signed the check. "You never told me what Peter will be doing tomorrow. I hope it's something he can do well enough to impress rather than depress."

Edmund tamped down the green-eyed monster that roared to life whenever it sensed how much she liked his alter ego. Peter might not look or sound like Edmund, but he was still Edmund underneath. Besides, if she developed an attraction and friendship for his alter ego, she'd realize Edmund could understand her world. That she could fit into his. It was a harebrained idea, and probably coming at the worst time because of the TV show, but Edmund never shied away from going after what he wanted. Lana was under his skin in a way none of his previous girlfriends ever had been. He had to take the risk. She toyed with her water goblet as she waited for his answer. He crossed his fingers she'd forgive him.

"Since you told me how good you are at training, I found Peter the perfect job. He'll be inspecting hotel rooms with you."

Chapter Nine

Despite the positively divine pillow-top mattress and high thread count bedding, Lana tossed and turned most of the night. Why would Edmund put Peter with her? Was he punishing her for their awkward dinner? The end of the meal hadn't been as bad as the beginning, but she knew he wasn't happy with their "date." Perhaps some of her restlessness was that she still craved his touch. Wanted his kisses. But she was not a woman who easily gave into her desires.

Lana double-knotted her work boots. She'd eaten a room service breakfast of scrambled eggs, bacon and toast. Since she'd quit early yesterday, she knew she had to work more efficiently today. And if Peter couldn't catch on? She couldn't worry about that. She could only control what she could control. She'd survive Edmund's challenge. She was an excellent trainer. She and Peter would have a great day.

Lana took the freight elevator to the Grand's lower level. Using her phone, she began checking her email as she made her way to the employee entrance. Then she ran into a solid wall.

Two hands steadied her. "You really need to start watching where you're going," a lisping voice said.

She gripped her phone like a lifeline as her head jerked up. Was Peter even taller today? "Peter! What are you doing here?"

Big teeth dominated his sheepish grin. "Waiting for you. I figured we'd go over together. Mr. Clayton suggested it."

"He did?" *Edmund, what are you playing at?* "I'm glad you're not fired."

"Me too. I'm excited to be working with you today."

Wishing she'd grabbed a cup of coffee, Lana led the way to the UTV. The temperature hovered in the midforties, meaning the snow was mostly melted. She noted a hint of sun peeking from behind some clouds. The forecast had lowered the chance for additional snowfall. She climbed into the side-by-side, and the interior seemed to shrink as Peter filled the entire space.

"They didn't give you one of these to use?" Lana asked as she drove the service road to the Chateau.

"No. Lachlan likes to use this time to go over the day's itinerary."

"Lachlan thinks he's far more important than he actually is." Lana rounded a curve. "Between you and me, he rubs me the wrong way. He's too Hollywood or something."

Peter laughed. "A good description. What type of guy do you like, if you don't mind me asking?"

Was the UTV heater working overtime? Beneath her puffer coat, she felt hot, really hot. "Oh, I'm not dating. I'm focusing on my career. I'm trying to save enough to go to Paris."

"But if you were? What type of guy would interest you?"

Edmund's image came to mind, and Lana shoved it aside and focused on the road ahead. Once both hotels were open, dozens of vehicles would use this service road so that guests would never be disturbed by seeing staff move between one hotel and the other. Today they were the only ones on it. "Why do you want to know?"

The space was too tight for him to shrug, so his tone cajoled instead. "Humor me. The moment we get there you'll be bossing me around and I'll probably mess something up. I'm not trying to ask you out. Just making conversation."

Lana shrugged off the strange disclaimer. "Want some advice? You should be showing confidence on the job site. You have brains. You can do the physical stuff. It's not that hard. Fake it until you make it."

"I admire how you're so confident."

Her hands turned the wheel as she splashed through some standing water. "I want someone who's honest. Open. Not afraid to be himself. I want the love my parents have. That's my answer."

Peter shifted but was too big to get comfortable. "They must be wonderful people."

She spared him a quick glance and found him looking at her. "Oh, they are."

"I overheard someone say you have a younger brother."

"Yes. Ryan. I'm going to his basketball game tonight. I'm not missing it for anything." Lana turned down the heat. Almost there. She needed out of this UTV, as Peter's closeness was making her jittery.

"Basketball's one of my favorite sports. I played some in high school, but baseball was my true love. I try to get to a basketball game now and then. Being there in person is much better than watching on television."

She shot him a glance. He appeared serious. "Would you like to go with me? It's a high school game, so not very exciting. But it'll get you out of the hotel if you don't have anything else to do tonight."

What had made her blurt that out? What was she doing? *Being kind,* she tried to convince herself. Helping someone in need, like she'd been raised. "You could meet me there. No worries if you have other things to do."

"Like contemplating my failures? Your offer is definitely better. Count me in. I'd be honored to accompany you. Thanks for the invite."

They'd reached the Chateau. Lana parked by the loading dock. "I don't see Lachlan's vehicle."

Peter seemed pleased. "That means we'll have time to work before he arrives. You can show me what to do before the cameras get here and interrupt everything."

Lana liked that idea. "That's perfect. I hate being on camera. I'll let that stay Keith's job, especially as they've already paid him. I'll show you the ropes, but it's important that you realize one thing. Once I train you, you're on your own."

By noon, Edmund decided that Peter excelled at quality control. Part of the reason was because Lana had been a great teacher. Edmund had also discovered that she'd meant what she said—once she'd trained Edmund's alter ego, she'd disappeared. As for the job he currently was doing as Peter, one could say Edmund had been doing quality things his entire life.

Basically, Peter's job was simple. He went into a hotel room with an iPad, went down a comprehensive list and ensured every item placed in the room was located correctly and without flaw. In the final weeks before the first guests arrived for the soft opening, beds would be made with freshly washed linens, toiletries placed and all furniture dusted and floors vacuumed. By that point Lana and her team would be long gone, off to another hotel.

While he worked undercover in his Peter costume, Edmund became even prouder of how the Chateau had turned out. A few years ago, when the Conquering Claytons, as Edmund's father and uncle were known, had started their master plan for the area, they'd had wanted to bring the glory of the Napa and Sonoma Valleys to the Midwest. Since then, Clayton Holdings had transformed this part of Missouri Wine Country into a national tourist destination. They'd done it in a way that had benefitted not only the town, but the entire region.

Companies needed continued growth to thrive, or at least Clayton Holdings did. That was why the Chateau sought to be the most luxurious hotel experience in the Midwest. Each winery had a different theme, and each hotel also had a niche. Built first, The Grand Hotel had a PGA championship golf course, a world-class spa and swimming pools that fit seamlessly into the lush landscape. The Chateau was the ultimate in privacy and discretion, created for those who wanted to get away. Each of the thirty-seven rooms had its own feel.

A Hollywood filmmaker celebrating his fiftieth wedding anniversary had booked the entire place for his immediate family, with the overflow guests at the Grand. He'd purchased a week's stay in May.

A descendent of one of St. Louis's beer barons had done the same. She would have her June wedding in the conservatory. Like the Biltmore and the houses at Newport Beach and on Long Island, The Chateau allowed guests to experience the life of a bygone era, but with modern comforts, top-notch amenities and high-speed Wi-Fi.

Edmund glanced up as Lachlan gave a dramatic sigh.

"Edmund, Peter, whatever, this is so *boring*." Lachlan waved at Ben, sending the cameraman away. "There's no drama watching you press on a tablet. This is not making for good TV."

"We still have to film Peter's scene with Billie. Let's go do that," Edmund suggested.

Billie was the Grand's housekeeping supervisor. She'd been working double shifts for the past week ensuring that Cederberg Interiors had correctly laundered, pressed, inspected and stored the bedding. Still to complete were the towels and dining room linens... The list was endless.

However, Lachlan dismissed the idea of filming Billie outright. "Later. Right now I want you to interact with Lana. She's much more interesting, wouldn't you say?"

Edmund's heart rate increased. He and Lana had had a full half hour together before everyone else arrived. They'd talked the entire time as if they'd been old friends. Of course, she thought she was with Peter, which gave Edmund twinges of guilt. "Lana doesn't want to be filmed."

"All women want to be on camera," Lachlan insisted.

"Then you don't know the right women," Edmund shot back. "When she taught me how to do inspections, Lana told me she didn't have any desire to be on this show. That's why you're dealing with Keith."

"We could have used footage of her training you. You need to be clearing these things with me." Lachlan was clearly miffed. Even if she was eccentric, Edmund thought Margot Van Horn was a lovely person. Her grandson was a dolt. Edmund couldn't believe her genes ran in this man.

"Your show is going to be boring," Lachlan said. "You need to give me something."

"I'm not giving you Lana when she doesn't want it," Edmund said. Especially after the awkward exchange in the lobby after dinner, something akin to, "Well, this has been nice," and, "I'll text you." Edmund didn't remember his and Lana's exact words. But he could remember every detail of how he and Lana stood there before they'd each laughed self-consciously and turned away. He'd gone toward the private penthouse elevator and she toward the main one.

He had to convince her to give another chance, which would not happen if Lachlan and Edmund forced her on camera. When he'd sat in his suite last night, Edmund had come to realize he wanted something more than sex with Lana. He wanted a deeper connection.

Not that he could tell Lana that truth yet. Edmund normally wasn't scared of anything. Not even Veronica and the viral video fallout had made him quake in his boots. Veronica's actions had been akin to Edmund being stung by a bee—it had made him angry, annoyed and given him some temporary pain.

Lana's outright rejection would wound him deeply, even if he didn't fully understand why. His head hadn't fully processed the reasons. Or maybe he'd locked them away— because after all, they'd just met and it was far too soon to feel like this.

This morning, when he'd squeezed into the UTV, his left arm had brushed against hers. He hadn't felt her skin, but the touch had made him extra aware. So had her scent and her smile. When she'd invited Peter to watch the basketball game, he'd jumped at the chance because he wanted to spend time with her.

He knew he was courting danger. But he couldn't help himself. He wanted the friendship she showed Peter even more than the lust she'd shared with Edmund. He hated that Peter seemed more her choice. Lana wanted a guy who was "Honest. Open. Not afraid to be himself." She wanted a love like her parents. He'd meet them tonight, and he found himself nervous about the prospect. Edmund, for the first time ever, might have found the one person he couldn't resist who could resist him. Who didn't want to be a part of his life.

"Lana!" Lachlan shouted her name as she walked by. He

MICHELE DUNAWAY 143

pointed at Peter but directed his words at Lana. "I want to film you and Peter interacting. This inspecting stuff isn't cutting it."

"No." She didn't hesitate or consider Lachlan's request. Her answer was immediate, earning even more of Edmund's admiration. He drank her in, enjoying the way she stood up to Lachlan's demands.

Lachlan brought out the big guns. "You have to do it. You signed a waiver."

"But not for what you want. I checked. There's no amount of money that can get me to be on your show." Lana folded her arms, the iPad pressed against her chest.

Edmund tried not to snicker as Lachlan's ammo missed the target. The fact Lachlan had thought threatening Lana would work showed he didn't know her very well. Edmund put the back of his hand to his upper lip and pretended to scratch the underside of his nose. The mustache he wore as Peter did itch something fierce.

Thwarted, Lachlan's lips puckered. Then he smiled and changed tactics. "Peter's doing a great job with inspections. That's because of you."

Lana didn't soften. "I'm glad you approve. He helped me get back on schedule following yesterday's debacle after your production company kept getting in the way. We do have a hotel to open."

Lachlan's smile slipped. "We also have a show to film, and he's now doing too great of a job. I'd hate for him to lose because his show is boring. You saved him once. Won't you save him again?"

That line formed in Lana's forehead. "I didn't think he was being judged on how exciting his show is."

Lachlan tried to reel her in. "It's all part of the process. Ratings, darling. He needs them."

"I'm not your darling," Lana snapped.

"Lachlan, if she says no, she means no. You don't need to badger her." Edmund had had enough. He sent Lachlan a warning glance that the man ignored.

"I'm only working in your best interests," Lachlan defended.

Lana stepped back, eager to escape. "I told Mr. Clayton that I didn't want to be filmed. Take it up with him."

"Believe me, I will." Lachlan waited until Lana moved out of earshot before rounding on Edmund. "You need to get her on camera."

"No means no. You need to respect that." Edmund shook his head, then pressed his fingers to Peter's wig to ensure it remained in place.

Lachlan wasn't going to be dissuaded. "You need to worry that if your show sucks, you're not going to be buying my grandmother's hotels. Same for if you don't cooperate. Justus was much better at this than you."

Edmund had no idea if that last remark was true, but the jab landed. "I'll see what I can do. But if she says no, it's no."

Lachlan smirked. "Mr. Clayton saved your job yesterday. I'm sure he can find a way to *persuade* her."

"Stop making it sound so unsavory," Edmund shot back. He was already deceiving Lana more than he was comfortable with. "You may think you have the upper hand because you're producing this show, but you're forgetting one thing. These are *my* hotels, and the contract gave me complete control over the episode."

"If there's no episode, you don't get *my* hotels. It would be wise if you didn't forget that." The producer gave an exaggerated eye roll.

Lachlan was a classic example of nepotism gone bad,

and Edmund itched to wipe that smug expression off his face. "You know what, Lachlan? Don't push me. It might just be worth losing some hotels to put you in your place. Trust me, I'd enjoy it."

Everyone in business knew not to push Edmund, and Edmund hid his victory smile as Lachlan sobered. If Lana didn't want to be filmed, it wouldn't happen on Edmund's watch.

After Peter had gone to meet Billie, Lana hadn't seen him again. She kept looking though, until she learned from Keith that Peter had returned with Billie to the Grand so he could learn about the Grand's laundry operations. Lana glanced at her iPad. She'd made amazing progress today. She could leave in fifteen minutes and have a guilt-free evening with her parents and Peter. She was making some notes on the whiteboard hanging in the breakroom when Keith entered.

"Hey, Lana. Lachlan said he wants to talk with you tomorrow. He'll probably find you first thing. Wanted you to be prepared. He gets on my nerves."

"Yeah, he does." Before she could say more, Lana's phone pinged with a text from Edmund. Had a nice time last night. You said next time you're picking the place. You up for doing that tonight?

Lana quickly sent back, Have a previous commitment. My brother's basketball game.

Edmund's reply appeared quickly: No worries. Hope it's a winner.

A few seconds later, another text came in from Edmund. BTW, Lachlan said you're refusing to participate in filming. I told him to respect your wishes. He shouldn't bother you again. If he does, let me know.

That was nice of Edmund. She appreciated that he'd backed her up. Lana typed quickly. Thanks.

She added a smiley face, but not the blushing one or the one with the wide, toothy grin that reminded her of Peter. Just the regular smile emoji. She watched her screen, but Edmund didn't text again. She tucked her phone in her coat pocket and noticed Keith was still standing there. "Sorry. I didn't realize you were waiting for me."

"Who was that?"

Lana shoved her phone into her tote bag. "Just a friend."

"Uh-huh. You had a giddy expression on your face."

Lana waved a finger at him. "I did not. It was a friend. That's all. Besides, I can't do long distance, and our jobs keep us on the road."

"As long as you weren't texting Lachlan. The man seems to have a thing for you."

Lana shuddered. "He doesn't have my number, and he's never getting it."

"Smart girl," Keith said. Lana arched a brow, and Keith grinned. "Sorry. Can't help but be your work dad. My girls are grown and living their own lives. I see you more than them."

"You want to head back over? I've got my brother's game so I'm leaving now. I'm taking Peter with me. He's just sitting in his hotel room. He really should get out."

"Was that the friend you just texted?" Keith asked.

"No. Someone else. You could go to my brother's game if you want. Anyone can go. Well, excluding Lachlan. He's definitely not invited, nor are his cameras."

Keith chuckled. "As much as I like basketball, the idea of sitting on bleachers in a high school gym holds little appeal after a long day of being on my feet. I want a beer and sports on TV. Have fun. Hope your brother's team wins."

"Me too." After making sure she had her belongings, Lana drove the UTV to the Grand and freshened up in her room. Because of her mom's insistence that they "weren't going to make the poor man Uber," Lana met Peter in the lobby at six-thirty. He'd changed into a different pair of jeans and a new flannel shirt. The first few buttons were undone, revealing a white thermal t-shirt underneath.

Peter fell into step beside her as they went outside under the heated portico. "Thanks for inviting me. I appreciate it."

"You're welcome." Lana pointed to an older model GMC Yukon as the SUV drove into the circle. "That's my mom. You sit in front. It'll be more comfortable." Lana opened the back door and climbed in. "Hey, Mom. This is Peter."

The moment everyone's seat belts were secure, Lana's mom put the SUV in gear. The drive to the high school took fifteen minutes. Admission was five dollars for those who didn't have sports passes, and Peter covered his and Lana's tickets. "Least I can do."

Lana's dad had saved them seats behind the home bench and about eight rows up. From there, they had a clear view of the court. "It's a good crowd for a Tuesday night game," Lana's mom said before she began talking to the parents of one of Ryan's teammates.

"Bringing back memories?" Lana asked Peter. He sat to her left.

Peter removed his coat and set it next to him in the sliver of space between him and Lana's dad. "Is it just me or do all high school gyms smell the same?"

"It's floor varnish and sweat," her dad said. He reached his left hand over and introduced himself. As Peter and her dad began talking sports, Lana felt unaccountably pleased by how well the two men got along. Team warm-ups ended, and the MC announced the starters, including Lana's brother.

After the national anthem, her mom elbowed Lana and leaned closer. "He seems nice. Is he single?"

"Mom," Lana protested. "Don't. He's just a friend, and I'm using that loosely as I've known him exactly two days. He's the subject of the show that's filming at the Grand. Stop trying to get me to settle down."

"I just don't like that you're alone."

For some reason Edmund's handsome face came to mind, especially the way he'd smiled at her over plates of delicious food. "I'm not. I was out last night. We had dinner."

"Anyone I know?"

While Peter spoke with Lana's dad, Lana filled her mom in, leaving out the sexual details, of course. "That's why it can't work."

Her mom's fingers rummaged in a red-and-white-striped bag of freshly popped popcorn before she passed the bag to Lana. "Well, I can't say I'm not disappointed you won't be seeing him again. Don't give me that look. I can't help that I'm old-fashioned. I'd love some grandchildren to spoil at some point."

"You're going to be too busy traveling to Ryan's college games. Stop rushing things."

"What are you rushing?" Peter caught this part of the conversation as the referee blew the whistle.

"Grandchildren," Lana's mom filled in helpfully. "I keep hoping Lana meets someone nice and settles down."

"Mom!" Lana's embarrassed indignation was real.

Peter laughed. "That's every mother's dream. My mom feels the same way and tells me all the time that she's not getting any younger. Do you want kids, Lana?"

"Someday." Lana's eyes tracked the action on the court.

Ryan's teammate had missed a shot and Beaumont High was on defense. The other team scored first, eliciting groans from the home crowd. "You?"

"Definitely. But I'm not in any rush, much to my mother's consternation." Peter gave Lana a smile, one she returned.

"Sounds like your mom and my mom would agree on that," she told him.

Lana and Peter rose with the home crowd as Ryan dribbled toward the three-point line. His rainbow shot bounced off the rim and Beaumont lost the rebound. Everyone settled back on the bleachers as one of Ryan's teammates fouled. After substitutions, players gathered for the foul shots.

"So how many?" Peter asked as the crowd began to yell "air ball."

Lana turned to him as the first shot hit the rim. "How many what?"

"Kids. How many?"

"I don't know. One? Two? If I have more than one, definitely closer in age than Ryan and I are. This is the first basketball game of Ryan's I've ever seen."

"You could move home," her mom said.

"Mom!" Lana protested. "Enough."

The visiting team scored, and Ryan claimed the rebound. The crowd rose to its feet, and seconds later Lana's brother had added three points. "He's really good," Peter said.

"I don't know much about the sport," Lana said, her gaze never leaving the action on the court. "But he looks good out there."

"Trust me, he's got the it factor. Now they just have to win."

By halftime, Lana was a bundle of nerves. How did her parents sit through Ryan's games week after week? Lana wanted Beaumont to win so badly she'd gripped her knees. "Is it always like this? They can't seem to get a break."

"Previous teams were much easier," her dad said. "There's still another half left."

Beaumont struggled with turnovers. The home team never took the lead, but thanks to Ryan and his teammates, the deficit had never exceeded five points. The team could easily turn things around, provided Beaumont came out of the locker room believing they could do it.

"Shall we stretch our legs?" Peter asked.

"Sure." Lana realized how stiff hers were as the crowd left the bleachers during halftime. Peter followed her as she led the way into the school commons, a two-story multi-purpose area almost the size of the gym they'd left. During the day the area also served as a cafeteria, but tonight the lunch tables were folded and moved against a far wall, allowing for the Winter Guard to work on its choreography. The guard didn't use music but rather counted out loud as they synchronized their steps.

"The school never really sleeps, does it?" Peter asked.

"Maybe around eleven. That's when the janitors go home." They approached the snack bar where parent club volunteers sold cookies, sodas and popcorn. She pulled some money out of her pocket. "I'm getting a bottle of water. Want anything?"

Peter reached for a wallet fraying at the edges. "You should let me pay."

"My parents would have my hide if you do. You're our guest."

Peter pointed to the rows of candy on the back counter. "Peanut M&M's would be great."

His choice gave her a sense of déjà vu. Surely he couldn't know. "Those are my favorite. Good choice."

He gave her a big goofy grin, one she returned. "Look at what we have in common. They're so much better than the plain ones."

"Most definitely." Even more aware of Peter's presence, Lana paid for two packages of peanut M&M's and two bottles of water. She passed Peter his portion. "My second choice is the peanut butter ones. Then plain."

Peter ripped into the yellow packaging. "What about the caramel? Or the pretzel ones?"

She drank from the bottle and swiped a hand under her lips to catch a loose droplet. "Good, but not enough to entice me. But you know what does? There's a bag that mixes peanut, peanut butter and plain. That's the best of all worlds."

"I'll have to remember that. Now I know how to tempt you."

They moved to a less crowded part of the commons, ripping into their candy and putting pieces into their mouths. Lana tried not to stare at Peter's huge teeth. He towered over most of the people there. "What do you think? Is this like you remember high school?"

"I don't think our student section dressed like their grandparents."

Lana grinned. "Your school didn't have home game theme nights?"

"We were too cool for that. Did you see those costumes? There were kids with walkers in there."

Lana laughed. "Beaumont goes all out. When I'm old, I hope I can move like those kids do."

"That's for sure." Peter uncapped his water and sipped. "Thanks again for having me. I really appreciate it."

She poured more candy. "It's been fun getting to know you. You're not exactly what I thought you were." She'd been pleasantly surprised and found herself liking him more and more. "I thought you were some guy trying to find a workaround so he could be on television. Have you ever noticed how so many of those shows have the same people on them? Like there was this dating show and the potential dates all had IMDb pages. That's why I stick with movies."

"You're exactly like I thought. Kind and generous. And beautiful."

Lana felt her face heat, and she wagged a forefinger at him. "Flatterer."

Big hands lifted in mock protest. "Hey, you bought me M&M's. I have to repay you somehow. Compliments it is."

Lana laughed. "Well, if M&M's is all it takes for endless compliments, how many bags do you want?"

"Dozens. That way we can be forever friends. Although, you're the type of woman a guy falls for."

"You are too sweet." Peter was fun. She also didn't believe he was serious. "I'll have to go to Costco or Sam's Club."

"Perfect."

Lana's heart gave a flip when she realized he was serious. He wasn't as attractive as Edmund—who was?—but she and Peter got along really well. Just friends, she told herself. Then why were they flirting? And what did she plan on doing about it?

Lana's mom approached. "Second half is about to begin."

Already the crowd was moving back into the gymnasium. Saved by the buzzer.

Chapter Ten

As the second half began, Lana made sure there was plenty of bleacher space between her and Peter. Not enough to fit another person, but enough for their coats. They made a good barrier. She reminded herself that this wasn't a real date. It was her brother's high school basketball game. Peter had nothing better to do. She was being friendly. That was all. She was not attracted to the guy who looked like the model on the paper towel packaging. Certainly not in the way she was attracted to Edmund.

She did like Peter, though. Not in that like-like way when she'd been a student crushing on the popular guy. Not even like when she'd met her ex-fiancé at the local four-year college. Not like when she'd swooned over Trey/Edmund.

She liked Peter because he was real. He was a nice guy who treated people with respect. He had a great sense of humor, and at one point Lana's dad had even pointed to Peter and given Lana a thumbs-up behind his back.

Peter had that special something. When he'd told her tonight he wasn't doing the show for the money but rather for his family, this time she believed him. Family mattered to him, especially his younger sister. They were talking about her now. "You wouldn't believe the amount of pressure she put on me to do the show," Peter said. "She finds the whole thing rather funny, especially because it makes me uncomfortable. She says I don't get out of my comfort zone enough. That I'm too stuck in my ways."

"I'm understand that. I'm stuck in a loop myself," Lana admitted. "Exactly when do we know to get off the carnival ride? When is it good enough? Do you ever feel like you're never satisfied? Because I do."

"That's what makes you great at your job."

Peter knew exactly what to say, making Lana appreciate him even more. "But as my mom likes to say, a job doesn't keep you warm at night."

"Do you want to be kept warm at night?" Peter held up his hands before shoving them back into his lap. "Not that I'm volunteering."

She kept hearing those words or something to their effect. First from Edmund, now Peter. A sliver of disappointed déjà vu shot through her. Her ego might like it if he hit on her, even if nothing came of it. "I used to think I didn't need anyone. I was having an adventure. Then I met someone. And he's..." She paused. Heaved a sigh.

"Your secret is safe with me."

"It doesn't matter. Each of us travels too much for work. And I've got plans. Goals. Dreams to achieve. My mom wants me to settle down, but whenever I think about giving up traveling, the walls seem to close in."

Lana glanced down toward her mother, who, for this half of the game, sat on the other side of Lana's dad. "Sometimes I wonder if there's something wrong with me."

As Lana slapped a hand over her mouth, it took everything Edmund had not to gather her into his arms.

"I can't believe I said that to a total stranger," Lana said. "Just ignore that."

As guilt powered through him, it took Edmund every ounce of willpower not to blurt out who he was. Edmund wasn't a stranger, but Peter was. When Edmund had wanted to get to know Lana better through his alter ego, he hadn't expected her to share these types of confidences, secrets she'd never tell Edmund, especially as he'd figured out who she meant when she'd said she'd met someone.

"I won't use it against you," Edmund said, making a promise both he and Peter would keep.

"My inability to be satisfied and settled is common knowledge. You heard my mom. It's what people want from me. It's why I broke things off with my ex. I realized we didn't suit. Not long-term. He was a John Mellencamp song, just with vacation at the Lake of the Ozarks and not the Gulf of Mexico."

"'Pink Houses.'" Edmund knew the song.

"Yeah. Google the Richard Marx song 'Satisfied.' Even though it's from 1989, it's my mantra. I grew up with his stuff on repeat since my mom loves him. She saw him recently in concert at the casino."

Edmund reached into his bag of M&M's and extracted several. Lana had already eaten hers, and Edmund poured some into her hand. "That will be us someday, you know, going to concerts of musicians we loved when we were this age."

"Let's hope we both have someone to share it with," Lana said. "You know what really bothers me though? How easily replaceable I was to my ex. Not that I want him back," Lana added hastily. "Simply that I was so easily forgotten. As if I didn't matter at all."

"He sounds like a grade A idiot. You deserve someone who will give you the sun, moon and stars."

"But what if I made a mistake and I'll never find some-one?"

Edmund understood that fear. "There are worse things than being alone," he told her. "One is being with the wrong person. And look at it this way. If you made a mistake, you wouldn't be here with me."

Edmund watched as she filled her mouth with M&M's. Had that been the moment she'd become so desirable? When he'd watched her eat candy on the plane? He had turned into one of the guys in those "I met my forever on the plane" stories.

"What if this is a mistake?" Lana gestured wildly. "Maybe in another universe my life is different."

"Well, since there's probably not a rip in the space-time continuum, I'd say you're pretty safe from being a mistake, much less making one. You're awesome, Lana. This morning you told me to be confident. So fake it until you make it. And tell you what, when you do, I'll have your back."

Lana crushed the empty plastic water bottle, and the plastic crinkled. "Do you always know the right thing to say?"

If he'd said the right thing, he would have told her he was Edmund, not Peter. He would have ended this farce and let the chips fall where they may. He sensed it was already too late for him to come clean. "Far from it. But with you it's easy."

Lana had never met someone so easy to talk to. It felt as if she'd known Peter forever. Long ago, in middle school, a friend had accused her of overlooking the geeky boys for the cute ones. The rebuke had stayed with Lana. She could never have talked with Edmund like this. He was everything women flocked to, having looks and money. But Peter was the better guy.

A shout and the crowd jumping to its feet stopped Lana from thinking too much. The game, which she and Peter had watched as they'd talked, had been within three points for most of the fourth quarter. She rose as Ryan scored to tie the game. When Lana sat back down, her mom reached across her husband and grabbed Lana's hand and squeezed.

"Ow."

"I'm sorry. I just get so nervous," her mom apologized as she let go. "If they don't win, they're eliminated."

"I promise to attend more of his college games than I did high school." Lana rubbed her fingers. Play continued and the clock wound down. Beaumont blocked a drive and gained offensive control. With another two-pointer, Beaumont took the lead. As the teams rushed to the opposite side of the court, Ryan stole the ball. The home crowd began screaming, reaching a crescendo as Lana's brother reached the line. Lana held her breath as the clock went under four seconds. Both of Ryan's feet left the ground, and the ball swished through the net exactly as the buzzer sounded. Crazy didn't even begin to describe the elation on the gym floor as the team and student section rushed out to congratulate her brother.

"Incredible. That had to be at least a thirty-inch vertical jump," Peter said.

"I have no idea what that means, but my brother being incredible is an understatement if there ever was one." Lana exhaled the excess adrenaline. "I can't believe they won!"

"That's my boy!" Lana's dad announced to the crowd as other parents approached to high-five her parents. "All one hundred ninety-five pounds of him."

"Does that mean something special I should know

about?" Lana asked Peter. Peter shrugged and gave her a loopy grin that made butterflies take flight in her stomach.

Beaumont shook hands with the opposing team and headed into the locker room. The gym began to empty.

Her mom gestured toward the doors. "Shall we? You both have an early morning, don't you?"

"We do." Lana half sensed, half felt Peter's hand guard her back as she made her way down the ancient bleachers. Inside the car, Lana leaned her head against the seat back and listened to her mom and Peter discuss the game and Ryan's college options.

"Thanks again for inviting me," Peter told her mother once they arrived at the hotel. A valet hustled over as Peter exited.

Lana's mom leaned so she could see out the open passenger door. "We're so happy you joined us. Don't be a stranger."

Peter bent his head so he could see her mom. "I won't."

"Love you, Mom. Talk to you tomorrow." Lana stepped away before her mother said something like how much she'd liked Peter. She'd probably text it later anyway. Lana and Peter watched as the taillights receded.

"Shall we?" Peter indicated she should enter before him. Then he paused. "But before we do, I had a great night."

"Me too," Lana said. She shivered as the wind blew under the portico. The temperature had dropped.

Peter noticed. "Come on, let's get inside where it's warm."

They went through the first set of sliding doors and then through the second. Lana began to unwrap her scarf as they entered the lobby. Then she stopped so short that Peter had to edge around her. Lachlan was leaving the bar. He saw them and stepped into their path, cutting them off from reaching the elevators. "Don't you two look cozy. Where have you been tonight?"

"A high school basketball game." Lana's irritation flared. Lachlan's arrival was like someone bursting a balloon. He was the last person she wanted to see.

Lachlan crossed his arms. "You should have let me bring the cameras on your date."

Before Lana could snap at Lachlan, Peter mimicked Lachlan's stance. At mid-six feet, he towered over the shorter man. "And get all those consent forms signed?" Peter asked. "I don't think so."

"Well, when you put it that way, perhaps the game wouldn't be a good idea. But I still need visuals that will entice the viewers. Did you ask her?"

"No. Why would I? She gave you her answer earlier."

"Maybe she's changed her mind, since you're so cozy and all."

Lachlan's smile annoyed Lana, and she faced Peter. "Ask me what, Peter?" Lana asked.

Lachlan answered instead. "To be on camera. What we filmed today is boring. In order for Peter..." Lachlan coughed out the man's name as if he were catching his breath. He gathered himself. "In order for Peter to win a bonus, he has to have ratings. Getting ratings means having drama. Watching him click an iPad all day today was not good television. But the way the two of you interact? Maybe we should add a little showmance to liven things up."

"No," said Peter at the same time Lana said, "What would that involve?"

"A showmance? I'd think that would be obvious." Lachlan smirked.

"I meant being on camera helping him train," Lana corrected coolly. "You said Peter's work today was boring. You're not faulting my training, are you?"

"Of course not." Lachlan turned smooth as butter. "But

the audience didn't see you training him. Just what he was doing afterward. Click. Click."

Lana heaved a sigh. "Do iPads even click?"

Lachlan rolled his eyes. "Does it matter? His episode is going to be change-the-channel boring."

"You don't have to do this, Lana. I told him no," Peter said.

"Would it help you out if I did?" Lana didn't wait for Peter to respond before rounding on Lachlan. She resisted poking the producer in the chest and telling him how annoying he was. "You need footage of me training Peter in order to use what you have and make it look less boring, right? Is that what you're asking me for?"

"Yes. At the minimum."

Before Lachlan could add more, Lana interrupted. "Mr. Clayton said I can do what I want, that it's up to me. We can shoot that scene tomorrow morning before Peter goes off to his next job. Which is?" Lana gazed at Peter, whose forehead featured a deep wrinkle of confusion. His nose even contained wrinkles of consternation.

"Valet for half a day. Bellman the other half," Lachlan said.

"Great. Parking cars makes for nice visuals. Same for loading luggage. Plenty of opportunities to get footage of things that aren't boring. So no need for a showmance. I'll meet you at the Chateau at eight. I'll give you thirty minutes of my time."

"Lana, you don't have to do this," Peter protested. "The show will be fine."

She placed a hand lightly on his arm. "Friends, right? I'll see you tomorrow. Now I'm going to go text Mr. Clayton. He and I need to chat."

Lana strode toward the elevator and, reaching it, pushed

the button. Thankfully the doors slid open immediately. She stepped inside and pressed her keycard to unlock the lift. She allowed herself to look across the expanse of lobby after she pressed the button for her floor. Peter and Lachlan seemed to be arguing. The doors closed, and Lana slumped against the wall.

Then she reached for her phone and sent a text to Mrs. Cederberg before sending one to Edmund. He needed to know what she'd agreed to. Hopefully he'd be okay with her decision, because the last thing she wanted was the wrath of Edmund Clayton III.

As Lana strode off, Edmund gritted his teeth and checked his temper. He wasn't a violent man, but he'd like to wipe the marble floor with Lachlan, or at least punch the smug grin off his face. "I cannot believe you did that. I told you not to ask Lana. I don't want her involved in any of this."

"Too late now. She's agreed." As if suddenly aware of Edmund's ire, Lachlan took a step back. "Let's be real here. You want to win. Justus wants to win. My grandmother's batty, but I love what she's trying to do for my career. I need this chance to make great TV. Do you think I want to be producing this type of show for the rest of my life? Hell no. I want to be Spielberg. Or Christopher Nolan. Or the next Wes Anderson. My family's money can only get me so far. Work with me. You want hotels. I want film credits."

Edmund was well aware they were standing in the middle of the lobby, in view of everyone and those ever-watching security feeds. He wanted to yell several expletives, which honestly was so out of character for him that the thought of doing so shocked him. Fish out of water? More like a man trying to balance dozens of spinning plates about to crash. His phone pinged.

He pivoted, hiding the screen from Lachlan. Lana had texted, Hey, back from the game. Ran into Lachlan downstairs. Need to talk to you. Are you in your penthouse? I'll come by in 10 minutes.

Then another text: Wait, you might not be alone. Umm, if you're with someone, just don't answer when I knock. I'll know to go away.

"Damn it." Edmund growled out the words. "We're done here. I'll see you at eight."

Edmund went into the main elevator and keyed Peter's floor. He texted Lana, Give me 15 minutes. And yes, I'm alone.

He raced inside Peter's room, stripped off his clothes and dumped the contacts into the solution. He tore out the dental partial that modified his bite and his voice. He yanked off the rubbery nose piece and tossed aside the wig. He ran his hands through his own hair to ensure no pins remained. He peeled off the mustache, soul patch and sideburns. Those always left his skin chafed, but tonight he couldn't do anything about the redness beyond rub some lotion into the spots where the glue had been. Quickly he changed into his regular dress clothes.

This changeover was the worst part of the entire undercover outfit. Having to move between suites took time and energy, and he'd have to be back here bright and early tomorrow morning so he could be at the Chateau by eight.

Lana demanding to see the boss that first day had necessitated even more subterfuge. Peter wouldn't be staying in a penthouse, and Edmund wouldn't be in a regular room. Besides, in his Peter disguise, he'd had to make several selfie-style confessional videos. He poked his head out the door, saw no one and made his way quickly across the hall to the service elevator. He took it down to the first floor and made his way to the bar. Thankfully Lachlan had gone on his merry way. "Woodford Reserve. Neat."

"Yes, Mr. Clayton." The bartender made haste and Edmund left a hundred-dollar bill as a tip. Then he made his way to the private elevator. When the doors slid open to the hallway beyond, he saw Lana knocking on the door to Penthouse A. She wore the same clothes as earlier.

He called out to her. "Hey, I'm here. I was downstairs. Sorry I wasn't waiting when you arrived." He swiped his keycard and held the door open so she could go first.

"Did I interrupt you?" She seemed nervous.

He lifted his glass. "I was in the bar getting a drink. Proof I wasn't shoving someone out the door."

"Maybe you shoved them out of the bar."

He didn't even like that she might believe that. "Not my style. When I told you I wanted you, I meant you and no one else." Edmund flipped a switch, and the lights in the living area joined those already lit in the short foyer. "Have a seat."

Lana instead wandered around the room. "This is really nice. I haven't seen what the penthouses look like."

Edmund sipped his whiskey, and heat bloomed across his chest. "We want the Grand to win all the stars and diamonds."

"My room is lovely. One of the nicest I've ever stayed in. This suite is like a movie set, even more opulent than the one at the airport hotel."

"Airports are usually full of businessmen passing through. The Grand provides a resort experience. Totally different hotel grades."

She went to the window. "What views do you have? Ah, you're lucky. Both the golf course and the lake."

"And the river valley, not that you can see the river because of the distance and the thick trees along the bank." Trying to control his libido and raging emotions, he sipped more whiskey. "Why are you here, Lana? After last night's dinner, I got the impression that you hoped we wouldn't run into each other again. Not that I'm not glad to see you."

"Well, I'm not here for sex." Her voice cracked.

Edmund wished he could tell her the truth. Instead, he had to tread carefully. "As much as I enjoyed having sex with you and wouldn't mind repeating the experience, you're not the type to go to a man's room for a nightcap. So tell me why you needed to see me so urgently that it couldn't wait until morning." Even though he already knew. She was here about Peter. Peter, whom Edmund was starting to hate.

"I'm sorry it's so late. Although it's not even ten, and you were at the bar, not sleeping. You're probably the type who works all night anyway, especially when you're on the road." The words rushed out, another sign she was nervous.

He tipped his glass toward her. "You know me so well. You're here, so tell me what you want."

"It's about Peter."

"Did he do something else wrong?" Edmund somehow managed to appear curious as he waited for her to tell him she'd agreed to be on camera. And if he didn't need to keep this farce going, if he didn't need to win these hotels, he'd tell Lana the truth this instant—any legalities be damned— so they could have a laugh and maybe even fall into bed just through that door.

Well, he hoped she'd laugh. Somehow, he didn't think she'd be as amused as he was.

"No, it's not Peter. It's me. They want me on camera."

"I told you that you don't need to be. There is no reason

for you to be uncomfortable in order to help Peter with his show."

"Lachlan says it's necessary."

"The producer is a jerk." Edmund sipped more whiskey to keep from spitting out more vile things, especially after the conversation he'd had with the man in the lobby several minutes ago.

Lana paced. "He says the footage they have is boring."

"Do you want some water? Wine?" When she said no, Edmund gestured to a love seat, and Lana sat. He edged onto a cushion on the couch perpendicular from hers, set his drink down, manspread his knees and dug his elbows into the top of this thighs so he could rub his palms together. "What's in it for you?"

The question shocked her. "What do you mean?"

"Why do you care so much about a man you just met, one who's only after fame and money? You must care if you're willing to defend him and badger me into keeping him from being fired. Now you're willing to allow yourself to be filmed. I genuinely want to know the reason."

He did. That part wasn't a lie. He'd had a great time tonight—well, Peter had—because Lana had opened up to Peter in ways she never had with Edmund. It was crazy to be jealous of his alter ego, but he was. She might have given Edmund—as Trey—her body, but she'd given Peter pieces of her soul. Didn't she know how much that cut him? Of course, she couldn't know, but Edmund did. Slice by slice, she'd dissected pieces of him, sacrificing their chemistry for friendship with Peter, a man who didn't really exist. A man whom she obviously liked far better than the one who sat before her now. "Just be straight with me like you always are."

Lana rubbed a spot on her arm. "Maybe I'm helping him

because someone helped me when I was down. He's easy to talk to. I don't know."

"Maybe you like him," Edmund suggested. "Maybe he's under your skin."

Her denial whooshed out. "Not like that. Lachlan suggested we arrange a showmance, but it's not like that. And I said no."

"Lana, be honest with yourself," Edmund said gently. "Perhaps there's a connection there."

"Yes, there is." Lana's admission hurt his heart. "Then again, there's also a connection between us, one much different from Peter. And neither matters because our lives are too different, both yours and mine, and mine and Peter's, for anything to work out between me and either of you. He's got an agenda with this show. You have your job opening hotels. I'm going to be traveling. So even if I wanted something, it can't happen."

"You keep telling yourself that, but other people manage to make things work."

Lana scowled. "I'm not going from your bed to his. I'm not that person."

"You want something real, like your parents have."

"What if I do? Is there anything wrong with that?" Lana tilted her head and studied him. He wondered if she might suspect he was Peter. If she asked, he'd tell her the truth. That wouldn't break his vows to his sister or the show's NDA.

"No. You shouldn't stop until you're satisfied. Until you've got what you want. That's important, wouldn't you say?" After what she'd said to Peter, Edmund had played the Richard Marx song while he'd changed. He understood what she was looking for. Knew why she was so driven to succeed. He was the same way. He waited for her to pick up the clues he dropped. *Come on, Lana. Figure it out.*

"What if I don't know what I want?" He hated the way her lip quivered. "Besides Paris. I'm for sure going there someday."

Edmund resisted his desire to touch her and hold her close. "I told you there's nothing wrong with wanting more. Whatever you want, it's your choice, Lana. I'm letting you take the lead, even if you choose that this thing between us goes nowhere. I don't want to be an ogre."

"Peter works for you. It's awkward. And I don't know if I even like him like I do you."

Edmund's heart celebrated but he kept calm. "I can't make the choice for you. I've already told you I'm not going to be the big bad boss. We're friends enough that I want you to be happy."

Lana jumped to her feet and began to pace. "But that's the problem. What if it might be you who makes me happy?"

"I make you happy?"

"I don't know!"

Shock made Edmund stand. He shoved aside his conscience that berated him to tell her she could have both Edmund and Peter, that they were one and the same. Instead, he gathered Lana to him and inhaled the sweet scent of her perfume. She fit in his arms perfectly. Felt so right. "Lana, do you know what you're doing to me? I'm going crazy wanting you. I want to get to know you better. Work with me here."

Lana rested in his arms. "We can't turn one night into more. Then again, I feel like I'm Elizabeth rejecting Darcy. I wonder, am making a mistake?"

"I have no idea what you're talking about," Edmund said.

"Doesn't matter. Darcy feels things about Elizabeth that are contrary to everything he knows, his entire nature.

That's the best description of me right now. I want you, but I know the reasons are wrong. Maybe that's not quite it. This week has messed with my head. And it's only been a week. I have to be realistic."

She reached up and rubbed a spot above his lip to the left of his nose. "You had some lotion or some…" She rubbed her finger and looked at the end. "Sticky stuff?"

Edmund wiped his face with his left hand. "Must be from the package I opened earlier. You know how they use that rubber stuff to keep things secure to the back of the box?" Not quite a lie. His facial hair pieces did come prepackaged.

"That glue is gross. Takes forever to get off your fingers. You have to roll it in a ball."

"Exactly." Glad she'd bought his excuse for the mustache residue, Edmund captured her flailing hand. His fingers rubbed hers to ensure the sticky vanished. "You were asking me what we're doing. Because what I'd like to do is kiss you and never stop. But you're still conflicted. I can feel you trembling in my arms, so I'm letting you decide."

"I'm so confused. Maybe my decision is that you should make the decision."

He kissed her forehead. "Clever, but no. I respect you too much. How about we talk tomorrow afternoon? You can tell me how filming went. I'll watch out for Peter when he's over here. Make sure he's fine."

Her eyes rounded. "You'd do that? You're a better man than I've given you credit for."

Edmund was a cad for lying. "Of course."

"Thank you. I'm sorry I took you away from the bar. I'll see you tomorrow." She pulled away from his embrace and headed to the door.

Edmund's arms missed her immediately. "I have to video chat with my sister anyway. Sleep well, Lana."

Edmund waited until the elevator doors closed behind her before he went back into the suite and drained the remaining whiskey in one gulp. What was he doing? He shouldn't have let her leave. He should go after her. Tell her the truth. To hell with the consequences or waiting for her to follow the breadcrumbs.

His mobile began ringing as a video call came through. His sister's face filled the screen. "You don't look well. What's wrong? Spill," Eva said. "Tell me everything."

So he did, from the beginning. Eva listened, only interrupting when she wanted him to clarify. "That's why I need to tell her who I am," Edmund finished. "I can't keep living this double life."

"Listen to me. Tomorrow is Wednesday. You finish filming Thursday. You can wait one more day until you're done. There's nothing to be gained by telling her tonight. She's going to be mad at you no matter what."

"We don't know that. Maybe she won't be. I know it's only been a few days, but there's something real between us."

"You aren't thinking straight. You think your breakup with Veronica was problematic? Lana may not be a psycho social media influencer out to land a billionaire, but that doesn't mean the public won't hound her. What do you think will happen when they get ahold of the undercover boss love triangle? You're doomed. Wait until filming has wrapped. Circle back later, once you've seen how the show goes. Big brother, you know I love you, but your relationships always end in disaster. You need to focus on the prize. You want Van Horn Hotels. As much as I dislike

Lachlan, he's right. Go for the end goal, then after you get that, go after the girl."

Edmund went to the window and gazed out over the darkened landscape. "She won't want me then."

"Then she doesn't deserve you. You're filming an undercover show, and Dad's hyped about finally acquiring Van Horn. Stop getting distracted by a pair of legs."

"She's much more than that," Edmund snapped. "She just seems to like Peter better."

"Which tells you all you need to know. You and she are oil and water. They don't mix long-term. You have to constantly keep shaking them for them to stay together. After this week is over, once you're back to your own lives, you'll figure out if this is real or not. You'll be able to think clearly."

"I want it to be real," Edmund said. "I'm not ashamed to admit it."

Eva leaned closer to the screen. "You know what? I'm coming out there. Your producer thinks the show needs drama? Well, here I come. This Clayton needs to check out our fabulous candidates. See you tomorrow, big bro."

With that, Eva's face disappeared from the screen. Edmund immediately sent Lana a text. Eva is coming into town. Be prepared for the inquisition. I told her about you.

All of it? Lana shot back with a worried emoji.

Edmund worried his lip and sent, Not the intimate details, but yeah. She knows that we had dinner and met on the plane. I'm sorry in advance if she tries to run you through the gauntlet. If she does, I'll be with you every step of the way.

It felt like eternity until her answer came back, one word: Fine.

He waited, but nothing more came so he liked her message and sent back, Sleep well. She liked his message, signaling she was done with their chat. He didn't pursue it further.

Thursday afternoon. He'd tell her then. Even if she hated him for it.

Chapter Eleven

Wednesday morning, before she'd even gotten to the job site, Lana had butterflies. Sure, she was nervous about being on camera. But it was ridiculous to have a sense of anticipation forming in her stomach because she was about to see Peter.

As she crossed the threshold into the Chateau, a feeling of wonder accompanied her nerves. The Chateau hadn't skimped on any of the details that made it special. Besides the guest rooms and common spaces, Clayton Holdings had spared no expense in creating spaces that made it easier and safer for employees to do their jobs. In the kitchen, chefs had extra prep areas, stoves, storage and the highest-grade appliances. Management had ample room to work. Various employee breakrooms created comfortable spaces to eat and relax. Whatever his flaws, Edmund Clayton's hotel chain was one of the best for a reason.

She'd love to see this place when it was up and running, but she'd be long gone by then. She'd received a text from Mrs. Cederberg already outlining her next assignment: San Diego. That city would definitely be warmer than Beaumont in March. As she was thinking about the clothes she needed to pack, Lachlan strode into the breakroom. "Here you are."

Lana gave the contract addendum a cursory scan before signing. "Where do you want to film?" she asked him.

"How about one of the rooms you still have to check? I'm not here to interrupt your work."

Lana bit back the "Could have fooled me" and pasted on a pleasant smile. As her mom always said, you caught more flies with honey than vinegar. No use antagonizing the guy who had the power to make her look bad to millions of TV viewers. She had to trust Edmund wouldn't let that happen. More butterflies took flight thinking of him. The fact that he wanted a relationship with her was mind-boggling.

Speaking of, as she and Lachlan walked upstairs, a text arrived from Edmund. Good luck today. And would you please join my sister and me for dinner tomorrow?

Lana chewed on her lip but let it go before she ruined the lipstick she'd added for the camera. She sent back, When you ask so nicely, how can I refuse?

She could sense his smile when she read his response: Come to the penthouse around five.

She entered Room 36, which contained an oversize living room, sitting/office area, bedroom, bathroom and kitchenette. When combined with Room 37, the space would be a two-bedroom suite totaling almost nine hundred square feet. Lachlan left her standing there as he went to discuss angles with the cameramen.

"Hey, Lana." Peter shoved his phone in his pocket. As he smiled at her, the flicker of guilt she thought she'd seen in his expression vanished. "Thank you again for agreeing to filming. You didn't need to, and I really appreciate you for doing this."

His words warmed her, so she touched one of the furnishings instead. "This is lovely. Looks like we saved one the best rooms for last."

"It's a gorgeous space," Peter agreed. "Cederberg Interiors outdid itself."

"Save your chitchat for the cameras." Lachlan gestured for Peter and Lana to move into place. "Now we'll start. Action."

Lana swiped open her iPad, but before she did much more, Lachlan yelled out more directions. "When I say action, you need to talk. Get closer," he told her. "Do something. Don't just look at your tablet. Act natural. Do what you did yesterday."

That sounded much easier than it was. "Okay." Lana blew out a breath and readied to start over.

"Hey," Peter said gently. He gave her a friendly, reassuring grin. "You got this. How would you start if you were by yourself?"

His words helped her focus. "I like to work from the door to the window. That way the view is the last thing I get to see. It's sort of a reward."

Peter pointed. "Then let's start in there. That's where you were when we met, right? At least before I hit you with the mattress. You can't look any worse on camera than I did that day."

Some of Lana's nerves vanished. Had it been only a few days since they'd met? "Let's hope not."

"You'll be fabulous, because that's who you are." She and Peter stepped inside a bathroom bigger than her childhood bedroom, which helped, as the room seemed to get smaller once they entered. "Work your magic. Show me where you start."

"I don't know if I'd actually call it magic."

"Everything you do is," Peter said.

She dipped her chin so he couldn't see how his loaded words impacted her. She swiped to the bathroom inventory check sheet. "I start with the tile. I ask myself, is this what the decorator picked out?"

Peter leaned over her shoulder, so close she could smell his aftershave. Her nose wrinkled. How had she never noticed that he wore the same kind as Edmund?

Lana pointed to a picture on the iPad. "The tile is correct. I've only seen it wrong once, because the builders have their own process to ensure accuracy. Next I ensure that the seams are caulked correctly and that the fixtures are the chosen ones."

Peter had moved closer to her. "Doesn't the construction company do the same checks?"

"Yes. They do their own set of quality control. But another set of eyes never hurts, and my boss is particular. She wants her vision enacted perfectly. It's the details that matter. Like if she picks out a Kohler Numi 2.0 toilet, my job is to ensure an Innate model wasn't installed instead."

Peter was inches away, the fringes of his breath reaching Lana's ear as he watched over her shoulder while she inspected the shower faucets, the toilet and the sink. Lana suppressed a quiver of awareness similar to the one that had made her initiate another round of lovemaking with Edmund that fateful Saturday night.

"As we work down the list, you can see that the countertop matches the pattern chosen. There are no chips. This room also has a claw-foot tub. The shower has two rainfall showerheads, both from the correct manufacturer and both matching. Heated towel bars. Etcetera."

She caught Peter's reflection. She felt the wink he gave her in her toes. "Mirror." Lana strangled that word. Overcome by feelings she didn't want, she thrust the iPad into Peter's hands. His large fingers caught the tablet without fumbling. "We're done in here. You do the next part."

Ben had squeezed into the bathroom to capture her and Peter's conversation, and as if suddenly noticing he'd been filming, Lana pushed past Ben and into the main portion of the suite. Peter followed at a distance, stopping at an ornate desk. He towered over the piece, his presence shrinking the room to almost a pinpoint as he checked the piece of furniture against the list. He held out the iPad. "Did I do it right?"

Lana glanced at his work. "Yes. Good job. Now do the rest."

When Peter smiled, Lana's awareness meter chimed a red alert. "Lana, you told me you love your job because it allows you to travel. How long do you stay on-site?"

He'd thrown her a softball opening for the cameras, and Lana grabbed it like a lifeline. "I'll leave once the furniture and fixtures are inspected. The soft goods, like linens, bedding and towels, are already with the Chateau's housekeeping staff. They'll service these rooms and have them ready before the first guests arrive for the soft opening."

Calming her racing heart, she led Peter over to a portion of the wall that looked like paneling. Lana slid open a hidden set of sliding doors. "What do you see here?"

"Minifridge, pod-type coffeemaker and a tiny sink. This is the bar area separate from the kitchenette."

She rose on her work boots to peer over his arm as he checked off items. "And?"

"The crystal decanter set is missing a glass."

"Which means you fill out that box to the right of the item. That creates an inventory list alerting us we need to bring in a new one."

"You have a good eye."

"It's not the most glamourous job, but it's important, especially at this level. The Chateau guests will expect the best." More blood rushed to her head from being in such close proximity, and Lana was grateful when Peter began moving around the rest of the room. Staying a safe distance away, Lana hovered like a mama bird with her fledgling chick. "You're doing great."

"I don't want to let anyone down. Several of Mr. Clayton's hotels across the country have Michelin stars. That's the standard he's going for here. Even if the Michelin people don't come to Missouri." Peter gave a nervous laugh as if he'd revealed too much. "Or so everyone who's working on this project tells me. What do I know? I just want to make these things as nice as can be for the guests."

After inspecting the sofas and living area, she and Peter made their way into the bedroom, where the huge, four-poster, king-size bed created a focal point for the decor. With her hormones already in overdrive, Lana hovered in the doorway of the corner bedroom. "Don't you want to see the view?" Peter asked.

The view was her favorite part. Lana made her way to the windows, pressed a button and the sheers slid back. Another button retracted the blackout shades. The curtains on the wall could be closed as well, but for practical purposes they were mostly ornamental and held by tiebacks.

"How is it?" Peter's closeness sent hot breath into her ear and shivers down her spine.

Room 36 overlooked the front of the Chateau and a series of terraced French gardens. Despite the brown foliage and melting piles of shoveled snow, Lana could see the symmetrical outlines of walls and gravel paths. Ice glittered in the reflecting pools. The ornate benches designed for sitting and bird-watching awaited spring. She'd seen this same view from other rooms on this side of the building, but for some reason today's view felt more intimate. Perhaps it was because she shared it with Peter.

Lana resisted the urge to press her nose to the glass since that would leave a mark. "It's going to be beautiful in the spring, like a mini botanical garden. It looks like the photos I've seen of Versailles."

"That was the idea," Peter said.

She turned toward him. "Really? That's interesting. I had no clue."

He seemed momentarily uncomfortable. "Yes. Someone told me that."

"Huh." Minus her check sheet, she hadn't studied the plans for the hotel. Her job was to go in, check things off and move on to the next. Why bother falling in love with things she couldn't have, or places she would never stay in again? But a slice of Paris in Beaumont? Suddenly she wanted to see the hotel in the spring and summer.

"Cut." Lachlan's voice made Lana jump.

Lana shook herself. A winter view of a garden she'd never visit shouldn't affect her so much. Nor should the man next to her, whom she'd lose touch with the moment she traveled to her next assignment. She moved away from both him and the window. "Is that it? Can I go?"

"We have the footage we need," Lachlan announced with a flourish. He pointed to Peter. "Let's head back to the Grand."

"Give me a minute," Peter told him.

Lana would have run from the room, but Peter still held her iPad. Instead, she watched as everyone else filed out, leaving them alone.

"Filming can be difficult, but you were great. You okay? You seemed to get lost there for a moment." Peter's concern touched her, making her highly aware she was wanting things she couldn't have. Love. Permanence.

She gave him a reassuring smile that didn't come close to meeting her eyes. "I've got a few rooms left, so I need to get started. I had planned to stay here through the weekend, but I'm needed in San Diego on Monday. An office building this time. I've never done one of those. I decided to leave Saturday night."

"Won't your parents be disappointed?" Peter asked.

Lana began backing toward the door. "Ryan's team is headed to state, and they'll be busy with that."

"How about you meet me for lunch tomorrow?" Peter asked.

"Thank you for thinking of me, but it's not a good idea with all I have to do. Good luck with the rest of your filming."

His offer was tempting, but she had her next assignment, and escaping these feelings was the smartest plan. He must have sensed her hesitation and indecision, because he tried again.

"Maybe a quick drink this afternoon? I have a busy night planned. Can you spare some time before you visit your parents? Say four o'clock at the Grand bar?" Peter handed her the iPad. "Just one drink is all I ask."

Lana could work him in, especially when both of them had evening plans. "I suppose I can spare an hour. I want to hear about your bellman training."

Peter grinned. "See you then."

After Lana left the suite, Edmund stood for a few minutes staring at the empty doorway. He hadn't been imagining the sexual tension zinging between them, especially every time they stood close. Even without sheets, he'd wanted to tumble her onto that mattress and pleasure them both. Repeatedly.

Thankfully Lachlan had called cut. Once he was finished filming and back in Portland, and a suitable amount of time had passed, he'd figure a way to send Lana to Paris. He'd seen the longing in her eyes when he'd told her about the gardens.

She deserved to see the real thing. He'd put her up in the most luxurious suite in central Paris, on one of the most famous streets in the city's first arrondissement. As part of the show, he was already doing things for Jimmy, like paying for his degree and his engagement ring. Edmund would be sending his head of housekeeping on a seven-night cruise with her entire family. His employees would find out their good fortune when he filmed the reveals tomorrow afternoon. Today he had two more people to work with and the interview.

Lana deserved to be pampered. She had saved Peter's job. She deserved a vacation at one of his hotels for her part in the filming. He could give her Paris. Not because they'd had sex, but rather because she was the nicest, most genuine person he'd ever met. If he were her man, he'd spoil her daily. He'd lamely told her that first night that they were like two ships passing. Already he felt them slipping away from each other. He hoped he could adjust course before they got too far apart.

"Why are you still in here?" Ben entered the room. He picked up the light meter he'd left behind. "Lachlan's already back at the Grand. He said you can ride over with me."

Edmund made his way toward the door. "Just thinking for a minute. I'm opening a hotel. Lots of moving pieces to consider."

Ben shrugged. "Yeah, and you got this scene with Lana thrown into the mix. You guys did great. The chemistry was obvious."

"It's not a showmance," Edmund insisted.

Ben held up the meter like a shield. "I'm not saying that's the effect Lachlan was going for. I know you don't like him, but he's not a bad guy. Just one under a lot of pressure as he tries to get what he wants. Aren't we all under that pressure at one point or another?"

Edmund was constantly under pressure. Deciding both cameramen probably also needed a bonus when this was over, Edmund and Ben returned to the Grand. Still undercover as Peter, Edmund changed into a hotel uniform and moved behind the valet stand.

"I'm Toby," the freckle-faced college kid working there said. "Wednesdays aren't high check-in days, especially in winter. We won't put away a lot of guest cars today. Most of the clients will be here for our afternoon high tea or to visit the spa. In and out."

Larry filmed the entire exchange, including Peter finding out about Toby's college dreams. Following that, Peter worked with the bellman, which meant Edmund was there when Eva arrived.

She stepped out of the Lincoln Navigator that had brought her from the private airport in Chesterfield, which was about forty-five minutes to an hour away, depending on traffic. Edmund noted how everyone snapped to attention. While the staff had been deferential to today's guests, the tone changed when a Clayton was in the room.

Both cameras filmed her arrival, catching Edmund's humiliation when his sister told Peter to "Be careful with that bag" after he'd loaded her three suitcases onto the rolling luggage cart. She looked at him as if he'd done it wrong. To add insult to injury, her Yorkshire terrier poked its head out of Eva's purse and barked. "Shh," she cooed. Eva removed her sunglasses and peered at Edmund. "You do have those, yes? What's your name?"

His sister was enjoying toying with him. "I'm Peter, ma'am," he said, using a term he knew she hated, because saying ma'am made her sound old. Two could play at her game. He bit back a smile when she glared at him after his "Shall we go inside, ma'am?"

Mr. Smith greeted Eva the moment her knee-high boots touched the lobby floor. "You have the penthouse next to your brother. He's in a meeting right now or I'm sure he would have greeted you himself."

"Oh, he's always busy with something. Right sweetie?" Eva cooed at her dog.

"We're so glad to have you with us," Mr. Smith said. "Peter will bring your luggage to your suite and ensure everything is to your satisfaction."

Eva shot Edmund a smirk. "Ah, yes, Peter has been helpful so far. You run a world-class hotel, Mr. Smith. I'm sure my brother is extremely pleased." Eva didn't glance at Peter, but Edmund felt her mirth. Her dog, Princess, yapped its agreement.

She stepped into the elevator, and the addition of Ben and his camera, plus the luggage cart, made for tight space. As they made their way skyward, Eva said nothing, concentrating on looking at the ceiling as she absently stroked Princess, who kept barking as the poor dog wanted Edmund's attention. Ben fiddled with his phone.

When they reached the penthouse floor, Ben stepped out first so he could film Eva and Peter leaving the elevator. Edmund didn't even glance at his penthouse door as they passed by. Ben walked backward as Eva strode toward the door farther down the corridor. When she reached Penthouse B, she waited for Peter to open it. Ben backed in first, and after he reached an appropriate filming spot, Eva walked into the room and said, "I always love coming here. Everything is always as perfect as would be expected of a Clayton hotel."

She watched as Peter took her suitcases off the luggage racks. Edmund noted that the kitchen area already had bowls of food and water waiting for Princess. "Would you like me to call housekeeping and have them unpack for you, ma'am?" he asked.

"Thank you, but I can handle that myself." Eva set Princess down so she could find her wallet. Instantly the dog raced to Edmund and began sniffing his pants. Then Princess started barking and jumping on Edmund's leg. "Look at that. She likes you."

Edmund knew the dog loved him. He loved her, too. "May I?" After Eva nodded her permission, Edmund lifted the dog and cradled Princess in his arms. He had to hold her out slightly so she didn't lick at his fake facial hair. "What a sweetheart."

"You're so good with her." Edmund's sister didn't blink an eye as she withdrew a folded hundred-dollar bill from her purse. "Hard to believe that I heard you almost didn't have a job here. Then someone named Lana stepped in, I heard?"

Edmund gritted his teeth, making the partial dig in. Trust his sister to go for the jugular immediately. "She did. I'll be forever grateful."

"I'd like to meet her. Can you arrange that? I always like to reward exceptional customer service." Eva had the audacity to look innocent. She knew Lana would be joining them for dinner tomorrow, and that tonight Lana was seeing family.

"I'll see what I can do. How about four fifteen in the bar downstairs? Will that work?"

Eva exchanged the hundred-dollar bill for her pet and the room key packet. "I'll see you then."

"Cut!" Edmund almost jumped out of his skin upon hearing Lachlan's voice. Where the hell had he come from? Lachlan clapped his hands. "That was perfect."

Eva gave a little bow. "Thank you."

"What the hell was that?" Edmund demanded of his sister as Ben lowered the camera. "You don't need to meet Lana on camera. Bad enough you stayed in character in the elevator."

Eva grinned. "Of course I want to meet her. I told you that I'm bringing the drama. We'll film our drink. It will be perfect."

Edmund whirled on Lachlan. This was not acceptable. Edmund wanted a private moment with Lana as Peter. He needed a way to pave the way to the big reveal. He wanted her to know before anyone else, because the moment the first employee left Edmund's office, no amount of nondisclosure agreements would keep the secret that Edmund had been undercover as Peter. "My drink with Lana as Peter is not for public consumption."

Lachlan shrugged. "You'll be sitting in public."

Eva set Princess on the floor, and the dog went to find its kibble. "We all know it's not a showmance. But this will humanize you and tie the entire show together. Lachlan, will you leave us?"

Eva waited until Lachlan and Ben left the suite before stripping off her wool peacoat. She dumped the garment on top of one of the suitcases, and Edmund caught it before it fell off. He hung it in the closet. "Eva, you can't do this. She's going to hate me more than she already does."

"You can tell her it was all my fault tomorrow when you do the reveals. Oh, and Jack and Sierra will join us for dinner tomorrow. And Michael."

Edmund scoffed. "Michael's coming here? I'll believe that when I see it."

"Mom and Dad had something to do with it. He was in the press again. You know how they hate it. I think Dad has had enough."

"Whatever." Edmund had bigger things to worry about than dealing with his playboy brother who never seemed to know where the office door was. "I assume Liam is off adventuring."

"He takes full advantage of being able to do good. Besides, after losing Anya in that hiking accident? We can't fault him. He blames himself enough. He needs time to grieve."

"It's been two years," Edmund pointed out. Then again, he should cut his brother some slack. Edmund had never been as deeply in love as his brother had been. While Edmund had feelings for Lana, Liam had wanted to marry Anya. Had been ready to propose.

"Shall I make a reservation for La Martina?" Eva asked.

Edmund shook his head. "Lana and I ate there already, so can we go somewhere else? And make it casual. We're pretty overwhelming. Let's not scare her off. What about Miller's Grill? That seems to be a popular place."

"I'll ask Jack. He'll know. You really like her, don't you?"

"Yes. I want to convince her that we might have a future. But first I have to convince her to go out with me."

Eva tucked her short hair behind her ear. "I can't wait to meet the woman who has my brother in knots."

"Just don't be a pain in my ass." Edmund gave Eva a quick kiss on her cheek.

She waved a finger. "If you call me ma'am again on national TV, I'm firing you myself. I'm twenty-five. I'm not our mother."

"Yes, ma'am. I'm glad you're here, sis." With that Edmund grabbed the luggage cart and scooted out the door before Eva lobbed something soft in his direction.

Realizing he should tell Lana what was going on, Edmund stopped and sent her a text. My sister Eva is in town and already met Peter. Be prepared for her to crash your drinks meet up, along with the film crew. Sorry.

Lana's response came when Edmund was in the freight elevator. Fantastic. I'm glad you gave me a heads-up. She added a vomit emoji that made Edmund smile.

He sent her one last text. Just found out myself.

There, that wasn't lying, was it? Edmund checked that his phone was on silent before shoving it into the front pocket of Peter's work slacks. He found Lachlan and the crew in the lobby waiting on him. "Shall we interview the bellman now?" Lachlan asked.

"Yeah. Let's get this over with." The sooner everything was finished, the better. Edmund was tired of the subterfuge.

Chapter Twelve

When Lana arrived in the doorway of the Grand's bar, she could see Peter sitting on a stool chatting with the bartender. The scene gave her a jolt, and she did a double take. For a moment she thought it was Edmund sitting there. He and Peter had such similar postures that she could have sworn that Edmund and Peter were related, that was, until Peter turned.

Then the difference between the two men couldn't be clearer. Peter had blond shaggy hair compared to Edmund's wavy cut. Along with the deep five o'clock shadow gracing his jawline, Peter had a goatee, thick eyebrows, thick sideburns and a big mustache. Edmund might have some evening stubble, but on him it had been casual and sexy and surrounding full, kissable lips.

Peter's upper lip stuck out, giving him a smile almost too big for his face. His deep brown eyes didn't have the mysteriousness of Edmund's gray ones. As for clothing, no way would Edmund wear a t-shirt, flannel and Levi's as Peter had this morning. Or his current outfit of uniform slacks and a dress shirt buttoned to his wrists. At least he'd stripped off the coat that screamed "Let me help you with your luggage!"

The irony didn't escape her. This space was off-limits

to employees, meaning if Peter wasn't part of TV show he wouldn't be in here. Edmund, however, would be right at home hobnobbing with the rich and entitled guests who frequented the space. Life wasn't fair, Lana mused. How had one man gotten such exceptional good looks and wealth, but not the gregarious personality? How did the other have the easygoing, affable personality but not the movie-star looks?

"Hey," Lana greeted Peter as she slid onto the stool to his left. "How'd the rest of the day go?"

"Good. I made three hundred in tips."

"Is that good?" It seemed like a lot but Lana had never worked for tips.

Peter rolled his broad shoulders. "I have no idea. Toby, the college kid I worked with, said it was a slow afternoon."

Peter had a longneck bottle of beer in front of him and tipped it toward his mouth. "What can I get you? They have a good pinot noir."

"Did I tell you I liked pinot?" Her forehead wrinkled with a strange sense of déjà vu. She was getting confused as to what she'd told Peter and what she'd told Edmund.

Peter studied the edge of the label he was peeling from the bottle. "Maybe? Or maybe I'm repeating what the bartender said. They mostly serve Clayton vintages."

"Including the Missouri ones," the bartender said as she placed a square black cocktail napkin in front of Lana. She wore the same type of slacks and shirt as Peter, but she had a black vest buttoned up over it and a nametag reading Jillian. "We have the Jamestown Norton if you'd like a red that's local."

"You know what, that sounds lovely." Lana adjusted her position so her legs didn't come into contact with Peter's. They both remained quiet as they watched Jillian open a fresh bottle of Norton. When she put the glass in front of

Lana, she indicated Peter's beer bottle. "Do you need another one?"

He shook his head. Lana sipped the delicious wine and surveyed the crowded bar. "What time are the cameras swarming?"

"Four fifteen. I figured we could have at least fifteen minutes to ourselves. I'll be honest. I'm ready for them to leave me alone. Lana, listen, I need to tell you something about the filming." Peter paused as if contemplating what to say next. Before he could continue, Lana heard a strange female voice calling her and Peter's names.

"Lana! Peter! Here you are!"

"Of course she couldn't wait," Peter grumbled.

Lana turned as a woman breezed into the room, Lachlan and his cameras in her wake. This must be Eva, Edmund's sister. She had a dark, French-cut bob that showcased diamond studs that Lana had no doubt were real. She wore a tan sweater set and a brown plaid skirt that skimmed her knees and touched brown knee-high boots that had thick two-inch heels.

Lana put her hand out, and Eva took it. "Nice to meet you, Ms. Clayton."

"Call me Eva. All my friends do."

Lana had no illusion they would be friends, but she played along because the cameras were rolling. "Nice to meet you, Eva. How was your flight?"

"Fabulous. I heard my brother was on your flight and that you were lucky you landed when you did, what with the airport closing. I'm glad you were both able to find rooms for the night."

"I was too." Lana didn't like the gleam in Eva's eyes that said she'd deduced exactly what had happened between Lana and her brother. If Edmund was sitting where Peter was, Lana would throttle him. Then again, if she and Ryan had been closer in age, maybe they'd share things too, like who they were dating or sleeping with. She had no idea if Ryan even had a girlfriend. How pathetic was that?

Eva turned her attention to Peter. "You didn't have any trouble getting into town, did you?"

"The roads were clear when I traveled to Beaumont."

Lana heard something tight in Peter's voice, a tick she'd never heard before. As if Eva had noticed it, Edmund's sister nailed Peter with a pinpoint gaze. "Did you actually see anything of Beaumont? Did you come straight here or do some sightseeing in St. Louis? You told my brother," Eva turned back to Lana, "that he had to see the Gateway Arch."

Lana's head swiveled as Eva faced Peter again. There was an undercurrent happening that Lana didn't understand. "Have you been to the Arch, Peter?" Eva asked. "I have. It's one of those things you *must* do if you're in the area."

Peter's lisp became more pronounced. "I wanted to be prepared to work for you, so I came straight here."

"Have you two met before?" Lana asked.

"Of course," Eva said smoothly. "I've been involved since the casting. And we can't have Peter not seeing something of the area while he's here." Eva's dog stuck its head out of her purse and gave a bark. "Lachlan and I were talking about the show and we agreed we should showcase some of Beaumont as well. You know, beyond just the hotels."

Lana sensed Peter was as surprised as Lana was by this change of events. He said, "I thought we were done filming." His thick brows knit together so they appeared as one.

Eva was a human bulldozer, and she pushed ahead. "Lachlan told me you went to a high school basketball game last night. But there's no footage of it."

"How's that relevant?" Peter asked, and Lana found herself surprised. Peter's forceful tone contained a hint of warning.

"Could someone stop and explain what is happening here?" Lana asked. Peter seemed agitated, which wasn't good. Eva was a Clayton. Basically, his boss.

"One of the things the show likes to do is to show some of the town," Lachlan intervened smoothly. "We haven't done that yet."

Eva's gray eyes were similar to Edmund's, as was the smile she directed at Lana. "One of the reasons I agreed to participate in a televised competition was because it would provide PR for the Beaumont Grand and the Chateau. But the Clayton family has made huge infrastructure improvements across the entire county. Jack, that's Edmund's and my cousin," Eva added for Lana's benefit, "has been working on revitalizing the historic downtown. Have you been there?"

"I grew up there. My family lives on Third Street," Lana said. "I saw the changes as we drove in."

Eva clapped her hands, and Princess yapped. "Really? Then you know all about Wine Down Wednesdays at the La Vita è Vino Dolce wine bar?"

"I haven't lived here for two years, so I haven't been." Something was up. Lana could feel it.

"But you like wine." Eva pointed at Lana's glass. "Let's move this party to the self-service wine bar. That way you and Peter can walk down Main Street on the way. It'll make good footage and be good PR for the town. Let's get out of this stuffy place. You and I are much too young for it."

"I'm supposed to visit my parents." Lana offered her excuse. But as if fate had conspired against her, her phone pinged. "Excuse me." Lana read the long text from her mother. Ryan was headed off to study with friends. One of her mom's friends had slipped and fallen, and her mom was taking over a casserole. Oh, and Lana's dad was going to bed early because he had to get up in the middle of the night to pretreat the roads because there was a chance of ice tomorrow morning, and the highway department didn't want to come off looking unprepared like that one time everyone still talked about. Her mom asked if they could reschedule. Perhaps Friday night? At Ryan's next game?

"Everything okay?" Peter leaned over as Lana typed a reply saying that yes, Friday should work fine and she'd call her mom tomorrow.

"It looks as if my family had things come up, and they're canceling tonight's plans." Lana pushed aside the hurt. They lived full lives here. No matter how much her family cared, she'd left the nest. When she dropped into town for visits and major holidays, she worked around their schedule. "I suppose I'm free."

Princess barked again, and Eva shushed the pooch. "Great. How about we regroup here in twenty minutes?" Eva pointed at Peter. "You need jeans. Something bar casual, not clothing saying, 'I was learning to be a bellhop today.'" Eva flicked a glance over at Lana. "You're perfect just as you are. You can stay with me while Peter changes."

As Peter slid off the stool to Lana's right, Eva slid onto the stool to Lana's left and set her purse on the bar top. Eva pointed at Lachlan. "Cameras off and go enjoy your break."

To Lana's surprise, Lachlan did exactly what Eva wanted. Lana watched him leave. "How did you do that? He's been annoying me for days."

As if the two were coconspirators, Eva invaded Lana's space and her perfectly manicured fingers patted Lana's forearm. Then she signaled the bartender and asked for a glass of club soda. "One of the conditions of the contract is that Clayton Holdings has final approval of all the footage Lachlan wants to use. And he thinks I'm cute. Unfortunately for him, I do not return his feelings. But manipulating them can be useful. Now, tell me about you and my brother Edmund. I hear we're doing dinner tomorrow."

Lana stared, stunned. "You don't waste any time, do you?"

Eva didn't miss a beat. "It saves time. When you're the baby in the family, you have to learn to work every advantage. When you're a Clayton, it becomes doubly important." Eva wasn't the least bit apologetic, and Lana had to admit she admired her confidence. "So...back to my brother."

"How about you tell me what he said about me and I'll fill in the gaps," Lana said. "You know, to save time."

Eva laughed at Lana's use of her words. She lifted her short glass filled with club soda. "I can see why Edmund likes you. He's such a stick-in-the-mud. You must be very special to have broken him out of his shell."

Lana doubted she was special to a man who dated social media influencers and socialites. "It's clear he's told you some things, but I'm not giving you details."

"Touché." Eva leaned forward. "But just between us, tell me. Who do you like best? Peter or Edmund? Have you kissed Peter? Because I know you kissed Edmund and probably much, much more. Now, don't be upset. He didn't tell me. It was what he didn't say that let me figure it out. I know my big brother well. And your face gets this dreamy look whenever I say his name. *Edmund.* See? Like that."

Lana felt herself flush, but pride meant she had to deny her feelings. "It does not. Besides, we aren't dating."

"Who? Peter or Edmund?"

"Your brother. I don't even know Peter. As for Edmund,

I haven't told anyone about our night. I don't want any loose lips. You know, the kind that sink ships." Or that passed in the night, like they had both thought they'd be.

Eva appeared confused. "What ship are you talking about? Are you and Edmund a ship? Like Bennifer? Let's see. Edlana. Lanamund."

"What? Stop that. Those are terrible." Lana drained the last of her Norton in one sip. "He shouldn't have said anything to you at all."

Eva's nails tapped along the bar. "He had to tell me. You know, legal stuff and all that."

"I thought you were VP of PR."

Eva shot Lana some serious side-eye. "Did you see his viral breakup video? Who do you think coached him on how to respond? And if he told me about you, it's because he likes you enough to break his rules. He wants to protect both of you."

"I had no idea who he was. The guy I met on the airplane said his name was Trey. Then I learned he was actually Edmund."

Eva lifted the glass and twisted it, the glitter in her nail polish catching the light. "Trey's his nickname. You know, because he's the third. And because Edmund is so old-fashioned. It's not a name you shorten, like Ed or Eddie. He told me because I refuse to see him go through a PR nightmare ever again. He's my favorite big brother. Liam and Michael are awesome, but I don't have the same bond with them. You could be good for him. Piece of advice though. He's not good at showing his feelings. He can come off cold."

"So he told me," Lana said. She knew Edmund not as an iceman, but as a warm, generous lover. He had layers. Depth.

Lana sighed. "Even if he does let me in, our worlds are

too different. The square footage of his penthouse is bigger than my childhood home. He snaps his fingers and everyone jumps."

"Which is why you like Peter better." Eva gave an understanding nod.

"While Edmund is far easier on the eyes, Peter is much easier to talk with," Lana admitted.

"What if Edmund could talk to you like Peter?" Eva asked.

"I doubt that's possible. Peter is an ordinary, working-class guy wanting to get ahead. That's me and my family. You have a dog in your purse that's wearing a diamond-studded collar."

"Princess. Isn't she adorable?" Eva took the pup out and cuddled her. "Just because I can afford to give her good things, doesn't mean I'm insensitive to how others live. I take her on lots of walks and her feet touch the ground." The dog licked her cheek, and Eva reverted to baby talk. "But not when there's snow, right, sweetheart? We have booties for that."

Lana picked up her empty wineglass before setting it down. She waved off a refill. "Thank you for proving my point."

"Tell me, have you kissed Peter?"

"No. Why would I? I haven't kissed Edmund since that night either."

"Why not? Are they not worth kissing?" Eva shot Lana a you're-crazy look, which Lana ignored. Thank goodness the cameras were gone.

"Even if they are worth it, I don't go around kissing people if we're not going to be in a relationship. That night with Edmund was totally out of character. I don't even know why I'm telling you any of this."

"Because you like my brother and I'm easy to talk to. My mom said I was born talking."

Lana stared but couldn't help but smile. "Your family really likes hyperbole, don't they?"

"You have absolutely no idea how much. Oh, here they come. Quick. If Peter wanted to kiss you, would you?"

Lana shook her head, her answer instantaneous. "Absolutely not. And don't put me in that position."

"I promise I won't." Eva crooked a finger. "Pinkie swear."

Even though it was childish, Lana twisted her finger around Eva's. "I want you to know I take pinkie swears seriously. You best not try to make me kiss Peter."

"Oh, you have no worries from me." Eva released Lana's finger and tucked Princess back into her purse. "Peter is the last man I want you to kiss. I'm one hundred percent on Team Edmund."

Highly aware of Lana, who was quietly sitting beside him in the back of the hotel's town car and staring out the window, Edmund turned his attention to the passing scenery. He was grateful Eva and the cameramen rode separately.

When Edmund had arrived back to the bar, still in his Peter getup, Lana and Eva had been making a pinkie swear. Edmund had no idea what had happened, but something had. A tension now existed between Lana and Peter that hadn't been there before. Lana seemed lost in thought as they traveled to the wine bar, so he left her alone.

When they reached the town of Beaumont, the driver took them on a short tour. The quaint town looked like a movie set, except it was real. Lana, as if tired of the silence, began acting as a tour guide, narrating this part of the trip. "Main Street is divided into two parts, north and south."

By now Edmund knew Lana well enough to hear her

nervousness. What exactly had Eva said to her? Lana continued narrating as if nothing was amiss. "Beaumont is your quintessential Missouri river town founded by the French in the late 1700s. Then the Germans arrived. They're the ones who started growing grapes and making wine. North Main is mostly restaurants and bars. There are a few eateries on South Main, but the dining district is along this stretch. After we cross this street and pass the bookstore, we're on South Main. My parents told me that Jack Clayton bought a lot of these buildings and has really made sure they're in top shape for being as old as they are."

Despite their car's excellent shocks and struts, Lana's words vibrated because of the brick cobblestones that were hundreds of years old. Hearing the vibration, she laughed, and some of the tension left. "When we were little, my friends and I would come down here on our bikes and ride them as fast as we could. We'd yell because it made our voices go like this." She demonstrated the shaky sound, making Edmund laugh with her.

"Sounds like fun."

She turned to face him. "It was. I wonder if they're still around. I lost touch with everyone once I started traveling. I'm not on Facebook very often. Do you have social media?"

"No. Don't have the time or inclination." Especially after Veronica, who was probably still trying to increase her followers and influencer status one way or the other once she'd bad mouthed him enough.

"Oh, there's the cookie store. Too bad it's closed. You have to try the chocolate chip. Phenomenal."

Since he was dressed as Peter, not Edmund, he simply nodded his agreement. If he were Edmund, he'd tell her that he'd eaten the cookies. They'd been served at his cousin

Jack's wedding and Jack had brought back a dozen or two every time he'd flown out to the West Coast for business meetings.

"I'll be sure to try them at some point." Edmund gritted his teeth, wishing he could share how his cousin had walked into the cookie store and found Sierra baking them. To hear Jack describe it, he'd fallen in love with her then and there. Not that their road to love had been easy. She hadn't forgiven him for what had happened between them in high school, and worse, he was trying to buy her dad's winery. Two strikes down, Jack had swung for the fences, hit a home run, won her over and married the woman of his dreams.

The hell with it, Edmund thought. He refused to do this anymore. He was going to tell Lana who he was. But the driver had parked at the curb, and Edmund's door was yanked opened. Lachlan stood there. He was too late.

"Larry is going to film you opening Lana's door. Then you'll walk toward the wine bar. Ben is inside. He'll film you once you enter."

"Okay," Edmund said. He turned to Lana. "Did you catch that?"

Lana rolled her eyes, a sentiment Edmund shared. "He's lucky I was once in a middle school play and can take direction, especially as I'm able to open my own car doors, thank you very much."

"Let me at least prove chivalry is not dead."

Lana grinned. "I didn't say I didn't like it. Now go. Don't keep Lachlan waiting."

Edmund wanted that smile directed at him, not Peter. "Your wish is my command."

Lana watched Peter circle the front of the car and come around to the back passenger side. Despite the heater blowing inside the vehicle, anticipation and nervousness made shivers run down her spine. Darn that Eva. Lana now battled with the idea that somehow there was a choice between Team Peter and Team Edmund. Despite this evening being about acquiring additional footage for the TV show, when Peter smiled and helped Lana from the car, it felt like a date.

Lana's foot wobbled as she stepped onto the uneven cobblestone sidewalk. Lachlan hadn't wanted them to wear their coats, claiming the garments would get in the way, so she'd left hers on the back seat. She wore a dark blue and white Fair Isle sweater, a pair of jeans and flat, waterproof leather boots that reached her knees. As Peter's firm grip steadied her, she shivered both from cold and awareness. She exhaled a puffy cloud of white. "Thanks."

"Anytime. Shall we go?" Peter offered his arm. Lana linked hers through his and ignored the camera in her face. After a short walk, they stepped inside the wine bar. Warmth greeted them. "Wow," Peter said. "I wish I'd thought of this concept first."

Located in a former storefront, the wine bar had a low-key, relaxed vibe. The interior of the hundred-year-old building had been gutted and the wooden beams refurbished and stained. The exposed brick walls rose a story and a half, making the smaller interior seem lofty and spacious.

"Too bad it's cold or we could go up on the rooftop," Lana said. "You should do that this summer. I've heard the view is one of the best in the city."

"Thanks for the idea. I'll remember that," Peter said, more for the camera's benefit than hers.

Following the lead of Ben and his camera, Lana and Peter passed the long, full-service wooden bar and walked to where an empty booth beckoned along the back wall. People sitting at tables stared as they moved through the bar, but thankfully the surrounding conversations didn't stop. If they had, Lana would have been even more self-conscious than she had been with Edmund the other night at dinner.

After those around them surmised that she and Peter weren't celebrities, the patrons ignored the spectacle of two cameras, a producer issuing directions and a woman with a dog in her purse who'd taken the last seat at the bar. Lana forced herself to relax. She viewed new places as an adventure. If she kept her focus on maintaining that attitude and not the man seated across from her, she should be okay.

A waitress appeared and gave them a food menu. She explained how the self-service pours worked and that they could order any type of beer, wine or cocktails from the full-service bar. Peter passed over a credit card and within minutes the waitress brought back two plastic chip cards. "Shall we?" Peter said. He and Lana slid out of the booth and made their way behind the main bar where eight self-service wine cellars stood.

Each of the temperature-controlled glass cases contained four bottles of label-visible wine. The process to operate the dispensers was simple. Patrons retrieved a clean wine glass from the shelf. They inserted their chip cards. Once their credits appeared, they could dispense their choice in either a two-, four-, or six-ounce pour.

She and Peter debated the wine choices before Lana chose a pinot noir from California. She watched as the chip card reader deducted the cost of her two-ounce pour from the card balance, and the exact amount of wine flowed from the spigot and into her glass. Peter did the same with his card, and once they had their wine, they clinked their glasses together in front of the wine cellars before walking back to their booth.

"I love this concept," Peter said. "You don't have to commit to a bottle."

"There are several local wines on tap, too." Lana set her glass down on the table before sliding into the seat. Peter sat across from her and adjusted his long legs to keep them from touching hers. She tried to ignore the two cameras she could see in her periphery.

Lana tucked her hair behind her ears. She'd worn it long and loose tonight instead of in its everyday ponytail. Hopefully she looked alright on film. "You know, this feels like we're in one of those 'which house should we pick' moments on that house-hunting TV show. Although, did you know they've already bought the house when they're filmed? The producers have them look at other houses anyway. I read that somewhere. You have to have already purchased something to be cast."

Peter sipped his wine. "Well, I can tell you the competition I'm in is real."

"Keith told me about last week's candidate. Said he could do the work but seemed too stuck on himself. The guys found him fake. They felt like he was auditioning for something. At least the guys know that you're trying."

Peter fingered the thin stem of his wine glass but didn't take another drink. "But he didn't get fired."

"True, but he didn't win any brownie points either. That has to mean something." Lana reached for her wine but checked the movement. She didn't want to appear like a lush on television. The one sip they'd taken by the wine cellars would have to do until Lachlan called cut. "You should be a shoo-in to win."

"It would mean a great deal to my family." Peter lifted his glass and studied the contents.

"Keith's my work dad. I hope you know he really is a

good guy. You'll like it here. Beaumont is a great place to live. In many aspects, it'll always be home." Lana realized that was a truth she'd long been denying. Her things might be packed away in her parents' basement, but their location acted as a tether, a way to maintain a connection.

The waitress returned with one of the venue's signature chocolate charcuterie boards, featuring everything from buttons to wafer cookies to chocolate truffles. Lana moved a few of the confections onto the square white plate in front of her. When she didn't lift one of the pieces to her mouth and instead set her hand on the table, her stomach rumbled its protest.

"Traveling as you do must make it hard to have a relationship," Peter said. He moved some chocolate to his plate, but like Lana didn't eat any.

"I have goals that I want to achieve before I settle down. This job will help me get there, same as your contest is helping you."

Peter captured her tapping fingers, swallowing them in his hand. "I'm glad you were part of my journey. Thank you for everything. I'll be sure to tell you what happens."

"If I don't see you winning on TV first."

Peter gave her a big smile. "Exactly."

When he freed her fingers, she moved her hand back to her section of the table. She was grateful Peter's gesture had lasted the correct amount of time to be viewed as friendly, not romantic. She reached for a Mint Meltaway and held it between her fingertips.

"Cut," Lachlan called. "Nice work."

"Thank God." Lana popped the square candy in her mouth, chewed and let the creamy center spread over her tongue. She immediately reached for another one.

"I have shivers, that was so good!" Eva approached with

the owner at her side. Lana noted Caleb hadn't changed much, minus the deeper laugh lines that came from aging. Lana had the same ones, which she tried not to think about.

"Thanks for letting us film here," Eva told Caleb. Lachlan, Lana noted, was in deep conversation with his cameramen. Lana washed the chocolate down with some wine, and the residual taste of the chocolate melting on her tongue brought out additional flavors of the pinot. No wonder Caleb had chosen to do dessert charcuteries in addition to the traditional meat and cheese options he also offered.

Lana's stomach rumbled its displeasure at eating nothing but Mint Meltaways. Chocolate and wine wouldn't be enough for dinner. While the wine bar offered a variety of flatbreads, that wasn't what Lana wanted. Since the blinking red lights were off, she downed the two-ounce pour and glanced at Peter. With everyone else in conversation, no one paid her or Peter any attention.

"Meet me by the wine dispensers." Lana scooped some of the candy into a napkin and put it in her cross-body bag. No sense in good chocolate going to waste. Glad neither she nor Peter had worn a coat, she slid out of the booth and grabbed her empty glass. "I'm getting another pour."

She went to the far side of the self-pour area and hovered as if deciding what vintage. Peter joined her. When he went to slide his chip card in the payment slot, Lana stopped him. "Do you have all your stuff on you? Your wallet and your phone?"

"Both are in my pocket." Peter wore a thick fisherman's quarter-zip sweater over a plain white crewneck. "Why?"

"Because we're going to go somewhere else and get some real food." Lana circled the bar until she and Peter were closer to the front windows and the exit. Because of the crowd, she could hardly see the booth where they had been seated. She grabbed Peter's hand, ignored the tingly sensation and tugged. "Come on."

Lana made a break for the front door and slid through. She sensed rather than heard Peter as he followed. She used what Edmund had called her "airport speed walk" until she reached the town car. When she knocked on the glass, the driver unlocked the doors. "We need you to take us to La-Belle's," she told the driver as she slid onto the back seat.

The poor man appeared confused. Peter leaned forward. "I'll give you three hundred bucks if you don't tell Lachlan or Eva Clayton where we are until we get back." He grinned at Lana. "My tip money."

"I don't want to get into trouble," the guy said as he took the bills Peter handed him.

"You'll be fine," Lana promised. "I know Edmund. He owes me one, and Peter just gave you his tip money to make your decision easier. We'll even get you a burger."

As the driver pulled away from the curb, Lana leaned against the leather seat and dissolved into giggles. She turned to Peter. "They're probably just now realizing we've ditched them. I hope they don't follow us. I'm sure these cars use GPS trackers."

"How do you know Edmund?" Peter asked as the driver turned up the music.

"We're sort of friends. I met him on a plane. We've had dinner together. I don't know how to describe our relationship beyond that. I travel too much. He's too busy with work. Friends seems a good description."

"Ahh." Peter leaned back against the leather seat. Their driver made his way toward the edge of town and parked in front of a nondescript white building whose car-filled parking lot hinted at the venue's popularity. "Where are we?" Peter asked. "What is this place?"

"LaBelle's Diner, operated by LaBelle's Dairy. Let's hope they have a booth free." Lana led them into a restaurant that appeared frozen in the 1950s. Black vinyl booths lined the walls. Chrome chairs with black cushions surrounded tables with black-and-white-checkerboard tops. A lunch counter ran down half the space with every stool full.

"The same family has owned this place for over forty years," Lana told Peter as they followed a teenage hostess to a booth located in the back. They settled in across from each other and studied the tri-fold laminated menus.

"What are you getting?" Peter asked. "What's good here?"

"I'm having a chocolate shake and a chicken sandwich with waffle fries. I also recommend the burgers. Everything is sourced locally. Even the potato chips. If you want, I'll go halfsies with you. You get a burger, I'll get the chicken, and we can share."

Peter placed his menu on top of Lana's. "Deal."

A teenage boy dressed in jeans and a LaBelle's long-sleeved t-shirt took their order. Peter removed his phone from his pocket, swiped, studied it and turned it face down on the table.

"Lachlan?" Lana asked. "I meant what I told the driver. I'll speak with Edmund if necessary."

Peter placed his arm on the table. "Lachlan got what he needs, minus tomorrow's footage. We're fine."

They chatted until their food arrived, and Lana cut her sandwich in half. Peter did the same, and they swapped. He took a bite of her chicken sandwich first. He groaned in appreciation. "This is good."

"LaBelle's tries to be as green as possible. They believe in sustainable farming. Those chickens lived happy, free-range lives not even three miles from here until they had one bad day. There are other families around here that are part of the area farm cooperative. It's responsible farming, not factory farming. Better for the environment and the animals. Sometimes the restaurant will be out of something and that's the way it goes. Anything not eaten is composted."

"Clayton Hotels told me they're trying to be greener. Did you know Vegas recycles ninety-nine percent of its indoor water?"

Lana dipped a fry in ketchup. "Not a place I've been to. While I don't gamble, I do want to see the Strip someday. And Hoover Dam and Lake Mead. I keep a list of where I want to go."

Peter reached for one of his crinkle-cut fries. His toothy grin had become practically irresistible. "Really? I can't wait to hear more."

Chapter Thirteen

Edmund bit into a thick, salty French fry. He listened intently as Lana talked about her travels, sharing things he hadn't heard on the plane. He checked his phone as it buzzed yet again.

"Someone really wants to talk to you," Lana said. She reached for her chocolate shake.

"It's nothing." Edmund quickly sent Eva a return text: Leave me alone. Then another: Will explain later. He relaxed when his sister liked the second text.

Lana stirred her shake with a long-handled spoon. "By the way, I'm buying dinner. No arguments. Especially since you gave up your tips."

No woman ever offered to buy Edmund dinner, but Lana had done it twice. He watched as she sucked on the end of the straw. Was it wrong to be jealous of chocolate ice cream? She gazed at him over the top of the rounded goblet.

"This has been great fun," Edmund said. "You had a great idea. I'm sure it comes from you knowing who you are and what you want."

"I fake it well."

She licked whipped cream from the end of the straw, and he swore his pants tightened. "Don't sell yourself short."

She blinked several times, the straw poised at the end of

her lips as she studied him. "I keep hearing that. Admittedly, this trip home has changed me. I love my job. My bonus will go toward my bucket list trip to Paris. But then after that, what's next? Sure, London. Sydney. Tokyo. But what happens when I've seen everything? *Can* I even see everything? What if I never do that typical get married, have two-point-five kids and a white picket fence thing?"

Edmund held the next fry midair. "Do you even want that?"

"When I left my ex, I didn't think so. I took pride in being independent and not needing anyone. Now, I'm thinking it might be nice to share a life with someone. Well, the right someone." Lana suddenly stiffened and covered the left side of her face with her hand. "Crap."

Edmund scanned the room but saw nothing amiss. "What's wrong?"

"Do you see the man who just entered?" Lana ducked even lower, sliding her legs farther beneath the table so they tangled with his.

Edmund located the guy. "The one with the baby in the car seat and the toddler?"

"That's my ex." Lana slunk down even farther so that her head wasn't visible above the back of the booth. Her hand came onto the table, felt around and snagged a fry. "He clearly wasted no time since we broke up two years ago."

"Do you still have feelings for him?" Edmund put the French fry into his mouth and watched as her ex waited for his carryout order. While Edmund didn't believe Lana still had feelings for her ex, Edmund wanted to hear the words. She'd turned him upside down and inside out. He'd hate to think she was still pining for someone from her past. Bad enough he was sitting across from her in his Peter disguise.

"No, thank goodness. We weren't suited. I know that now."

Edmund felt pure relief as Lana's gaze caught his. "I wanted the fantasy. Not that I want my life to be a movie. It's the idea of the romance. The grand gesture, you know? Is he still there?"

"He's just left with his order."

Lana pushed herself up. "I probably looked pretty stupid down there." She drained the rest of her shake. "Sorry about that. I didn't want to have one of those 'Lana, how've you been? What have you been doing?' conversations. It's not because I didn't want him to see me sitting with you."

"You don't have to explain yourself. You always have to remember you're enough, Lana. More than enough." Edmund found himself surprised by how insistent his tone was. But even as Peter, he wanted her to know that.

"I wish we had time to get to know each other better." Lana pushed her empty plate forward. "You've always been honest with me. No drama. No lies."

Edmund managed not to wince. He was living on borrowed time as Peter, who by tomorrow afternoon would cease to exist. Taking his place would be Edmund, the liar. The one who drama followed like a shadow. The one for whom business deals meant everything. The one who still needed to tell her the truth.

His phone buzzed again. He turned it over and saw another message from Eva. Don't you dare tell her. I know you. You're thinking it right now. DON'T DO IT.

"We should probably get back," Edmund told Lana.

Their server brought the check and the carryout order they'd placed for their driver. Lana snatched up the bill before Edmund could read the amount. "On me," she insisted, placing three twenties on the table. "Let's go."

Their driver thanked them for the food and returned them to the hotel. A valet opened Lana's door. Edmund met her by the lobby doors. She peered inside. "I don't see anyone. Maybe they went away."

Edmund's feet hurt from wearing Peter's terrible shoes, the ones with the lifts that changed his gait. "They could be stalking us from the bar. We should make a rush for it."

She grinned. "Okay. One, two, three. Go!"

She rushed through the lobby. Despite the sharp pain in his toes, Edmund kept pace. By the time the elevator doors closed on them, she'd dissolved into peals of laughter. He'd never heard a better sound. She slumped against one wall with him on the other until the car stopped on her floor. "I hate goodbyes, so I'm going to walk away and not look back."

"Fair enough." He'd see her tomorrow, but not as Peter. Hopefully she'd forgive him. Hopefully she'd see a future for them.

Lana kept one hand on the door-open button. "Good luck with your show. I'll watch for it." Then, before he could speak, she let the button go, gave him a backward wave and stepped through the doors, which closed immediately. Edmund rode the elevator to Peter's floor and changed out of his clothes. He had three texts from Eva demanding he find her when he got back, so he went to meet her.

"Where did you go?" she demanded when she opened the door to her penthouse.

"LaBelle's. A family-owned restaurant a short distance from here. Locally-sourced meats and cheeses. You'd love it. Best chocolate shakes ever. Even comes with one of those long, thin hazelnut cookies."

"I can't believe you ditched me!" She glared at Edmund when he shrugged. He wasn't sorry. Not one bit.

Eva scowled at him. "Tell me you didn't reveal the truth. Family first, remember? Eyes on the prize."

"I wanted to, but the right moment never came up." He'd come close though, in the car to the bar and then at La-Belle's. She needed to know. He couldn't keep lying.

Edmund ran fingers through hair that was sticky from being underneath a wig. He wanted a long shower to wash off the day's grime. Tomorrow, after one final appearance from Peter, the employees would be called into a conference room at the Grand to discover their good fortune and meet Edmund.

"Lachlan and I decided that you should do a reveal with Lana too," Eva said. "Offer her a trip. Pay for her brother's college."

"I don't think she should be part of the show," Edmund said. His phone vibrated. Lana had texted, Are you awake?

Eva leaned her hip on arm of the couch. Princess yapped, and she scooped her up. "Why not? Lana signed the paperwork. I think you're underestimating her. And we need to win. And let's face it, while I like her and can see why you do, you know whatever this is won't work out. I love you, but you'll revert right back to being a workaholic."

"Maye. But even if I don't, putting her in the show feels as if I was using her this whole time. She's different. She paid for dinner tonight. Refused to let Peter pay because he tipped the driver to steal us away. My relationship with her is already tenuous enough because of the subterfuge. If I'm to have a chance, I have to come clean, not buy her off." Edmund texted Lana back, Am up. Why?

Lana's reply came quickly. I need to see you. If it's okay.

Edmund jerked a hand through his hair, but it remained plastered to his head. So much for a getting a shower. Lana was more important. Give me five minutes. Am with Eva.

Eva peered at him. "What is it? You look like you've seen a ghost."

Edmund's focus was on his phone, watching as Lana liked his message. "Lana's on her way. Whatever happens next, you stay out of it. Do not interfere. Do not let Lachlan interfere. I don't want to lose her."

"Wow. Where's my cool, aloof big brother?" Edmund shot her a look, and Eva raised a hand in surrender. "Okay, okay, as long as you don't tell her until the reveals, we won't film one of her. We can't have anyone knowing until after we've filmed Peter's final segments. Surely you can wait eighteen hours. If you agree to that deal, I'll handle Lachlan."

Edmund's temple throbbed. "As long as it doesn't hurt her. If I think anything is, I'm telling her and that's that."

Eva set Princess on the floor, and the dog scampered off. "I've never seen you act this way. You must really like her."

"I do." Edmund headed toward the door.

Eva intercepted him. Her warning gaze made him pause. "Just be sure you know what you're doing. We don't need another social media blowup."

Edmund flinched. "You know that's the last thing I want. Lana's not like that. But I still don't know if she's choosing me or Peter."

Eva placed her hand on Edmund's arm. She gazed at him. "Let's hope she tells you she's Team Edmund."

"Thank you for seeing me." As if trying not to lose her nerve, Lana rushed by Edmund and moved to the middle of the suite. He'd never seen her in such an agitated state. Edmund ensured the door was locked before he approached.

"Let's sit down, and you can tell me what's going on. Does this have to do with the filming?"

Lana collapsed onto the love seat. She twisted some of her sunset-colored hair around her finger. "I'm done with that. I did the training stuff this morning."

Edmund grabbed two bottles of water and handed her one. "Was it meeting Eva? My sister can come on rather strong."

"She's blunt. She asked me..." Lana stopped, uncapped the water and sipped. She gathered herself. She gestured with the bottle. "Thanks. I needed this."

"Do you want some wine? I have some over on the bar."

Lana's hair swished over her shoulders, reminding Edmund of how those red strands had spread over his pillowcase. Her lips wrapped around the bottle as she took another sip. She wiped under her lower lip. "I'm good. I'm just a bundle of nerves. I'm not usually like this."

"Except when planes take off and land." She'd clutched his hand, and he hadn't wanted to let her go.

Lana gave a short laugh. "Okay, well, besides that. Even when I saw my ex tonight, I wasn't in these kinds of knots."

Edmund settled onto the couch directly across from her. "Would it help if you started from the beginning?"

"I don't even know when that is." Lana set the bottle down. She gripped her knees. "You know your sister crashed my drinks with Peter."

Fraught with his own nerves that he refused to show, Edmund loosened his grip on his plastic bottle before he squeezed it too tight. "How did that go?"

"Actually, we ended up at La Vita è Vino Dolce on Main Street. Then Peter and I ditched the cameras and made a run for it."

Because he had promised Eva he'd keep his secret, Edmund simply encouraged Lana to keep talking by prompting her with, "And?"

"He gave his tip money to the driver to speed us away. We went to LaBelle's, a diner on the outskirts of town. We split a chicken sandwich and a burger."

He resisted leaning forward to place a hand on the knee she bounced. "Sounds delicious. But Lana, I don't know why you feel you had to come and talk to me. We've never said we were exclusive, nor are we in a relationship. You don't owe me any explanation of how you spend your time."

She nibbled her lower lip. "It's about what Peter and I talked about. It made me think of you."

Edmund's breath hitched. He could replay every single one of their conversations. She worried that she couldn't have it all. She wanted the grand gesture. The romance. Was worried it would never arrive. He reminded himself to play things cool. He'd promised Eva eighteen hours. Tomorrow he'd come clean with Lana and give her the grand gesture so that she'd forgive him, and someday they'd laugh about this as the story of how they met. "And?"

"Your sister asked me which of you two I liked better. She asked me, if Peter asked to kiss me, would I let him?"

"Would you?" The words came out on a cough. Edmund took a long drink. "Sorry. Got something caught in my throat."

"I told her I wouldn't because I don't go around kissing people if we're not going to be in a relationship. I'm certainly not the type to sleep with one guy and then kiss another." Lana sipped water and recapped the bottle. "Thanks for telling her *everything,* by the way. That was quite a blindside. Although, if I'm being fair, she did admit she filled in the blanks and was trying to protect you from another viral video."

"My sister lives in fear of viral videos."

Lana palmed her thighs. "Well, I can understand. That's

one reason I'm here. I don't want to appear on camera looking like I'm dating Peter. I don't want to have the world see
me in some fake showmance, and I certainly don't want to
look like a fool. Most of all, it's important that whatever
Lachlan does with the footage, I don't want you to think
that I used you. You were the one who agreed to allow Peter
to stay on."

Edmund rose and went to the window. The world outside seemed cloaked in still and quiet darkness. He didn't
want her to see the emotions on his face until he got control of them. Composed, he turned back toward her. "Lana,
if anything, I've used you. You're on camera and will be
promoting my hotels. I will not let Lachlan make you appear like a fool. Minus a dinner at La Martina that I ma-
nipulated you into, you've been perfect. I'm the one who's
acted inappropriate toward you. I'm the one who's been a
cold, selfish jerk. To be honest, I'm jealous of the fact you
like Peter better than me."

"I…" Lana joined him at the window. "There are so
many parts of him that I like. But since we're being honest, most of me likes you better."

Hope flared, only to die when she said, "But our worlds
don't work together. We don't make sense. Your sister asked
me if I was Team Peter or Team Edmund. Your name
popped into my head as the answer."

Edmund found himself on tenterhooks as a sliver of
hope returned. He wanted her to pick him. To be with him.

"My instinct was to choose you," Lana rushed on, as
if the admission cost her. "The realistic part of me understands that we can't make one night into a lifetime."

"But what if we could?"

She shook her head. "I walked away from Peter tonight,

and, because I hate goodbyes, I didn't look back. I already agreed to go to dinner with you tomorrow."

"And?" Edmund felt stuck on that one word, as if his entire future depended on it.

Lana pushed strands of hair behind the ear that he'd nibbled until she'd moaned with pleasure. How much simpler things had felt that first night.

"I don't know if I can go to dinner. I don't want to spend time with your family and then have to say goodbye to them or you. This is why I don't form deep relationships on the road. I hate goodbyes, especially the kind that sting. Or hurt. When I'm on the road, I can say goodbye all day and not feel a thing. You've made me feel things. You've made me want things that I buried deep."

"What if we don't have to say goodbye?"

Her lower lip quivered. "You know that's not possible. We have places to be. Careers to follow. Dreams to chase."

Edmund's heart bounced like a seesaw. He wanted to make her feel all the good things and none of the bad. "I'd like you to be at dinner, but you can skip it if you want to. I want you to be comfortable, Lana. As for the rest, if I can procure a hotel room out of thin air, can you at least entertain the fact that I might be able to find a way to make things work? That neither of us has to sacrifice anything to get what we want? That we can both be satisfied, but together? Can you do that for me?"

She placed her hand on his arm. "Will you give me tonight to think on it? About both dinner and us?"

"Of course." He'd give her whatever she wanted.

She removed her hand, and he missed her touch. "It's bad enough always saying goodbye to my family. They look at me with such longing that I feel guilty for wanting to have a life of my own. This is why I slipped out of your bed. No muss. No fuss. No investment."

"It makes sense." He didn't like it, but he understood. Edmund remained rooted, afraid if he moved, she'd vanish.

"When I saw my ex tonight, he had a baby and a toddler with him. What would I have said if he saw me? That I escaped my small town and its traditional expectations, but at the same time, that life on the road can be lonely? I don't want him. But maybe I do want what he has. Like why couldn't that be me? Why don't I get to have it all?"

Edmund took one of her hands in his, the one with the butterfly tattoo. Then he reached out and cupped her cheek. "You will have it all, because you are incredible and deserve it. You can do anything you want." He couldn't help himself. "I have it on good authority that Peter crushed on you pretty hard."

"He's staying here, in Beaumont. That's a no-go. Not even worth starting."

Edmund swiped a finger over her lips. "I can be anywhere you are. You blew into my world and rocked it to the core. Can't you tell how much I want you? How much I'll move heaven and earth to keep you?"

"I want you too." Lana fingered his sleeve. "But I'm afraid. Your life is a fishbowl. I'm a nobody. I'm afraid you'll find me lacking."

"Never."

"You can't make that promise," Lana said. "We were both engaged, so we know firsthand how relationships crash and burn. What if we're simply a flash in the pan? When I texted you and asked to come up here, I planned to swallow my pride and ask for one more night in your bed. I wanted to wake up in your arms at least once."

Edmund's lust warred with his heart, which battled with

his conscience. He couldn't make love to her again, not until she knew the full truth about his deception as Peter. "I want nothing more than for you to wake up in my arms every day. But Lana, I can't tonight. There are things I have to tell you, important business dealings I'm not at liberty to share until tomorrow."

"That project you're dealing with."

"Yes. I'll be working on it most of the night." Not exactly a stretch. "Whether or not you come to dinner, will you meet with me tomorrow? Let me tell you everything then?" He pressed his forehead against hers. "Can you do this one thing for me, or am I asking too much?"

She tilted her head and moved her lips to his. The kiss was his undoing. He threaded his hands into her silky hair. His mouth plundered hers, his tongue exploring every crevice. He imprinted her to him knowing that he'd met the one woman with whom he wanted a future, but feared he'd have to let go of forever. The kiss deepened, and it took everything he had not to slide his hands under Lana's sweater. To somehow step back and disengage when she pulled at his shirt and tugged it free from the waistband of his slacks. "Lana."

While not his intention, his saying her name was like dumping a bucket of cold water. She broke the kiss she'd initiated. "I'll go," she said, backing away.

"Lana, look at me."

She froze. Her amber gaze sought the floor first before it found his.

"I want you more than I have any other woman in my life. I want to make things work. I'm completely under your spell. Remember those projects? Let me finish them. Then I can be yours and nothing will stand between us. Work is the only reason I'm saying no to making love to you right now. Please believe that."

"Okay." She didn't appear convinced. He couldn't let her leave this way.

He crossed the distance and used his thumb to stroke her cheek. "Give me until tomorrow afternoon. Let me move all the pieces into place, and I'll explain everything once I've met the deadline."

"Is there someone else?" Her face took on a bittersweet, faraway expression. "I'd understand if there was. It's not like we…"

He cut her off with a gentle kiss. In good conscience, he could not make love to Lana tonight, no matter how much he wanted to do so, especially after that kiss. "There's only you. I'm one hundred percent Team Lana. Until tomorrow."

One more light kiss, this one to her forehead. As she stepped into the elevator, it took every ounce of his strength not to go after her.

Lana flopped onto the bed in her hotel room, rubbed her temples and tried to make sense of everything that Edmund had said. While she understood deadlines, she had no idea what Edmund's projects were. *See,* her brain told her, *this is just one more reason that we can't be together.* He was a VP aiming to be CEO. Not only was he a public figure, but he had business dealings that kept him working past nine to five.

But she liked Edmund anyway. Like Mr. Darcy with Elizabeth Bennet, he'd grown on her. He wasn't as proud or arrogant as he originally seemed. Could they make things work like he'd suggested? Could they figure out a way to date? And if they were successful, then what? Where would they live? Would she still travel? Could she give up the adventure? Would she be satisfied? She'd drive herself crazy if she kept up all this thinking.

She took several cleansing breaths. Her mom would tell Lana that she was putting the cart before the horse. Speculating on unnecessary tangents long before anything even existed in reality. Lana had always been too much in her head, trying to play chess on a board set for checkers.

Control what you can control, she reminded herself. That's all she could do. Tomorrow she'd find out what he meant. She pressed her lips together, still puffy from his passionate kiss. She couldn't help herself. She sent him one last text, which he hearted: 100% Team Edmund.

Chapter Fourteen

The next morning Edmund's alarm went off at five. His eyes felt glued shut and his ears full of cotton. This week had been one of the most exhausting of his life. He hadn't gotten much sleep last night, especially after Lana's text that she was Team Edmund.

He'd almost texted her back, told her that he'd changed his mind, and invited her to please come back or let him go to her room. Instead, he'd tackled an inbox full of crisis after crisis. While he had left people in charge, the buck stopped with him and his sign-off had been needed on several items. By the time he'd finished with those issues, it had been 1:00 a.m. Insomnia kept him tossing and turning until three.

He made a pot of strong, black coffee, checked even more emails and ate the room service breakfast delivered to the suite at exactly five thirty. Just a few more hours and he could tell Lana the truth. He had no idea how she'd take it, but prayed everything would turn out okay. He meant what he'd told her. He wanted to see where things could lead. She was his forever.

Around six, Edmund went to Peter's room to transform himself one last time into his alter ego. Edmund filmed the selfie-style confessional using the speech Lachlan had emailed. By seven he was downstairs at the front desk to shoot the final footage. Along with other service requests, he'd help guests check out. While many used their television screens or the Clayton Hotel app, Edmund found it eye-opening how many travelers still wanted personal service and a printed receipt. Front desk clerk would serve as Peter's last role, and during his training, he chatted with Macy, the morning supervisor. Macy had worked for Clayton Hotels first in Illinois, then she'd met and married someone who lived in Beaumont.

"It was a love at first sight sort of thing," she told him. "I used to be at the Clayton Hotel in Chesterfield, but jumped at the chance to work closer to home and have a six-minute commute instead of forty-five. We've got six kids between us in our blended family. Can you believe that? But when you love someone, Peter, you do what it takes."

"I'm starting to realize that," Edmund said. All morning he kept watch for Lana, glancing up any time someone who slightly resembled her walked through, even though he knew she would be at the Chateau doing the final walk-through.

"You make everything look so easy," Edmund told Macy as their shift came to an end.

Macy laughed. "You'll get the hang of it."

"Cut! Good, we're done here. Macy, thank you." Lachlan handed her a check, which she discreetly tucked into her front pants pocket. "Peter, it's already noon, so let's do the final footage after lunch. Say, one? Then that'll be a wrap."

"Fantastic." Edmund was beyond ready to be done with Peter and this getup. He'd already moved Peter's bag to his suite. The Grand had a big convention over the weekend with guests arriving starting today. No sense in keeping the room as a storage space when it was needed for paying guests. Edmund started to leave the front desk for the back office when he heard a familiar voice.

"Edmund? Edmund, is that you?"

Damn. "I'm sorry, you must be mistaken," Edmund told his cousin Jack. "I'm Peter with guest services."

Jack noticed Ben and Larry adjusting their cameras. "What the hell is going on?" Jack demanded. "And was that Lachlan Van Horn? Where's he going?"

"Mr. Clayton, why don't you come with me to Mr. Smith's office?" Edmund asked, aware of Macy's curious gaze. Edmund pointed. "If you'd follow me…"

"Thank you, *Peter*, but I know the way," Jack snapped. "After all, it's my family's hotel."

Edmund reached Mr. Smith's office before Jack did. Because of the number of people moving through the office hallway, Edmund held a finger to his lips, the universal sign for don't speak. Jack didn't appear happy, but complied. Still in his role as Peter, Edmund told Jack, "Mr. Clayton, your cousin Edmund has requested you meet him upstairs in Penthouse A. If you're ready, I'll take you to see him. Unless you have an objection, we can use the service elevators."

"I can't wait to hear about what my cousin has to say." Jack added a roll of his greenish-blue eyes. While the two cousins had some similar features, like their noses, Jack took after his mother. Edmund noted his cousin's wavy brown hair had grown out even longer since he'd moved to Beaumont. He'd always had a cheekier smile than Edmund. Jack was a charmer, whereas people described Edmund as more classically handsome and cold. Basically, Jack was a friendly Mr. Bingley compared to Edmund's brooding Mr. Darcy. Edmund still hadn't read the books or seen any of the movie versions, but he'd read an internet synopsis. Same for the other movies Lana had mentioned. He'd wanted to truly understand what she meant about grand gestures and happy-ever-after endings. He got it now.

"I can't believe you came into town and didn't tell me you were doing…whatever this is," Jack said once the elevator doors closed.

"That's what tonight's dinner was for. I've been working undercover for a TV show. That front desk role was my last. I'm filming the reveals at one. If you hadn't interrupted me, I would have already been up here changing clothes. You're ruining the schedule, and you almost blew my cover."

"You're blaming me? Perhaps if someone had filled me in on everything then I wouldn't have ruined it. And what were they thinking? I haven't seen you in a costume this terrible since you were in high school. I thought they were supposed to give you a makeover or something."

"My appearance wasn't my choice, and the makeovers you're thinking of are for a different show." Edmund entered the suite. He kicked off the offensive shoes and began to pull off the mustache that had itched the entire morning. "This costume is such a pain. This whole show has been one. Just the reveals left to shoot, and then the nightmare is over."

Jack snatched a bottle of water from the minifridge and sat on the same love seat Lana had occupied last night. "Why don't you tell me why you're even doing this dumb thing in the first place, and in my hotel, of all places."

Edmund arched a fake, thick eyebrow before peeling it off. "Our hotels, you mean."

"Whatever. Just because I stepped away—for my wife, I might add—doesn't mean I'm not still a family stakeholder. And going undercover doesn't sound like you. Who talked you into this idea? Eva?"

Edmund pulled off the other eyebrow. "It has to do with Van Horn Hotels. Mrs. Van Horn wants to launch her grandson as a Hollywood hot shot and figured making me and Reginald Justus jump through hoops by going undercover on Lachlan's show was a good way to get Lachlan some exposure. Our dads know about it, as does Eva, but that's it. If I get the higher rated show, we get to buy Van Horn."

While Edmund was talking, he sent an SOS text to Eva, telling her to come to the suite pronto.

Jack shifted and made himself more comfortable. "That explains why Lachlan was here bossing around a film crew. I've been hearing rumors, especially after last night, when there was a TV crew down on Main Street, so I came over today to find out the truth. You look ridiculous, by the way. And sound even worse. And what's with those Baby Billy teeth? And good grief. Your nose."

"It's this stupid partial. It takes a few minutes to take out unless I want to rip out the inside of my mouth."

Jack shook his head. "I can't believe you came into my own backyard and didn't tell me what was going on. These are my neighbors. My town. I could have kept a secret."

"We kept the circle small, and you quit the company." Even to Edmund's ears, the excuse sounded lame. He tugged the nose off, and his eyes watered.

"That doesn't mean I quit the family. My businesses here support everything in our master plan for the area. And since my wife's family lives in Beaumont, it was easier for me to remain in town and let you take over. You're a workaholic. I'm not anymore, because being married gives you different priorities."

"Then why are you mad? You're not even part of the Van Horn acquisition."

"I'm angry because had you trusted me, I could have helped you. This is where I live. I'm a member of the chamber of commerce. As long as whatever you're doing doesn't upset the balance of the universe, or Beaumont, then it will be fine. But how was I to know? You never told me anything. You always do what you want, Edmund, and to hell with the consequences. In hindsight, it's a crappy thing to do, keeping me out of the loop. You need to trust people. That's your biggest flaw. You don't have to be so cutthroat all the time. You're so tightly wound right now that I'm afraid you might snap."

"Yeah, well, there's a girl, and that's another reason I'm on edge."

"Really?" Jack gazed up at him. "Do tell."

"She knows me like this. *And* as Edmund. It's a mess."

Jack shook his head. "Edmund, jeez."

Edmund tossed the black plastic glasses on the table. "It was never my intention to keep things from people, but that's the nature of the show. I need to take off the rest of this stuff and take a shower. I've got to be dressed and down in the conference room in less than an hour."

Eva burst in then. "Edmund. What are you doing? Why haven't you changed already?" She glared at Jack. "You! You always ruin everything."

Jack, who'd stood to greet Eva, paused. "What do you mean? I didn't do anything. I didn't even know about this. How can I ruin it?"

"Rumors are already swirling. You called Peter Edmund and now the front desk staff is gossiping. You're going to blow the reveals. And Edmund, you need to hide. I tried to stop her but she kept insisting. We really need to stop giving contractors all level access."

"Stop who?" Edmund paused before reaching the bedroom. "Why am I hiding? What did you do?"

"Eva? Are you up here?"

Edmund knew that voice. He cringed as Lana pushed open a door that hadn't fully shut behind his sister. Behind her, Ben held a camera aloft, and its red light blinked ominously. Behind him stood Lachlan. It was Edmund's worst nightmare coming true.

"Damn it! This is not supposed to happen this way." Edmund pointed to Lachlan and Ben. "Both of you! Get the hell out."

Peter stretched out his arm—no, Edmund. No. Peter *was* Edmund, Lana realized—and his big hand blocked the camera lens. Within seconds the door thudded closed, as Edmund had backed both Ben and Lachlan out of the penthouse. As Lana assessed the scene, a cold sense of foreboding traveled from head to toe, as if she'd just realized she wasn't watching a horror movie but was starring in one. As if her entire world had been a cruel joke.

Jack Clayton stood in the center of the room, a half-empty bottle of water in his hand. He wore jeans and a Henley. Eva, sans dog, wore a horrified expression, her wide mouth open as she rapid-fire apologized to her brother. To Lana's ears, Eva's voice sounded like Charlie Brown's teacher: garbled and indecipherable. She got the gist that Eva and Edmund were arguing.

Edmund wore Peter's uniform, minus the polished shoes lying on their sides a few feet away. Peter's brows, mustache and soul patch were gone, as were his thick black glasses and his huge nose. His teeth still protruded. He still had the blond bowl cut. His face kept morphing—anger mixed with guilt, then shame mixed with trepidation—a series of emotions flashed over a face Lana knew but really didn't.

"What is this? What's going on?" Her words sounded far away, as if the scene itself hadn't come into focus. Then everything clicked: the cameras. The firing. The various jobs. Edmund's ease reassigning Peter. The boss was in disguise. Undercover.

Which meant all those conversations... All those moments they'd shared...

Lies. Each and every one of them.

From the very moment she'd met him on the airplane, when he'd been flying in coach as if he were a common man, Edmund had lied to her. Acted like someone he wasn't. And whenever he was himself, he'd known her intimate secrets because he'd heard them while pretending to be someone else. Lana's lips quivered. "Whatever game you're playing, it stops now."

She somehow found a way to make her feet move. They'd felt glued, rooted to the floor, from the moment she'd walked into the room. She headed to the door.

"Lana, wait. Please." Hearing the pleading in his voice, she stopped.

Jack gave Edmund a reassuring pat on the shoulder as he exited the suite. Eva hovered for a minute. "Lana. I'm sorry. Listen to him, please. This is my fault. All of it. I told him he couldn't tell you. Blame me. Don't blame him." She mouthed "sorry" to Edmund as she left.

"I should go too," Lana said, although she didn't move. What was it that made her want to put herself through more emotional torture, like that time she'd asked her sixth-grade boyfriend why he'd dumped her, and he'd simply said, "You aren't pretty or cool enough," straight to her face?

Edmund ripped off his sideburns and let them fall to

the floor. "Don't go. Give me a chance to explain? Please? Will you wait while I get out of these clothes and take out these awful teeth?"

Lana bit her lip to the point of pain in order to ward off the mixed feelings flowing through her. She wanted to rage. Cry. Scream. Hide and lick her wounds. Eat endless tubs of Ben & Jerry's Phish Food ice cream and watch rom-coms where there was a guaranteed happy ending. "Give me one reason I should stay."

"I told you last night I wanted to explain. Please let me tell you the truth."

"Will it even be the truth?"

"That's fair," Edmund said. The wig came off, and with it a few strands of Edmund's hair. He appeared more like himself, minus the lines of concern creasing his forehead.

Lana folded her arms and braced herself. She was a strong, capable, independent woman, even if at this moment she felt her heart was bleeding out onto the floor. "I really don't know if the truth matters at this point. You lied to me."

"And I feel terrible about it. I care about you." Edmund appeared like a lost puppy, and Lana lost her cool. He wasn't the victim of a deliberate falsehood; she was. Her voice notched upward as her words burst out with more anger than disbelief.

"You *care* about me? Which you? Edmund? Peter? Trey? Who are you anyway? Besides a liar who's pretended he was someone else from the very beginning."

"I wanted to tell you. And I meant every word I said. Both as me and as Peter." Edmund raked a hand through his hair but the strands remained standing. "Do you know how many times I wanted to tell you? How hard it was to keep this secret, especially from you?

"But in the end, you didn't trust me enough to tell

me." Disappointed, she pointed toward the bedroom. "Go change. I'll give you five minutes to explain, and then I'm leaving."

"Thank you." Edmund disappeared through the doorway. Lana went to the refrigerator and removed a bottle of water. The cold liquid soothed her throat but did little to calm her frazzled nerves. She set the bottle down and noticed an unopened package of peanut M&M's, the extra-large, resealable sharing size. Tears threatened, and she turned the package away from her. She paced to the living room window. When Edmund returned, she was still staring aimlessly at the gray winter view.

"Lana."

As Edmund spoke her name in the voice she recognized as fully his, awareness shimmered. He was so handsome. Even without a shower, he looked every bit the vice president who would eventually be the CEO. He'd changed into pressed slacks, loafers and a white dress shirt. He adjusted a cuff link. "Thank you for staying."

"Why not? I already threw myself at you last night. What's a bit more humiliation?" She couldn't help the bitterness. Had she realized he was Peter…had she known he'd known all her secrets…she never would have come. What made matters worse was that she knew he knew it, and that's why he'd turned her down.

"I never meant to hurt you." Edmund stopped about ten feet away, as if afraid to get too close. His eyes were back to their normal gray color. As Peter he'd been wearing contacts, she realized. The show had done a great job with the disguise. She'd been as close to Edmund as a woman could be, but she'd bought into the reality of Peter hook, line and sinker. It had been the ultimate con.

His shifted his weight, as if knowing he was on quicksand. "I can't blame you for not trusting me, especially after what I did. Tell me how to fix this. I don't want to lose you."

Suddenly, Lana felt exhausted, as if she'd run a marathon. The tiredness went bone deep. Hope and promise had fled and left her instead with a sense of futility. She wouldn't ever have it all. None of her deepest, secret dreams would come true. She wasn't worthy; the universe only liked to tease her with a taste of happiness before taking it away.

Had she grabbed the bag of candy, she would have stress-eaten half of it by now. "I liked it better when I didn't know who you were," she said. She heaved a sigh. "Tell me why. The undercover stuff is pretty obvious. I've seen those reality shows. As long as the boss looks good, it's good PR, right? Hence Eva coming in and upping the drama. But why did you drag me into it? I wouldn't have done anything to help Peter if I'd known this was all some big setup, or realized the two of you were the same man. You were the one who came to talk to me."

"I'll own that. There you were, the woman I'd spent the weekend wondering about, the one who'd left. I couldn't believe my luck. Here was another chance. But I wasn't me. I was Peter. And you're right, I didn't have to get you involved. I should have walked away and approached you as Edmund. Then Eva…"

"Wait, you're not going to tell me it was your sister's idea," Lana snapped. She couldn't handle any more excuses.

"Keeping who I was a secret from you was a promise I made to Eva, one she kept reminding me about. If the show does well, we'll acquire Van Horn Hotels."

"A business deal." Lana tapped a finger on his arm. He appeared stricken. "You lied to me because of a *business* deal."

"Until I met you, my whole life was one deal after another. Last night, when you came to me, I wanted you more than I've ever wanted anything. But in good conscience, I couldn't make love to you, no matter how much I wanted you. Not when you didn't know the truth. At least that first night we were two strangers who'd agreed to remain such."

Lana sipped more water, mostly to give her hands something to do. What he said helped, but it didn't change things. He'd lied. She'd shared things with Peter she'd never told anyone. Edmund knowing those things created a power dynamic where he held all the cards. Would she have chosen Edmund at all, come to his room, if he hadn't known the right things to say to win her over? Just because he'd finally developed a conscience didn't excuse him.

Edmund moved one step closer. "Pretty much from the moment I met you, when you hit me with your shoulder bag, I fell for you. Then I found you working on my job site. And when you stormed into Smith's office all righteous about saving a stranger's job, you bowled me over. You, Lana, are what I want. I planned to tell you this the moment I finished the front desk job. Even before the reveals. Then Jack showed up. Then you came up here. Nothing has gone the way I wanted it to go."

Resignation slumped Lana's shoulders. She and Edmund were far too different. She liked people to be real, to be honest. The past week had been nothing but a lie. It was too much to bear, and she wanted to hide somewhere and lick her wounds.

"It's not like we run in the same circles, so we're not likely to see each other again," she said. "Tell the story however you want. I don't think I'll tell it at all, with the exception of how stupid I'm going to look on national TV. But then again, I've never really cared about things like that."

That was a lie, and they both knew it.

"Lana. Please don't."

"Don't what? Don't sell myself short? You and Peter did that for me, Edmund. You and this show. You let me believe the magic between us might be real. I can't forgive you for taking that away."

A rapid knock came on the door. Edmund moved and threw it open. "What?"

Lachlan stood there, irritation crisscrossing his features. "They're waiting for you downstairs for the big reveals. Let's go. Remember, you don't want to lose your chance to win some hotels."

"They can keep waiting. Give me a minute." Edmund slammed the door, and Lachlan's expression changed from irritation to surprise before he was out of sight on the other side. "Can we talk later? Please."

"What does it even matter at this point?" She'd been coming to tell him that she'd thought about him all morning. That the things Peter had told her the night before had resonated. That she couldn't wait to learn whatever it was that Edmund wanted to tell her. That after her final text to him, and after sleeping on it, she was still 100 percent Team Edmund.

A few minutes ago, she'd learned there never was a Team Peter. It had been an illusion. Edmund had been able to say the right things because he knew exactly what she was thinking. He'd been the one at the basketball game, the one at LaBelle's. Peter didn't exist.

Edmund waited for her answer. "It matters to me," he prompted softly. "You matter to me. I can cancel dinner."

"You go out with your family. How often do you see Jack? Eva? Didn't you say Michael was coming into town?"

By private plane, too, she'd bet. No wonder Edmund had been so uncomfortable in economy class.

Edmund tried one last time. "You're more important."

She rounded the sofa so that she didn't get close to him. She waved him off, trying to keep things light. "We'll catch up later. Go film the reveals. Don't keep them waiting. I can let myself out." She pointed at the door, which reverberated from Lachlan's renewed banging. "Go."

Edmund threw open the door to the suite. "Stop hitting the door. You're an ass, Lachlan, and this is your fault."

The room lost some of the tension as Edmund followed Lachlan into the hall. From her vantage point, Lana lost sight of them quickly. "You okay?" a voice asked.

Eva stood in the doorway, a worried expression creasing her face. Her dog poked its head out of her purse.

"I'm fine." Lana wasn't, but what was one more lie added the mountain created this week.

"Do you want to talk? He really does like you, Lana. Blame me, not him. He kept wanting to tell you."

"I know. He told me. Eva, I have work to do. Can we talk about this later?" Two more lies. Lana was really on a roll.

Lana slipped through the suite door and, using the regular elevator, she pressed the number for her floor. Once safely inside her room, the tears began to fall. Then she wiped them away and began to pack. She couldn't stay any longer. Not when there was nothing left to say. A relationship built on lies couldn't last. She had goals. A career to build. A trip to Paris in the fall.

She chose a number from her speed dial contacts and inhaled a relieved breath when the call connected on the first ring. "Hey," she said. "I'm finished here. I'm going to call a car to pick me up and change my flight. I'm ready to leave."

On the other end of the line, her boss's voice came

through loud and clear. "Are you sure you don't want to spend any more time with your family?"

"They're busy with Ryan and state basketball. I'd rather get a jump on the next project. Plus I could use some sunshine. There's a flight out in a couple hours. If I leave now, I should make it. I may have to run."

But what was more running? There was nothing here for her anymore. She liked Edmund enough that her heart felt like it was breaking. Part of her wondered if she should stay. But her head told her to do what she did best: run away and protect herself.

Mrs. Cederberg's voice was bright and cheery. "Then safe travels and enjoy San Diego."

"What do you mean she checked out?" Edmund bit back the shock and surprise. He schooled his features into neutral as he stared at Macy, the front desk clerk. She'd been delighted to discover during the reveal that he was sending her and her family on an all-expenses paid, island-hopping trip to Hawaii for two weeks. Each one of his employees had been surprised and pleased, including Jimmy, who kept repeating "Dude, this is too much," followed by an apology for calling Edmund "dude."

This afternoon's filming almost made a week undercover worth it. Edmund had long ago stopped believing in Santa Claus, but this afternoon he'd felt like Santa himself as he changed people's lives for the better. Yes, in the end it was all done for ratings and a show, but his employees had acted like they'd won the lottery. He'd been delighted by their responses.

With the exception of one. And she wasn't his employee. She was the woman he was in love with, and he'd gone to find her the moment Lachlan had shouted, "That's a wrap!"

Eva would deal with Lachlan from here forward, reviewing the footage and ensuring the final product fit the standards of Clayton Hotels. Edmund's part was over.

"I'm sorry," Macy said. "She had a car take her to the airport. We had another couple going, and they didn't mind sharing the Navigator. This was about three hours ago."

"Thank you." Edmund stopped drumming his fingers against the countertop. He'd thought she was spending the weekend with her parents. As he walked to the elevator, he sent Lana a text. You left.

When he received no answer, he impulsively checked the airline schedule. A plane to San Diego had departed an hour ago. She'd be at least four hours in the air. He pictured her eating peanut M&M's and reading a romance novel. Eva was sitting in Edmund's suite when he arrived, her dog, Princess, curled up next to her on the love seat. "Eva. What do you need?"

She lowered her phone. "I wanted to see how you're doing now that filming is over."

He sat on the couch. "Lana's gone."

"What do you mean, gone? I just spoke with her a couple hours ago. She seemed fine. Where did she go?"

Edmund knew Lana had lied. "San Diego. I can't blame her. I should have told her the truth from the beginning. I shouldn't have kept things a secret."

"You need to go after her. Take the plane."

"She told me our worlds are too different. I've been deluding myself that she and I could make things work. I've known her a week. What kind of a fool am I to think that what I feel for her might be real?"

Eva's lip quivered. "For some, a week can feel like a lifetime. When you have a connection like the two of you do, you can't let it go. I know I might not have believed it at first, but it was real. I saw it."

"Two ships passing have a brief connection, and then they go their separate ways."

"I'm really tired of all this ship analogy nonsense," Eva said, tossing her hands up in frustration. "You've always been an idiot when it comes to women, which is one reason I didn't trust this. I was wrong. If you aren't following her and begging for her forgiveness, what are you going to do? You need a plan. Some sort of groveling. Think! You deserve to be happy, Edmund. Do something."

Edmund gripped his knees as an idea formed. "I'm going to give her what she really wants. I'm sending her to Paris."

"And you'll meet her there? Like in the movie *Sabrina*." Eva's expression turned dreamy.

"Never seen it. And no, I won't be joining her. Paris is *her* dream. I need to let her go alone."

Even if she never came back to him.

Chapter Fifteen

The weather in San Diego couldn't have been more perfect. Highs were in the upper sixties, with lows in the mid-fifties. Lana didn't need a puffer coat, just a light jacket as she walked the waterfront Embarcadero along the western edge of downtown. The boardwalk hugged the San Diego Bay, giving her awesome views of the yachts docked there. She turned her face to blue sky and sunshine. The salt-tinged air soothed both her lungs and her soul. Her heart, however, remained broken. It would heal with time, she knew. As for how long it would take, that was anyone's guess. The trip had helped, as there were many sightseeing opportunities. She'd shopped in Seaport Village and taken a harbor cruise. She'd explored the USS Midway Museum and climbed aboard her first aircraft carrier.

At night, she'd curl up in bed and read books, foregoing romance novels for thrillers by Brad Thor, Daniel Silva and Catherine Coulter. On the night Ryan's team won the state championship, she'd watched the live stream. She'd cried buckets as students rushed center court and hoisted her brother into the air. She and Ryan had FaceTimed the next day for two hours. He told her he planned on committing to Kansas, since that was closer to home, just a four-hour drive from Beaumont. While he didn't expect to play much as a freshman, Lana told him it didn't matter. She'd attend as many games as she could.

As for Edmund, after two days of not answering his texts, he'd stopped sending them. While it was what she'd wanted, she had to admit that a small part of her wanted him to keep fighting for her, for them. But he hadn't, because him doing so was the stuff of fantasies, not reality. Neither of them could hang on to a dream forever, especially when it wasn't meant to be. Lana was nothing but a realist on that score.

Her phone rang with a video call, and Lana sat on a bench to answer it. Mrs. Cederberg's face filled the small screen. "I have a new assignment for you."

"I'm not finished here," Lana said. The San Diego project involved refreshing and redecorating a one-million-square-foot hotel and office complex located in the historic downtown financial district.

"It's Keith's turn to enjoy that lovely blue water I see behind you," Mrs. Cederberg said. "I need you on a plane. Get back to the hotel and pack. A car will arrive to take you to the airport in one hour. Anything else you need, buy once you arrive."

"Where?" Lana asked as her phone pinged with an incoming email.

"You can thank me later, but your fairy godmother is sending you and your family to Paris for spring break. Since they're already on their way to the airport, it's not like you can say no."

"Are you crazy?" Lana asked. "What are you thinking?"

Mrs. Cederberg laughed. "I'm thinking you deserve this. Go. Enjoy."

The call ended, and dazed, Lana headed for the hotel. Paris? With her parents? Maybe some dreams did come true.

Paris in the spring was a sight to behold. After a first-class flight with a connection in Atlanta, Lana found her family waiting at the hotel.

"I can't believe this," her mother said as she pulled Lana into a hug. "This suite is bigger than our house. It's beautiful."

Her parents had been put into a suite that had once been occupied by a famous Parisian fashion icon. Lana had a seven-hundred-square-foot suite that had once been occupied by a famous American author. Ryan had his own room, a junior suite. The entire cost of these rooms for a week was mind-boggling. Everything was the height of luxury, after all, it was the Hotel Clayton Paris.

While Mrs. Cederberg had claimed the trip was part of Lana's bonus package for a job well done over the past several years, Lana suspected the trip had been Edmund's idea. And while she might have initially thought to turn down the trip because of its generous benefactor, her family hadn't had a true vacation in years. She wanted this time with them, and everything had been prearranged.

There were spa treatments for her and her mother. The concierge had planned a complete museum and monument itinerary for each day. They had a personal tour guide who met them in the lobby each morning and sped them away via private car. Nothing was left off the list. They visited the Eiffel Tower, the Arc de Triomphe, the Louvre, the Musée d'Orsay and the Musée d'Art Moderne de Paris, which to Lana's delighted surprise had an Andy Warhol special exhibit.

To make things easier, the tour guide had selected their dinner destinations. Each meal contained multiple courses of delicious food. Because Ryan had previous plans he couldn't cancel, her family left two days before Lana's trip ended. She'd fly straight from Paris to the United States and arrive back on Easter Saturday. The extra time was enough for her to thoroughly visit Versailles. Her private tour guide had special access, taking her through parts of the palace far beyond those of the guided tours. Seeing the palace and its gardens took a full day, and she spent the next day at the Estate of Trianon, both outside and in. She'd loved seeing every single fountain.

"What was your favorite part of Paris?" her guide asked from the front seat as their driver whisked them back to Paris.

Lana leaned back against the seat. "I loved all of it. Paris is magical."

Wanting to relax the night before her flight, she enjoyed a delicious room service dinner and took a long walk along the Seine. It would be hard to leave, but she had Easter on Sunday and then a meeting with Mrs. Cederberg on Monday. Back in her room, she sent Edmund a text. Thank you for a magical week.

If she'd been expecting an answer, she would have been disappointed. Even the next morning, her phone remained silent, minus the notifications of her flight status. She flew to St. Louis via JFK, and once in Missouri, her dad picked her up at the airport. Unlike last time, there were no delays or hiccups.

Like a switch had been flipped, spring had arrived in Beaumont. Green growth vanquished winter brown. Daffodils lined the roadsides, and crocuses filled her mom's front gardens.

As was tradition, Lana's mom hosted the entire family for Easter dinner, and Lana diverted her grandmother's "when will you settle down" questions by regaling her with stories of Paris and her family's trip of a lifetime.

"Hey, Lana, isn't that show that filmed at the Grand airing tonight?" her dad asked. He checked his phone. "I'd set it to record, but we can watch it live."

"It's tonight?" Lana had tried to forget about the entire show and its eventual debut. "We don't have to watch."

"It's our hometown. Let's see how we made out," her mom said. "Besides, Peter was such a nice guy. What did you say his real name was?"

While Lana hadn't told her family about her relationship with Edmund, she had told them about him going undercover as Peter. They'd been surprised but accepting, especially since they'd liked Peter.

The show opened with an overview of Edmund Clayton III. Lana drank him in. He appeared larger than life on her dad's seventy-inch TV. Because he didn't have a wife to say goodbye to, he talked with Eva. Then he got into a car to go to the airport. Lana recognized the clothes he'd worn as the ones she'd stripped off Trey.

Next the show featured a quick overview of Beaumont, including a quick drive through the downtown historic district. Following that was exterior footage of both the Grand and the Chateau, the latter of which was just about to open officially following the earlier soft open.

After a commercial, the show moved to a standard hotel room, where Edmund transformed himself into Peter, gluing things on and shoving in the colored contacts. "It's my first day, and I admit I'm nervous," he said in Peter's lisp. "Will they recognize me? Will I be able to do this job? Because working with your hands isn't something that comes easily to everyone, and I admit, I've never had to do it before."

The footage moved to the Chateau, where Peter made a mess of everything from carrying mattresses to spackling walls. Mixed into this segment was Peter's conversation with Jimmy and another confessional. "Jimmy taught me about commitment to a cause," Edmund said. "He's an inspiration in how hard he works to take care of his mom and his girlfriend, so much so that he's put his own dreams aside. Another person I met taught me that standing up for what's important is paramount when there's injustice. I can't use enough words to tell you how inspired I am by her."

The show cut to a commercial. "Who do you think he means?" Lana's mom asked.

"Not sure," Lana replied, almost positive Edmund was talking about her. She was on pins and needles waiting to see if Peter's firing would occur, but that scene seemed to have been cut.

"He's doing a good job so far," her dad said.

"My friends tuned in once I told them I was watching," Ryan said. "Everyone's on social media commenting. It's fun seeing your hometown on national television. Do you think he'll mention us?"

The next few segments moved through Peter's time as a valet and bellhop. Lana leaned forward as Peter readied his next confessional. "I spent a great day meeting great people. I even attended a high school basketball game where Beaumont High won. I went with a new friend. She doesn't know I'm here undercover, and I wish I could tell her the truth, but I've been sworn to silence by my sister and the producers. Hopefully, by the time you watch this, Beaumont's team has won the state championship."

A slide inserted before the commercial congratulated

Ryan's team on its win. That elicited a huge cheer. Ryan immediately began messaging his friends.

"That was nice of the show to do that," Lana's mom said. She passed around a plate of iced cookies shaped like Easter eggs, bunny rabbits and ducks. Lana snagged one of the buttery, vanilla-flavored treats before they disappeared into Ryan's stomach. She followed the cookie with a glass of water as the front desk segment started. By the end of the show, Lana realized her footage had been cut.

At first, the thought of being sliced from Edmund's show made her angry. Then she realized she'd seen far more dramatic episodes of this particular TV program. Edmund had sacrificed his chance for higher ratings by doing a bland program. Eva ordering him about her suite as he carried her luggage was as exciting as the episode got.

To conclude the segment, each of the employees who'd worked with Edmund was surprised, shocked and grateful for his or her gifts. The camera panned to Edmund for one final confessional.

"When I started this journey, I never could have envisioned what transpired during my week undercover. First, the people of Beaumont welcomed me with open arms and made me feel at home. I wish you could have seen more of my week. I visited La Vita è Vino Dolce. LaBelle's. Aunty Jayne's Cookies. If you take one thing away from this show, I want you to know how much I love this town. It's special. I can understand why those who live here, like my cousin Jack, call it home. From the moment I stepped off the plane, I changed because of people I met. It's been a great experience, and I hope you come and visit one of our hotels and wineries soon."

Everyone clapped as the credits scrolled. "What a great

job," her mom said as the party broke up. Lana's grandparents left, and she went into the kitchen.

"I'll help you with the dishes," she said.

But when her mom shooed her away, saying, "I've got it, leave this to me," Lana went into the family room. Her dad watched the news. Ryan had gone upstairs to play video games. Her phone pinged. Mrs. Cederberg had sent her a text asking if she'd seen the show. Lana told her she had.

I have an invitation to the grand opening gala for you if you want it, Mrs. Cederberg sent. I'll be going. If you want to join me, I'll arrange your schedule so you're in town. Let me know tomorrow when you come by the office.

I'll think about it, Lana sent back as her emotions bubbled. To protect her from being in a fishbowl, Edmund had cut her from the show. He'd sent her and her family to Paris. Now that the shock had worn off from learning he was Peter, she could admit she missed their talks. Missed *him*. But he'd lied to her. Deceived her. Could she forgive him? Should she go to the gala and see him? What if she went and discovered he'd moved on?

Before she could talk herself out of it, Lana sent Edmund a text. Thank you for cutting the footage. I appreciate you protecting me.

She could at least tell him that. She waited, but nothing came in response. Then again, Portland was two hours behind St. Louis. Since it was Easter, maybe he was with family. Maybe he'd deleted her phone number. Maybe, just maybe, he'd met someone else. She had to consider that possibility.

An answer from Edmund finally arrived. You're welcome. Some of the footage was too personal. I've gone viral before. I didn't want that for you.

She sunk her teeth into her lower lip before writing, I'm sorry if you don't get the hotels.

He sent back, Sometimes we don't get what we want. As long as you're happy, Lana, I'm good with the way the show turned out. Take care.

Lana leaned back, debated what to say. She didn't want to leave things like this. She typed and hit send before she could stop herself. You didn't have to send my family to Paris. And yes, I know you were behind it.

It was another ten minutes before his reply came back. What would Mr. Darcy do? And yes, I watched the entire Colin Firth BBC version. Good night, Lana. Happy Easter.

She waited, but nothing more came following her reply of, Happy Easter to you too.

Lana thumped her hand on the couch. In the end, Edmund had given her everything she'd wanted. No footage and a dream vacation. How could she stay angry? "Damn him."

Lana's mom walked into the room, and her dad swiveled his head. "What? Bad news?" her mom asked.

"Tell me something. How did you two know you were perfect for each other? Like, how did you know that you'd be forever and ever soulmates?"

Her mom dried her hands on a dish towel. "Honestly, we didn't."

"She wouldn't give me the time of day, actually," her dad said. "Took me three times asking her out before she said yes, and that was for a group date where she practically ignored me."

"Mom!" Lana was shocked. "How did I not know this?"

Her mom set the towel down. "Because we want to set a good example. The truth is, even before we married, we knew we weren't a perfect couple. We loved each other, but your father frustrated me quite a bit in the beginning."

"I was a party boy with little ambition," her dad admitted. "When we met and I fell for her, your mom was way out of my league. I had to get my act together to even get up the nerve to ask her out, and she made me work for a second date. But I persevered because she was all I could see. But I didn't make things easy. And once we married…"

"I had to teach him life skills. Like putting down the toilet seat, among other things." Her mom gave a little chuckle. "It's funny now, but it wasn't then. But deep down, in my heart, I knew he was the one for me despite his flaws. Love is work, Lana. The best kind of work, but it's hard work. We've had ups, downs and all sorts of difficulties, but he's my world. This—" Lana's mom gestured around the house "—may not seem like much to some people, but it's what's inside a person that counts. Your dad is a good man, a great father and a loving husband."

"I might be in love with Edmund," Lana admitted. "But I'm not sure."

"The guy on the TV?" Her dad seemed surprised. "When did that happen?"

"Yes, the guy on TV," her mom answered, giving Lana's dad an "are you this clueless" roll of her eyes. "Why else would she bring him to Ryan's game?"

"Oh, yeah, I guess that was him. Just in disguise. Could do worse," her dad said. "He's a vice president with Clayton Hotels. That place in Paris was pretty nice."

"I did do worse," Lana reminded him. "Remember my ex?" Everyone shuddered. "And Edmund's on the road as much as I am. We'd never see each other. I don't know how we'd make anything work."

Her mom regained control of the conversation. "Lana,

ask yourself this. Is he the first person you want to talk to when you wake up? The last person you want to talk to when you go to sleep?"

Lana remembered their texts. "But he deceived me! He lied to me. All those talks, I don't even know if they were real. I don't care about his NDA or whatever. When I told Peter my secrets and it was really Edmund in disguise, he crossed a line. And remember Paris? Mrs. Cederberg told me the trip was a bonus, but I got the truth out of her. Edmund knew Paris was on my bucket list. He arranged everything."

"He must really like you," her dad commented.

Lana's mom shushed her husband's next words and drew Lana into her arms. She pushed a stray strand of Lana's hair off to the side. "Perhaps he could have handled things better. But whatever his reasons, I'm sure he regrets them. Paris seems like a pretty big apology though. That trip had to cost a fortune. Looks like you got a bonus, just like Jimmy and Macy. If you want, you might just get more."

"I've just worked so hard for my career. I can't throw it away."

"You won't, because you, my girl, are the smartest, most ambitious person I know. I'm so proud to be your mom. You saw a life outside of Beaumont and you grabbed it. It's okay to want other things. Your dad and I, we're proud of you every day. We're so lucky that you're our daughter."

A few tears brimmed in Lana's eyes. "How can I trust him though? Even if he cared, he was lying about who he was. I don't know how to reconcile that."

Her mom stroked Lana's back "He made a promise to his family. To his sister. Look at how he protected you with the edits. That has to count for something. You have to decide what you want. If he's it, go for it. If he's not, move on. We'll support you either way."

"What if I fail?" Lana asked. "What if the risk becomes too much? What if I work and work and am never satisfied?"

"Nothing good in life comes without failure. Ask Thomas Edison. Henry Ford," her dad added helpfully. "Your mother shot me down, Lana. But I kept trying. You have to decide if the risk is worth taking. No one can answer that but you. I'm the luckiest man alive because your mom took a risk."

"Perhaps you need to talk to Edmund," Lana's mom suggested "Nothing will happen if you don't. You'll remain in a state of inertia, always wondering, 'What if?' Clear the air with him. At least then you'll know how he feels. Then you can decide. We're here for you, whatever and whenever. Your dad and I love you exactly the way you are."

"Even if I don't move back to Beaumont and give you dozens of grandbabies?" Lana asked.

"Even if," her mom replied. "You, my precious girl, are perfect exactly as you are. You've always made us proud. We only want you to be happy. If that's circling the globe, so be it."

Her dad stood. "Can I get in on this group hug?"

"Of course," her mom said, drawing him into the circle.

They both hugged her until they let her go. Her mom gave Lana a pat on the arm. "There's a hint of a determined smile. Have you made a decision?"

Lana shook her head. "Not yet. But I'll figure it out."

Edmund had made some grand gestures and expected nothing in return. He'd done it simply because he cared, like Mr. Darcy. And had he really watched all five hours of *Pride and Prejudice*? Damn the man.

What did she truly want? What would make her satisfied? She didn't have the answer to those questions. She only knew one thing:

The next move, Elizabeth Bennet, is entirely yours.

Chapter Sixteen

There was nothing like a grand opening to bring members of the Clayton family out of hiding, and the afternoon ribbon cutting for the Chateau and the gala that followed were no exception. The entire family was present and dressed to the nines as their guests enjoyed the evening.

Edmund, however, wished he were anywhere else. The place reminded him too much of Lana, and the times they'd spent here when he'd been Peter. She'd been kind and generous, and he'd fallen in love with her so fast that his head had refused to acknowledge what his heart had known all along. "Is she coming?" he'd asked Eva earlier, when the doors to the ballroom had first opened. His sister had handled the invitations and RSVPs, and she'd shaken her head and told him she was sorry.

Since Edmund always did his family duty though, he smiled at the arriving guests. His father was here, along with Edmund's Uncle Jonathan, and Edmund's cousin Jack. Jack had of course brought his wife, Sierra, and she'd invited her sister Zoe and her husband, Nick Reilly. Edmund's mother was here, along with Edmund's siblings Eva and Michael. Michael already had several women vying for his attention, a crowd of single beauties hanging on his every word. Edmund found not one of them interested him in the slightest. Lana had ruined him for all others. He wanted her here.

Even Liam was in attendance, although he looked as if he wanted to be anywhere else. He wasn't even staying at the Grand or Chateau, but rather at an inn on Main Street. The last two years hadn't been easy for Liam, but hopefully he'd soon be ready to move on. Edmund knew his dad wanted Liam back in the family fold and working for the company.

Because keeping up appearances was important, Edmund faked having fun when guests came to chat with him. He held a champagne flute loosely, the stem resting between his third and fourth fingers like he didn't have a care in the world. The party was a success. Guests mingled in the ballroom and spilled out into the gardens. Tonight's weather was perfect.

A-listers from across the country had flown in, and gala attendees also included many of Beaumont's movers and shakers, and of course those who'd participated in the television show. Jimmy, his girlfriend and his mother appeared starstruck. Even Keith appeared awed. He approached Edmund tentatively.

"This place came out better than I thought it would ever look," Keith said. He tugged at the collar of his shirt. He appeared sheepish. "No hard feelings on having to fire you?"

Edmund grinned. "As long as there are no hard feelings your scene got cut."

"Nope," Keith said. "The missus wouldn't like me to look mean on TV. She told me some things aren't worth the money. Appreciate you giving us that weeklong vacation to Alaska."

As if on cue, Keith's wife appeared, and Edmund chatted easily with them both for several minutes. They told him they'd take their trip in July.

When Mrs. Cederberg joined the group, he congratulated her on a job well done and told her that he looked forward to a long and prosperous relationship between their two companies.

"Thank you for arranging for Lana and her family to go to Paris. After a week dealing with me and all the filming, she deserved a vacation," Edmund said.

Mrs. Cederberg didn't bat an eye, same as she hadn't when Edmund had suggested the trip and that he was paying for it. "She told me it was everything she wanted and more. The perfect trip for her family."

Edmund watched as Mrs. Cederberg went to rejoin her party. He was tired of waiting. He was going to call Lana. He couldn't wait for her to come to him any longer; it had been a week since she texted him on Easter. He needed to find out where she was. Go talk to her in person. He'd lay his heart bare, and if she rejected him... Well, he hoped she wouldn't. If she did, he'd deal with it then. But he'd not been this successful in business by playing it safe.

Eva appeared by Edmund's side. "Where are you going? It's time for your speech."

"I want to find Lana. I need to talk to her. You give it."

Eva appeared shocked. "No, it has to be you. Lachlan and his grandmother are here."

Margot Van Horn was in Beaumont? Edmund's brow creased. "Why? We lost. Our show didn't have the ratings or the online response his did."

Justus had filmed his show at one of his adventure tourism resorts. He'd pulled out all the stops. He'd gotten a Jeep stuck, and in the process of extracting the vehicle, had been covered head to toe in mud. He'd gotten into an argument with an incompetent groundskeeper after being drenched by malfunctioning sprinklers. He'd dealt with an employee accused of theft.

Edmund, after his fake firing, had wondered how much of Justus's scenarios had been real versus scripted, especially when the incompetent manager turned out to be not so horrible, and the employee hadn't stolen anything from the gift store, and Justus had proven the man's innocence to his boss. From every drama, Justus had emerged heroic. The only place Edmund had looked better than his rival was during the reveals. Edmund had been far more generous in his gifting than Justus had been with his employees.

"I'll help you escape and get out of here as soon as you finish your speech," Eva told him. "Just get up there and do it. Then I'll cover for you."

"Deal." Edmund set aside his champagne glass and made his way to a dais located at the end of the ballroom. He stepped in front of the podium. He'd opted for low tech, so he removed the paper from his jacket pocket and adjusted the microphone. He could see his father and mother smiling proudly at him. Michael and Liam both lifted their champagne flutes in encouragement.

"Greetings. I'm delighted to welcome you to the Beaumont Chateau, a Clayton Hotel flagship property. On behalf of my family, thank you, Mayor…"

As Edmund began speaking, he relied on years of ingrained leadership to deliver his remarks, especially as his heart wasn't in it. Normally he loved this moment. Watching guests *ooh* and *ahh* over a hotel, hearing the accolades and knowing he was part of the reason for them—that had once been enough. This moment usually represented his success. His triumph. Proof of his leadership. Both his father and his uncle were delighted with the Chateau. They'd loved the TV show. Edmund hadn't yet broken the news about Van Horn Hotels. He'd find a way to make up for his failure to land that deal. He'd find other avenues of growth. But he'd found himself unable to think about that now. All he could think about was Lana and what he could do to convince her to give him another chance.

Applause broke out after Edmund finished. He tucked the folded pieces of paper back in his pocket and made his way off the platform. The band began to play, and guests moved to the dance floor.

"Well done," Edmund's dad said, clasping him on the shoulder.

"Thanks." Edmund resisted snagging a flute of champagne from a passing waiter. He glanced around for Eva. The sooner he spotted his sister, the sooner he could sneak out and find Lana. However, Eva seemed to have disappeared. "I couldn't have done it without you, Uncle Jonathan, and Jack paving the way. I had a lot to learn. There's a lot of people who also deserve the credit."

"Well, well. Look at that. Humility. Who would have thought the great Edmund the Third would have developed that trait." Margot Van Horn stepped into the family circle.

"Hello, Margot," Edmund's dad greeted her. Margot accepted a kiss on her gloved hand from both Edmund and his father. "I was delighted to see you on the guest list."

"Saw it on Lachlan's show and wanted to see the place in person. You've outdone yourselves. Now, leave me alone with your son, will you?"

Edmund's mom took hold of her husband's arm and drew him away. Edmund gave a shake of his head as he watched them go. "My father answers to no one," he mused. "What power you have."

Margot laughed. "Only because I'm old and eccentric and have known him since he was in diapers. That's the secret, sonny. Keep them guessing. Looks like you learned something going undercover."

"I did. I also know we lost," Edmund said. "Eva monitored the social media and ratings. My show didn't do as well as Reginald Justus's did. I concede. I know you're selling to him."

"And now you're a gracious loser." Margot's brows rose. "My, my. How the mighty have fallen."

After losing Lana, there wasn't much left that could hurt Edmund. "As you said, I've changed."

The tiara she wore in her hair glittered when she nodded. "I know. I saw the footage you refused to have in the show. Lachlan let me see everything. Those cameras rolled nonstop."

Her sharp gaze pierced him. "What the hell were you thinking? Throwing out all that excellent footage? I expected you to win, Edmund. I wanted you to have Van Horn Hotels. Your grandmother was one of my good friends. I like your mother. I didn't want to have to sell to Reginald Justus."

Edmund stared at the older woman. She held a folded fan in her hand and rapped his forearm with it. "Seriously. What's gotten into you?"

"Love." The word came out because it was the first thing that entered Edmund's head. "I wasn't going to let the woman I fell in love with be embarrassed on national television. You said you saw the footage. So you know who she is."

"Then where is she? I certainly don't see her here." Margot stated the obvious without ever tearing her gaze away from Edmund's. "You tossed away a chance to own my empire because you fell in love. Are you crazy?"

"Yes. And when you put it that way, it sounds insane," Edmund admitted. "In fact, if you excuse me, I'm off to go find her and win her back."

"Not so fast. Are you telling me she's worth losing billions of dollars? That if I gave you a do-over, you'd make the same choice?"

Edmund resisted raking his hand through his hair. He drew on his inner resolve. The faster he ended this conversation with Margot, the faster he could leave. Finding Lana was his top priority. He knew where her parents lived. He simply needed a car.

"Even knowing the results, I'd do it again. If I did anything differently, I'd tell her who I was from the very beginning. I wouldn't have deceived her. She's worth more than your hotels. She's worth everything."

Margot rapped him with the fan again, but this time she smiled. "Good. You made the right choice. It's something Justus never would have done. Your actions show an impressive maturity I always knew you had. Your grandparents would have been pleased. I know I am. Reginald Justus and I could not come to acceptable terms. We have no agreement and will no longer be pursuing one. Therefore, I will expect to hear from your negotiators next week. My assistant will send you details. And Edmund?"

Edmund tried not to say, "Are you serious?" He couldn't believe it. He'd won. Clayton Holdings would buy Van Horn. He contained his excitement and said, "Yes, Margot?"

"Maybe you should let Liam and Michael run point on the acquisition. It's time, don't you think, to let your brothers share some of the limelight? I'd say you have other things to do. You said you needed to be somewhere else, yes?" With that, Margot walked away.

Edmund turned toward Eva, who'd materialized at his side. Her expression was incredulous. She shook her fists close to her body as she held in a squeal of delight. Then she threw herself at Edmund and gave him a huge hug. "I can't believe that just happened! Van Horn! Ours! I've got to go tell Dad."

Edmund grabbed her wrist so she couldn't leave. "Wait! You're supposed to be covering for me."

"Go out into the garden. I'll meet you by Aphrodite. Go! I can't cover for you unless you're out there. I promise I'll be right behind you."

Edmund watched Eva weave through the crowd. Then he turned the opposite way and headed toward the French gardens. Soft path lighting guided his way. Strategic fairy lights made the trees and shrubbery sparkle. Various fountains bubbled, the colored spotlights adding a romantic vibe. He passed several couples out for a romantic stroll. Music from the band drifted on a light breeze.

He made his way deeper, and then stopped as he reached the grand fountain of Aphrodite. The stone goddess rose tall, water pouring from the jug she held in her hand. Other streams of water formed arches around her. Playful nymphs laughed at her feet. The statue was an original masterpiece, commissioned for the Chateau.

As Edmund stepped closer, he realized he wasn't alone. A woman sat on the concrete lip, her floral ball gown draping to her feet. Her fingers played in the water, swiping back and forth. His heart leaped. He would have recognized her anywhere.

He realized Eva wouldn't be coming. Edmund inhaled the fresh night air and asked the universe for one more miracle. "Lana."

Upon hearing Edmund's voice in the semidarkness, Lana jerked her hand out of the water, the action sending droplets spreading over the dress that had been a Paris splurge.

She hadn't expected him for another ten minutes. Eva was supposed to text her when he was coming.

Lana scrambled to her feet, her ankle wobbling in the new pair of designer stilettos she'd bought in Paris. Edmund was there immediately to catch her. Her hand pressed against his tuxedo jacket, marking it with wetness.

"I'm sorry. I didn't mean to scare you." Edmund guided her to a bench and settled her down. He sat on the other end, and she hated the space between them. He smiled. "Are you okay? What are you doing out here? The party's inside."

Her heart pounded and hope flickered "I was waiting for you. I had this whole thing planned, but you're early. Not that it matters. You're here."

"Let me guess. Eva?"

As if confirmation, Lana's phone pinged. "I asked for her help. You've been so kind, with both the show's footage and Paris. I wanted to talk to you. And I wanted to see these beautiful gardens at night. It seemed right that I meet you here. But now I'm nervous," Lana admitted.

The fairy lights reflected in Edmund's eyes. "Would it help if I told you I'd already asked Eva to cover for me so I could leave my own party early and find you? I planned to show up at your parents' house and wait all night if needed."

"Oh, they're here. I'm surprised you haven't seen them."

"My only focus was giving my speech so I could leave and come find you. And here you are, in my garden. I missed you. The dumbest thing I did was not telling you the truth. I'll regret that for as long as I live. I hurt you, that was wrong, and I'm sorry."

"I'm sorry, too. Because of me, your show didn't win. You should have used the footage."

"No. I'd rather lose a deal than lose you. Can you forgive me for lying to you about Peter?"

"I'll forgive you if you forgive me for my reaction. Can we make that deal? Can we figure out a way to start over? I'd like that. I've missed you."

Edmund reached forward. "May I?"

She nodded, and he cupped her cheek. "I've missed you too. I love you, Lana, more than I love my hotels. I would give everything up if it meant I could be with you. I hope you can believe me. Especially when I tell you that right before I came out here, I learned that Clayton Holdings will get to buy Van Horn after all."

"That's fantastic!" Lana's relief was instant. "I never wanted you to fail. You're clearly on your way to becoming CEO someday."

"Not if doing my job means losing you. I love you, and I hope someday you can love me back. I won't have you living in a fishbowl."

Lana's heart swelled. She didn't know that could be an actual thing, but her heart felt as if it would burst because of how happy she was. She put her hand to Edmund's cheek, memorizing the texture of his light stubble. "As long as it's not all the time, I'm willing to compromise. I'm ready if you are."

"I promise you I am. We may be from two different worlds, but together, we create our own. I love you, Lana. You are what matters. You. Only you. I'm putting it all out there. If your feelings aren't the same, tell me and I'll leave you alone."

"Are you channeling Mr. Darcy, right now? I can't believe you watched the show."

"And a few others you mentioned. I want to make you happy. I want to give you the world if you'll let me."

She realized she still hadn't said the words. "I love you. All of you. Trey. Peter. Edmund. You are my love, because what's in here is all the same." She pressed her hand to his heart.

"My love. I like the sound of that. May I?" He lowered his lips to hers and kissed her gently. Desire burned through her as she explored his mouth, her tongue finding all his hidden crevices. His hands slid to her breasts. Heat began to pool low in her body. Then he shifted, stood and held out his hand. "There's a ball going on inside, and as much as I want to whisk you away and show you exactly how much I love you, I want to dance with you first. You're wearing a beautiful dress, and it deserves to be seen."

"You mean this silly old thing?" Lana teased.

He planted a light kiss on her lips. "That silly old thing is driving me crazy. Later I'm going to slowly take it off you and show you exactly what you mean to me. But like any proper gentleman, I'm planning on dancing with you first. I would be honored to have you accompany me inside. Are you okay with being the center of attention? I'm not ruining your big grand gesture, am I?"

"I'd planned to tell you I love you, and that as long you're by my side, I'm good with whatever comes next. I had music planned so we could dance out here, but it's clear that Eva stopped that as I don't see a violinist. That might have been overkill anyway."

"Nothing you do will ever be too much. You're everything to me. I can't wait to give you the world."

"And knowing that you hate sightseeing alone, I can't wait to show it to you."

Lana couldn't help herself. She kissed him thoroughly again. When they finally broke apart, he laughed and kissed her nose. "My love, you have yourself a deal."

Epilogue

"Ready?" Upon hearing her mother's voice, Lana turned from where she'd been staring out Room 36's window, watching the action in the French garden far below. Of all the rooms in the Chateau, this was Lana's favorite. Her mom gave her a huge smile. "It's time."

Her dad, so handsome in his tux, grinned and teased his daughter. "You can still back out, you know."

Lana rolled her eyes and laughed. Today was her wedding day, and she was giddily happy. "And let this fancy white dress I bought in Paris go to waste? Never."

Her dad kissed her cheek. "You've got a good man, Lana. I'm glad to officially welcome him to the family today. I love you, my girl."

"I love you too, Dad. Don't cry too much when you give me away." Laughing, her dad swiped the tear that had already formed.

Lana caught Eva's gaze through the mirror. "It's finally happening!" Eva squealed. "Only took you and Edmund two *long* years."

"That's because we've been so busy traveling," Lana reminded her soon-to-be sister-in-law. Following the Chateau's grand opening, Lana had adjusted her job with Cederberg Interiors to one that allowed her to travel around the world with Edmund. She'd made sure they had time to see the sights. They'd also prioritized family, including following Kansas basketball, often timing their work trips so they could be in town to watch Ryan's home and away games. When the team had won the championship, Lana and Edmund had been there.

The wedding planner rushed into the suite and clapped her hands. "Places! Places!" The planner made a quick adjustment to Lana's veil and then led everyone from the room. They headed downstairs, then lined up and began the short walk down from the Chateau, through a portion of the French garden, to the meadow where the ceremony would occur. A string quartet began Pachelbel's "Canon in D" as the wedding party walked down the white runner. Once the family was seated, and Ryan had escorted Eva to the front, Lana took her father's arm and gazed down the aisle to where Edmund waited.

The love she saw on his face made her want to run to him, but she maintained a steady pace. Finally, as the last notes of music faded, Lana Winchester married Edmund Clayton III, almost two years to the day of their reunion at the Chateau's grand opening.

They'd opted for a small wedding, which in their world meant only one hundred fifty guests watched as they made their vows. Despite the crowd, all Lana could see was Edmund. The rest of the crowd faded into the background as she joined her life to his.

She put a gold band on his finger. He added a diamond ring guard to his grandmother's engagement ring. He'd popped the question in London, while they were high above on the London Eye—the closest thing to the Arch there, he'd joked. The St. Louis landmark had been the first official tourist spot they'd visited—two days after the gala, when they'd finally climbed out of bed.

"I love you," Edmund told her at the end of reciting the vows he'd written himself.

"I love you," she answered at the end of hers. "I always will."

Later, after a long reception and an even longer night of lovemaking, they lay curled up in their four-poster bed. Edmund ran his fingers over her naked skin, making circles on a stomach whose flatness would soon reveal the secret only she and her husband shared. They were only at eight weeks and didn't plan on telling anyone until they'd reached twelve.

"I have one more present for you," Edmund said, his caresses creating delicious shivers along her sensitive skin. "Remember that house you liked here?"

"The Forest Glen property?" The three-story brick house was a historic Beaumont property located on two acres, high on a hill that overlooked the Missouri River, but still close enough to walk or ride bikes into the center of town.

"That one. You said one of your good friends used to live there, and that when you were a kid you'd swim in the pool and go through the hidden passageways."

"Yeah. I loved that house. It's a shame the current owners let it fall into disrepair. It needs renovation."

"Do you remember what else you said?" Edmund teased. "That if it ever came on the market…"

Lana sat up, joy filling her. "You bought it for us, didn't you?"

He nodded. "By the time this little one arrives, it'll be ready. I've already made you an appointment with Mrs. Cederberg, who wants you to know her design work is her wedding gift to us. I told her not to spare any expense. I know you haven't said anything about where you eventually wanted to settle, but with most of my family here and your family here…"

"You knew it would be here. You always know how to give me exactly what I need." Lana kissed Edmund thoroughly. She loved him more and more every day. Loving him was the best decision she'd ever made. Or as Edmund called it, the sweetest deal he'd ever made.

"You always said Beaumont was home," Edmund said when they came up for air. "My home is wherever you are. It seems like we're ready to settle down and have it all, picket fence included."

"Then welcome home, my love. Welcome home."

* * * * *